P9-CRV-025

BOOKS BY

REYNOLDS PRICE

THE FORESEEABLE FUTURE 1991

NEW MUSIC 1990

THE USE OF FIRE 1990

THE TONGUES OF ANGELS 1990

CLEAR PICTURES 1989

GOOD HEARTS 1988

A COMMON ROOM 1987

THE LAWS OF ICE 1986

KATE VAIDEN 1986

PRIVATE CONTENTMENT 1984

MUSTIAN 1983

VITAL PROVISIONS 1982

THE SOURCE OF LIGHT 1981

A PALPABLE GOD 1978

EARLY DARK 1977

THE SURFACE OF EARTH 1975

THINGS THEMSELVES 1972

PERMANENT ERRORS 1970

LOVE AND WORK 1968

A GENEROUS MAN 1966

THE NAMES AND FACES OF HEROES 1963

A LONG AND HAPPY LIFE 1962

THE FORESEEABLE FUTURE

REYNOLDS
PRICE

THE FORESEEABLE FUTURE

ATHENEUM
NEW YORK 1991
COLLIER MACMILLAN CANADA TORONTO
MAXWELL MACMILLAN INTERNATIONAL
NEW YORK OXFORD SINGAPORE SYDNEY

"The Fare to the Moon" first appeared in *The Southern Review*; "Back Before Day" in a limited edition from North Carolina Wesleyan College Press.

This is a work of fiction. Names, characters, places, and incidents either are the product of the author's imagination or are used fictitiously. Any resemblance to events or persons, living or dead, is entirely coincidental.

Atheneum
Macmillan Publishing Company
866 Third Avenue, New York, NY 10022

Collier Macmillan Canada, Inc.
1200 Eglinton Avenue East, Suite 200
Don Mills, Ontario M3C 3N1

Library of Congress Cataloging-in-Publication Data
Price, Reynolds, 1933–
The foreseeable future / Reynolds Price.
p. cm.
ISBN 0–689–12110–5
I. Title.
PS3566.R54F67 1991
813'.54—dc20 90–45463 CIP

10 9 8 7 6 5 4 3 2 1

Printed in the United States of America

FOR

HARRIET WASSERMAN

CONTENTS

THE FARE TO THE MOON 1

THE FORESEEABLE FUTURE 61

BACK BEFORE DAY 205

THE FARE TO THE MOON

ONE

As ever, she woke sometime before light. In the fall of the year, and with war savings-time, that meant it was just before five o'clock. The nearest timepiece in the house was his watch; and that was under his pillow still, still on his wrist. His brother would be here in half an hour; his overnight satchel was already packed—a clean pair of drawers, his toothbrush and razor, a Hershey bar she hid in a pair of his mended socks. There was nothing for her to do here now but make the coffee and watch him walk through the door, down the slope to his brother's car and then away.

She had halfway dreaded the news all summer; but when the letter came three weeks ago and he said "Well" and left it open on the table to read, she knew this morning would be the last. No way the Army would turn down a man as strong as him—not scarce as men were, this late in the war. When he had seen her pick up the letter, he stood at the screen door, watching the woods, and told her the ways you could beat the draft—all the foolish dodges he'd heard from scared boys. His favorite seemed to be vinegar and prune pits. The night before your physical exam, you drank a tall glass of white cider vinegar and swallowed three prune pits. Then you told the Army you had stomach ulcers; they X-rayed your belly, saw the dark shadows and the shriveled lining and sent you home with a sympathetic wave.

Without a word, she had bought the prunes and left them out on the shelf by the stove; the vinegar was always there in plain view. But he never mentioned the plan again, and last night she knew not to bring it up. Every bone in her body guessed he meant to leave. It made good sense, though it hurt like barbed wire raked down her face. She even guessed it hurt him as bad, but he never said it. And she wouldn't force it from him, not that last night. That was up to him.

After she brushed her teeth on the stoop and peed in the bushes, she came back in, damped the woodstove down, then shucked her sweater and dungarees, put on the flannel night shirt and crawled in beside him. She had lain there flat, saying her few prayers quick before he touched her. But he never did, not with his hands. Their hipbones touched and parts of their legs; but somehow the warm space built up between them till she felt gone already, that near him.

After five minutes he said "Remember, I set the alarm." He knew how much she hated the bell; it was one more way to say *You do it. You wake up and spare us.*

She had said "All right" and then "I'm thinking you'll live through it, Kayes." He had said many times that he knew, if they took him, he'd die overseas; and most of the times, he would laugh or sing a few lines of some hymn. But she knew he meant it; she said it to help him face the night, not because she was sure. And as far as she could tell, he had slept like a baby. She thought *I slept like a baby too, a mighty sick child;* but she also knew she had not dreamed once. That froze her as much as the cold dawn air—*If I didn't dream last night,* I'm *the corpse*—and she calculated they had the minutes to hitch up, one more farewell time. Her hand went toward him under the cover.

For the only time in the months he had known her, he stopped the hand with his own and held it. In another minute he said "Much obliged," then threw back his side of the cover and sat up.

It was still too dark to see him move; so before he could strike a match to the lamp, she thought *Except for this war, we'd stay right here. He don't give a goddamn for nothing but me.* Even without the sight of his face, she almost half-believed it was true. And early as it was in a chilly week, she was more than half right. It had been nearly true for six quick months. He had never admitted as much by day; but he proved it at dusk by turning back up at this door here, living her life beside her in private and sometimes in town and telling her things with his body by dark that, she almost knew, were meant to last.

When he finished the coffee, he poured hot water in the big tin pan, lit the lamp by the mirror and slowly shaved.

She sat at the table and watched every move. All her life, she envied men those minutes each morning, staring at a face they seemed not to notice, not trying to make it thinner or lighter, just taking it in.

Then he put on the first necktie he had worn since moving here; it had waited on a nail in the old pie safe. He took his change and knife from the shelf and portioned them out into several pockets. He took up the long narrow wallet and searched it.

She thought "Oh Jesus, now here it comes. Like every other white man God ever made, he thinks we can cross this out with money."

But he managed it altogether differently. He came the whole way to the table and sat again, in a fresh cold chair. He said "Please look right here at my eyes." When she looked, he said "You have been too good to me, every day. I will know that fact from here to my grave, wherever I find it. If I don't come back alive in time, remember I said I loved you *true*. I was sober when I said it, and I meant every word." He had still not smiled, but he leaned well forward. "Now give me both hands."

She had no choice but to spread both palms between them on the table, though she watched him still.

He laid two fifty-dollar bills down first; then he took off his watch and laid it on them. He had sometimes let her wear it on days when she doubted his promise to be here by dark.

She said "The money will help me a lot; thank you kindly. But you're going to need that watch overseas."

He understood she didn't mean that; she meant she thought it belonged to his wife, had been his wife's gift to him years ago. So he closed both her hands now, money and watch, and said "I bought that watch myself. It's yours till the day I walk back in here, claiming it again."

She had to nod, dry-eyed as a boy.

He stood up and, before he got both arms in his coat, a car horn blew way down by the road. He stepped to the door.

She stood where she was.

With a hand in the air, he kept her in place. "Don't let me see you in the cold," he said. Then someway he melted, silent, and was gone.

It was then that she knew the room was hot and dry as a kiln. She thought she was free to howl like a dog, and she sat there and waited for a moan to rise. But the car door slammed; and she heard it leave and fade completely away toward Raleigh with still no tears in her eyes, no moan. She said his name *Kayes* and waited again. But no, nothing came. So she stood and rinsed out both their cups and set them upside down on the shelf where they sat before he ever came here. Beyond her even, they had been her grandmother's and had sat unbroken in this same room long before she was born to meet this man that hurt her like this.

TWO

YOU COULD *call me anything—I used to answer.* But *from way before I remember good, every soul I knew but my mother called me* Blackie. *That was because my skin wasn't black. Mama was medium dark, a good walnut. And Red, Mama's aunt that mostly raised me, said my gone daddy was what they called* blue gum *that long ago, with skin so black his gums were blue. Most Negro babies are born real pale; but even with the kin I had behind me, everybody said I was born nearly white and stayed that way when most children shade on off, tan or dark. So somebody called me Blackie early, the way they called my fat friend Skinny Minnie; and Blackie hung onto my life like a burr—Blackster, Black, Blackheart. I answered.*

Even Kayes sometimes called me Black but just if he got mad or hungry—"Black, get your butt to the stove and start frying." *Mostly he called me Leah or Lee, Leeana, since Leah is my given name. Mama always said it came from the Bible. But when I got old enough to read for myself, the Bible said Leah was what Jacob got for his first wife when what he worked so long for was Rachel. It even said he hated Leah; and that set me back—I was meeting* stiff winds from a good many sides, without adding that. So I waited till Mama was gone one night, and then I asked Red. She said "Your mama can't read a soap box, much less the Good Book. What you think she know about some dead Leah? She just heard a preacher calling that name and liked the sound. Your mama would crawl to the moon for a sound—music in her bones; her daddy could sing."

There have been many people that took me for white. And they didn't think my name was a joke, or maybe it came from my straight hair. Red said I come here a nappy-haired baby; but it straightened out natural when my bosoms came. Half the men I know—any color you name—have tried to touch my hair, just for luck if no more, in serious fun. I been a clean person; I mean my skin. Even before I could hardly talk, in this cold house, Red said I would scrub in icy well-water before she had time to boil the first kettle—said "Black, you would flat-out polish your hide."

I would. And it paid. I don't mean I've yet took one penny for it. I'm way too proud and, till this spring, I never saw a man I wanted to have it. I mean my skin is the finest I've seen; and I've been up and down the land since 1919, when Mama lit out of here with me by the hand. First stop was Wilmington, Delaware. She stayed a few years; then came on back, too sick to take that winter they have. Watching her cough blood, I began to see I'd die someday. So I traveled a lot while I had strength.

Harlem, Springfield, Pittsburgh—you name it. And nobody, white or green, can match me, nobody I've seen; and I've seen a heap of shows. It's made me good friends, all up the line. Friends, I'm saying, not tomcats prowling—they'll eat any meat. Monied ladies in Packard cars, old men at clubs where I served meals, they told me time and again "You're splendid. Can I touch you for luck?" I tell em I'll touch them and then touch their hand or the back of their wrist. That does the trick.

It puts them at ease, almost every time, and I pass on. I've met little meanness, wherever I went; and the little I meet, I dodge in the road or slap up side the head bad, then run. So I was up North from eighteen to thirty, from the year Mama died down here with T.B. till fifteen months ago when Red broke her hip and sent for me. I hauled my precious skin on home, this ramshackle room, and kept watch with her till she passed on.

If I do say so, I did more than watch. Red got far more worse off than a baby, couldn't hold her water nor none of her mess. She thought I was my own mama most nights. She would lay me out for bringing men close as her Cape jasmine bush, under that window facing the road, and humping on the ground where Red could hear, when I hadn't even left the room.

I heard more of Mama than anybody knew. And God's my witness, till I got Red laid out in a casket in white satin pleats and deep in the grave, no man nor boy—not to mention hot women, and several have tried—ever laid more skin on me than a finger. I was one brown girl that had heard enough from two tails pumping. I'd take any music on Earth to that, any wreck or scream.

All through Red's last weeks alive, men would walk in here with hot fish dinners, chicken salad, peach pie. I'd thank them "profusely," as Red used to say, and ask had they heard any war news today? That would throw em for a loop! They were all 4-Fers with pus in their blood or, worse, they were hiding out from the Army. Till this war's over, I won't take that; I feel right patriotic someway. Back at first, I even had dreams of being an Army nurse and going to England when they were so bad off, bombs every night. I was still fool enough to think they could train you fast and ship you out. Every Negro I told said "Get your head tested, child. It ain't your fight. They don't want you." So I stopped telling my hopes and dreams. But my mind never changed, which is why I couldn't tell Kayes to shirk, even with that box of prunes I bought.

He came to Red's funeral with Riley his brother. When Kayes

walks in, nobody sees Riley; but he's all right or used to be. Red had been their grandmother's cook many years; and they were so welcome that one of my cousins, the big head-usher, set Kayes on the front row next to the aisle. When they led me in behind the casket, the only pew vacant was that same pew. So I nodded to Kayes, that was next to me, and sat two or three yards' distance down from him.

Make a long story short—he came on with us to the grave out back and saw Red covered. It near killed me and, swear to God, I thought he filled up. See, he had loved his grandmother much as I loved Red. She had raised him when his own mother left, run off with her own first cousin—a drunk—and left Kayes' daddy, Kayes himself who had just started talking good and Riley, an even younger baby. She left them, clean as a bat leaves Hell every evening at dusk. And Kayes' old grandmother, Miss Marianne, she took the whole crowd in and raised him right. Or at least the best she knew how to do, with my Red cooking every crumb they ate and washing and pressing every thread they wore. So sure, he ought to have cried at her grave.

What he did after that was walk halfway through the grove to his Chevy with Riley beside him. Then he stopped in his tracks like my eyes had shot him. I hadn't been watching him all that close—I was bent with the hardest grief I'd known, till this week now—but he spoke to Riley, who kept on going; and then he came back. When I saw him turn, I said in my heart "He's coming to me." I was dead-out wrong. It was still too early in the spring for flowers. But somehow, somewhere Kayes found a bloom—a white carnation that had seen better days. It was in his left hand. No other carnations were anywhere near, no wreath he could have stolen it from. I know I told myself "Black, he's grown it." I must have thought it bloomed that minute in his fist—big fist that had already bruised it some.

Anyhow not looking to me one time, he came right back to the edge of the grave, where Red's coffin sat with clods on the lid—two boys were standing there, waiting for me to move out of sight so they could finish—and he reached far down as his arm would go and let that one bloom fall on the dirt, where I knew Red's face was still looking up. I've never been partial to grown white people. Red and Mama both said you could trust them if you'd known them long.

I'd known Kayes Paschal since I was maybe four years old—Red bringing me to work some days when Mama was too sick to watch me and then was dead. I never had paid him that much notice. There at the grave though, I thought he looked good. Everybody but Kayes thought that and still thinks it. But sad as I was, he got no deeper into my mind or bosom than any tan man, not to mention the dark. I knew he married the banker's daughter that Red once said "could frost the sun," and she didn't mean with sugar.

But once I heard that flower hit Red's dirt, something snapped inside me in the midst of my chest. It takes a lot more than a white carnation to catch my eye. I didn't forget we were separate people, Kayes and me. I never once thought he'd speak to me, and I didn't dream I'd want it. But for some strange reason, I had held up good, right to that moment. You'd have thought I was some neat-dressed great-niece of Red's. But with Kayes coming back, giving Red that much, I said in my heart "Live through this, Leah, and you're guaranteed." I don't know what my fool mind meant.

It sure didn't think how hard his family had worked poor Red and for what slim pay, or how they'd drive her out every night to this piece of a shed, saying "See you tomorrow," when for all they knew she'd die in the night of cold or snakebite. All I understand, even today, is I took the first step forward to meet him. Kayes saw me moving and stepped on toward me. It wasn't till he put out his big hand that I saw the wide gold ring on his left; he was still mar-

ried to her. But it meant no more to me that day than a callus or a mole on his finger would.

Four days later though, as I was thinking I might better get my butt back North, I had stepped out into Red's yard to wash my hair in the sun. It was almost dry when something made me look toward the road. And here come Kayes again, walking the way he had to Red's grave, with his chin tucked down and leaning a little forward on the air, like a wind was trying to send him home. I said to myself "It's nothing but Kayes."

But once he got through the blackberry vines and spoke to the dog—they were friends, way back—I felt my eyes go straight to his hands. Big as they were that day by the grave, they had grown again. The right hand carried a brown paper sack (turned out it was three of the Hershey bars that Red used to want); the left hand that day was naked as mine. My mind said "Blackster, here it comes. Say no. You're too good for this." Even if no two people alive would believe a woman named Blackie was a virgin at thirty-one, I meant not to change, not for this white man I'd known all my life—gold ring or no. Turned out I was wrong.

THREE

Kayes's only brother was driving—Riley, three years younger but badly nearsighted and safe from the draft. He had married young, a plain girl tall as Riley and patient with all his shyness and fears. And they had two daughters, both smart and so lovely you might have looked at their pleasant parents and thought each girl was bought or adopted from a line of beauties or personally sent as a gift by God. As Kayes sat quiet in the car beside him, he thought *You're plain as boiled potatoes, but you sure got the luck.*

It was not self-pity, just the visible truth—look at Riley's wife, their girls, his money. Kayes and Riley had split their father's land with an amicable coin toss. Kayes got the better half and a hard-working tenant but lost money most years. Riley coined gold on sandy soil with a string of tenants no better than thieves. Look at his homely wife, not a penny to call her own and from poor country stock but a certified saint. Kayes's wife Daphne had money to spare from her banker daddy and blood so blue it could pass for ink; but her mind had shut when the son was born, named Curtis after her dead father.

Good as Curtis was, the boy drew all her care onto him. Kayes had guessed that things would balance out as the boy got older. But now he was fourteen, and still Daphne watched him like the first angel landed. So for that many years, except on unpredictable nights when her gate swung open with no complaint, Kayes was lonesome as the last tree standing on the moon itself. And full though he was of love and need, until he saw Leah that day at Red's funeral, he had touched no more than three other women. And all were white, all big young country girls that laughed at the end and went back to work with barely a word to prove he'd known them.

The Negro part had concerned him at once. When he turned away from Red's graveside, and Leah there behind him, he told himself "Forget her *now*." And he nearly succeeded. Despite the fresh sight of Leah's good face and his older memory of tales his friends told, long years back about colored girls, Kayes's mind soon turned to the things he must order for his tenant at the Feed and Seed—a load of cottonseed meal, one of lime, a case of formula powder for the baby (the tenant had four, none old enough to work).

It wasn't until he climbed the steps of his house an hour later and heard Daphne calling to Curtis—"Baby, *run*"—that Leah rose again in his mind, exactly as fine a face and bones as anybody left in the county, any woman. And before his hand touched the front-door knob, Kayes thought "I've known her since before she could talk." It was simply true but it meant a great deal, much more than he planned, from that week on till now today.

Riley cleared his throat to break the long silence. "You think they'll want you?"

Kayes was so far off, it came at him strangely. "Want me? The Army? They'd want *you*, Bud, if you weren't blind."

Riley took both hands off the wheel and bent to the windshield to search out the road, a blind driver. Dawn was in progress, a dull tin color, and the windows were still transmitting cold. "You used to have your old heart murmur. What happened to that?"

Kayes said "My heart ain't spoke for years." He did not mean anything deep or sad; but once it was out, he thought it through. It was wrong; he had spoke out to Leah, just now, in the room. Knowing they had less chance in the world than a baby left all night in the snow, Kayes had finally told her the weight she had in his mind and heart. He turned to the side of his brother's thin face. They had not shared secrets for twenty-odd years; but they'd never broke faith, never lied when pressed or failed one another's unending trust. So Kayes said something he had planned for days, "Riley, if I get killed over—"

Riley didn't look but his right hand came out accurately and brushed Kayes's mouth.

"No, old Bud, this has to be. If I come back in less than top shape, you'll be my executor; so you need to know. Daphne has got her own money, aplenty. Anyhow the law gives her a widow's share. Most of the rest goes to Curtis of course, but I put down five thousand dollars for you. Please give half of that to Leah."

"Leah?"

"Lee—Blackie—you know. Don't fail me, Bud."

Riley said "Absolutely." And when Kayes stayed quiet, he said "You really want to leave, don't you, Kay?"

Kayes nodded. "Yes, God—*leave* now awhile but not *die*, I guess." Then he chuckled.

Riley said "I'll be here to meet you, be sure. But where will you live?"

Kayes looked to his right. The sun, in climbing, had turned the pines from a near-black green to a color that made him think *Emerald*. As a boy Kayes collected the *most*, the *best*, the *scarcest* things; and somewhere he read that perfect emeralds were rarer than diamonds and cost more money. Though he was the least poetic of souls and cared less for money than a year-old infant, he looked at the pines now and thought "Countless billions." Then he wondered what in the world he meant. Well, surely he was trying to dodge Riley's question. So he kept on looking, counting pine trunks now.

Riley said "You understand Blackie will need to leave, if the Army takes you?"

Kayes said "Why's that?" He still faced outward.

"Assuming some white trash doesn't burn her house down, what will she eat? Nobody that knows about you and Daphne will give Black a job."

Kayes saw that was right. But he played the words again in his mind—was Riley hateful at all, out to hurt him? Did he mean to harm Leah? But in memory, the words played back straight and true. As ever, Riley had no grain of spite. So Kayes felt safe to look around—Riley met his eyes for as long as was safe—and said "O.K., I'll authorize you to pay her a wage to stay at old Red's house and fix it up. Paint the walls, mend the windows—Lee's smart with a hammer; she says she's worked, painting rooms up North."

Riley said "I don't doubt it. But Kay, that's not your house to fix. Nor mine, don't forget. Grandmother gave it to Red, long since, and the half acre round it."

It was news to Kayes; he thought the house was on Riley's half of the family land. All through his time out there with Leah, when his mind backslid, he told himself "My family's owned this house forever. Let any fool tell me to leave." He gave a little shake and tried to laugh. But Riley's profile was solemn again. So Kayes said "You might have told me that, months ago."

Riley said "You're a grown man. You chose your path."

Kayes waited a good while. "How lost did I get?"

"Beg your pardon?"

Kayes saw Riley now as he was in childhood, a serious boy who would answer you true—anything you asked. "How much have I broke?"

Riley knew they were in deep water now; he gave the question the thought it required. Then again he looked over, for the time he could spare. "Maybe nothing. Daphne's strong as an iron stake." He tried to end there.

Kayes pushed him on. "I've got a son—"

Riley nodded. "I'm his godfather. You forget that?"

"Have you talked to Curtis in all these months?"

Riley said "Every Sunday but Easter—he was busy."

"How much does he hate me?"

Riley said "A good deal. He's protecting his mother. You know how that is."

"Any chance he could ever feel better about me?"

To both their surprise, Riley suddenly laughed. "If you died a big hero, scaling the breastworks, shot in the brow, Curt might recover."

Kayes managed to smile. "I may oblige him."

"They don't have breastworks these days, Kay."

By now they had passed all the good things to see, the useful sights—trees and fields and low white houses in bare oak groves, the big hollow rock where a family was buried upright in a shaft, a mother and father and three young boys. Now they were coming to the fringe of Raleigh, where the town swelled out and killed the land from bedrock upward. Even the vacant ground was blighted, unwilling to yield. Kayes told himself "They are all better off, with me out of sight." He meant all the people who thought they needed to lean on him; he hoped they knew better.

Riley spoke as if each word cost thousands. "I guess this here is your best bet, a piece of the war. But I want you to know—I'll miss you terrible. You're a lot to me, Kayes; and nothing's changed that."

Kayes knew not to look; it would break them both. But he said "I guarantee I feel the same." And from there till they parked in front of the place where he and assorted men and boys would be examined for nothing but strength and the sense—if called upon—to die decent, Kayes thought about Leah.

Forget about Hitler and the wide Pacific, I could die this minute in full possession of all I hoped to find in life, whoever I hurt—and I stand ready to pay for them, two of the faces (I can't help Leah). One smart grown woman wanted *me. Just me in a room, no money, no stunts, no lifetime deal. No mention of what any blind man could see—we were different animals, her and me, not meant to plow in a double yoke, not here nor now.*

But we made it last for six whole months. Any hour on the clock, I could slide my car in off that road, below Red's pitiful piece of a house, and set my foot to the ground to climb those last hundred yards; and Lee would know *it. Some piece of her mind would know I was back and would raise her whole fine shape to meet me. Not a time, no single time I recall, did I climb all the way to the house without her walking to meet me or waiting in the yard with a cup of water or, if it was cold, in the window at least with oil light behind her and both eyes ready to smile me in.*

My skin. *She evermore used my skin. She was like a sensible squaw in the winter, kids starving around her; and then her man kills one last deer—Leah took my body and used every* part *to save us both, not a particle wasted. It was all food and* easement. *That's a word I'd never used but in farming, giving somebody an easement on land, to haul his crop across some corner of your woods or fields. But toward the end of the first whole week I stayed at Red's, I woke in the night and could hear Leah breathing like she was awake. She didn't speak though. The few other women I've known, deep in, would need to speak at a time like that, just to prove it was real. Lee was calm as ever. So a word just came to my lips, and I said it—*"Easement"*—and Lee said "True." I still* *think she understood all I meant, though we never discussed it by daylight. Never.*

Have I wrecked her too? Bud's right; some trash boys might try to scare her—the Cagles or some of the moron Coggins. But once I finally told her, last night, the possible mess I might leave her in, didn't she say "Where you think I been? *I didn't turn nigger this afternoon. All my life I* lived *for trouble—and child, trouble* came—*so I take my chances, like I took on you. Look what that got me." When I asked her* what?, *she said "Some* time, *a piece of time to think about in my old age, if I live to keep thinking and figuring out." Then she broke out smiling in the dim oil light, the smile that could give me all I lacked. And when I tried to say what to do tonight, if the Army kept me, she put both hands to her ears and frowned—a grown woman's frown, knowing all she knows. And speaking of pain, she out-knows me.*

Riley found a parking place in sight of the warehouse and killed the engine. He looked to Kayes and said "Can I come in?"

Kayes said "Thank you, no. They'd ship you straight to Japan by noon." It didn't mean anything but "Clear out please; let me do this right."

"But what if they fail your stiff old joints?—you've got to ride home."

The fact had really not dawned on Kayes; he was so sure of leaving. He thought it out, chose to skip the word *home* (where on Earth was that?) and then said "The bus'll stop right by Red's, if I ask it to. I won't need it though." He leaned over slowly and amazed his brother with a silent hug. When Kayes sat back, he looked to the panel clock; it was almost seven; he was in good time. He opened his door and said the last thing. "If you don't hear from me by dusk, please drive out to Red's and tell Lee I'm gone. If she needs to go on somewhere safe—maybe one of her cousins—I'll pay for your gas." He handed Riley the keys to his car.

Riley took them and nodded.

And Kayes loped away. Within three yards he told himself "I will never see that boy's face again." The boy was Riley, as ever in his mind. Sad as he knew he ought to feel, Kayes was light on his feet; and when a kid stood back to let him enter the building first, Kayes said "We're in the same rowboat, son. You first. After you."

The boy said "Yes sir" and took the lead with all the joy of a Judas goat at the slaughter pen.

For an instant as the boy moved, the side of his face looked like young Curtis—young as Curt anyhow, smart and distrustful. But still Kayes could laugh.

FOUR

SINCE IT WAS SATURDAY, Curtis had planned to sleep till ten, maybe closer to noon. Then he meant to find Cally, his friend with the rifle, and go squirrel hunting. But at eight o'clock, Daphne came to the shut door, waited a minute, creaked it open and said "Please, Curt. I need you today."

He could always wake on a dime, that fast; but he lay on and thought "You need somebody but I'm not the man." Beneath him, his dick was hard as a spike; he thought "I'll never get it down in time." But he said "What for?"

"What time did your father say he was leaving?"

Kayes had been at the west-side door of school yesterday afternoon as Curtis came out. The boy had seen the car, first thing, and was split between a taste for running straight to it with pleasure and the colder sense of his mother's pride—what she was still bearing and would need from him. He had seen his father only four short times in the past six months, and each time was worse than the one before. So Curtis walked over slowly now, opened the door and leaned in gravely. Kayes asked him to sit for a minute and talk. The boy obeyed but the talk came mostly from Kayes—he had already given Riley instructions to pay for anything Curt really needed. If the Army took him, he'd write letters weekly; please write to him.

All Curtis could do was nod "Yes sir" and wish it would stop. He loved this man so much and so deeply, so faraway back in the fourteen years that felt long to him. Bitterness poured up into his mouth now and nearly choked him. Curtis kept saying, time and again to himself, "If he just won't say that woman's name"—the only name Curtis knew was Blackie; and he heard that at school, not once from his mother. She'd die before speaking it.

When Kayes let up, the boy looked at him for the first full time and said "I've thought this through a lot. I hope they take you, I hope you come back, I hope it's *you* when you get here though." Kayes waited awhile, looking ahead, and then said "I thank you. And I'll work on it, son. But this may *be* me, right here and now." Then he gave Curt an envelope that, back home, turned out to be two fifties—new as if printed that morning. At the supper table when the boy's mother asked if Kayes had seen him, Curtis told her all of the truth he could risk, "Yes ma'm. He looked ready." She started the growling edge of a sneer; but Curt faced her down—no word, wide-eyed.

Now as he lay still, praying she would vanish, she held her ground and repeated "What time?"

"Ask Riley," Curtis said.

"*Uncle* Riley—"

"You know who I mean; he's got a phone."

"Don't be impudent, son—I slept at least two minutes last night. Anyhow I know Riley's driving him to Raleigh."

"Then you know more than me. I was sleeping fine."

"Curt, where is his car?"

"In Raleigh, I guess."

Daphne said "Surely not; he'd ride with Riley."

Curtis sat up suddenly and faced his mother. Her face, the face he served every day, was strung tight now and scarily pale. Still he said "Then I guess the damned car is at Blackie's place. He gave it to her." Curtis had never seen Blackie, not close at hand. But once her name was loose in the room, it threatened to stand her between them now, tall and stern and smelling like Kayes.

Daphne swallowed hard but concealed the shock. Finally she said "Is that a known fact, or are you just dealing in meanness today?"

Curtis said to himself "One more bull's-eye," and his face flushed red.

He turned to the wall, but he said "What now?"

She said "I've thought all night. By decent rights, that car is ours—"

"He's not dead, Mother."

"*Hush.* But you know full well the Army will take him."

"I don't, no ma'm."

Daphne waited. "Not a blemish on him, not to the eye."

Curtis said "His ear, that strawberry mark."

Before she thought, Daphne said "*No*, that used to be lovely." Then she heard herself and took a step to leave.

But Curtis said "We could drive out and get it."

"You and me? But who would drive it back? Baby, you aren't legal at the wheel, not yet."

"You got your key? I can drive as good as any two men; nobody'll stop us."

Daphne said "What if she's there? And what if Riley brings him back?"

Curtis's dick was calm for the moment. He knew he must take that chance to dress. As he threw back the cover, he said "I'll tell my father it was my idea; he still likes me. You can let me out on the road and head back. I'll handle the rest." As his mother turned to get herself ready, Curtis made his voice easy; but what he said was "My father's name is *Kayes*—remember?—not just *he*."

Daphne said "I can't say it." It was only a fact, not a plea for pity.

But all the way into deeper country, with Curtis sullen on the seat beside her, she gripped the wheel and thought little else. *Kayes, Kayes. I want it* all *back, those short first years we were good to each other. You can't want this; surely you're crazy. But none of your people have lost their minds; God knows, none of mine. And I can't blame liquor, which both of my sisters can blame in good faith—I doubt you've had three drinks in ten years—so here I've stood with no explanation to give the world, except to say you've lost your mind.*

All the women I know say that much already, when I'm not present—though ten days ago in this same car, Roe Boyd said, out of the absolute blue, "Daph, the fact that the girl's light-skinned as you *makes it all the worse." I pretended I missed it and Roe shut up. But I understood her—Kayes, if you'd gone to a coal-black girl, we'd have had this over long months ago and be back together, on the old right rails. Tell that to any three doctors south of Baltimore, and they'd sign an order in a New-York minute to strait-jacket you and cool you off till reason prevails.*

But you picked a woman no darker than I am, after two or three clear days at the beach. And stayed beside her in a house the wind can walk right through. I've been there with you, far more than once, to see old Red at Christmas and Easter. Remember I told you her roof was bad and you sent a man out with brand-new tin, and Red sent me two big dressed chickens, ready to fry? Red would die all over again, if she knew—you preying on a child she raised, a Negro that naturally thinks you're God or, if she doesn't, can't help herself; can't make you leave; may even die *for knowing you, if you leave today and the trash get at her.*

I'd *pray to die, if Curtis didn't need me. I've asked the Lord if I can pray for* you *to die in battle soon, in some brave act that cancels this and lets us lift our heads and move on. But I get no more from* God *than from you—not a word, not a look. I go to church and sit there waiting. It might as well be one dim coffin with me nailed down, alive and stifling and beating the lid; but nobody hears and no help comes.*

The nights I've lain awake and watched your pistol on the table, begging *me to pick it up and drive the six miles out to Red's and blow you and her to deepest Hell, some days at least before God does it. I've cursed the marksman lesson you gave me. Remember that? Remember* anything *we liked to do or pledged to keep on doing forever—like trusting, honoring, serving each other, come sun or storm?*

We were not back from the honeymoon for more than a month when you took me out that bright cold Sunday. I thought we were riding around, just looking. We passed the farm and waved at the tenants. I thought you'd stop and give the children the Tootsie Rolls we bought in town. But you pushed on, not saying a word, and finally took a sandy trail that sloped so steep downhill I thought we'd be in water any minute, deep in. I remember quoting St. Paul to myself, "Love hopes all things, endures all things."

I thought I was joking, whistling in the dark. And the sand did deepen till we nearly got trapped and you stopped cold in a thick bank of briars. I said "You want me to try to push?" You met my eyes like some rank stranger. And that was the time I first had to think I'd married a boy I'd never met, *much less really knew.*

Finally you said "I want you to learn something useful *for once." You always laughed at my fund of knowledge. Remember telling my father that Christmas "Daph knows everything but how* to breathe"? You reached down under your edge of the seat and pulled out the pistol in a clean white rag. It looked as big as a cannon to me. Till then I hadn't seen it—you'd bought it that week. Strange as you looked, I didn't feel scared, just puzzled as always. You got out then and beckoned me on. And what did I do but follow behind you in two-inch heels for what seemed a mile of ruts and briars? Then the brush stopped dead, we were in a wide clearing, the light was murky.

But you stood still, not looking at me, and fired six shots at a helpless pine. Then you reloaded and—still not meeting my eyes or speaking—you held it my way.

No choice but to take it. Well, I learned to shoot, at the same old tree. We must have killed it—maybe sixty rounds, most of them mine. Not a single miss. I could find the pine right now, if it's there.

Were we on Mars? Has any of this, these fifteen years, really happened, Kayes, or am I asleep? I thought I'd love you till both of us died. I thought it meant—the one weird day you taught me to shoot—that you had to love me. You wanted me, above all, to be protected in a world you already claimed was wild, though I didn't believe you yet awhile.

Even now, this close to Blackie's face, I beg you to live and come on in. I can say your name. I can even say hers; but here and now, in my private mind, I can barely say home. Come back to where you promised to stay. Everybody will know it was nothing but a nightmare. Wake on up, Kayes. There may be time.

FIVE

THE CAR was there, parked just off the road in a patch of young cedars. The path to Red's ran uphill from it; and by the time Daphne pulled to the shoulder, smoke was pouring from the chimney up there. For an instant she thought "They've burnt it." Then she thought "She's burning up things of his." But she knew both were wrong. And Curtis was reaching to open his door. So she said "I'll drive on down to that sycamore, turn and then follow you on home. Drive slow and easy; and if a patrolman stops you, I'll explain you're helping your mother."

Curtis had got his door wide open, and one leg was out. "Mother, I'm a lot better driver than you. You better hope I'm near if *you* get stopped." He finally looked back and halfway grinned.

But Daphne had seen a flash of green. The door of Red's house had swung back silently; and somebody wearing a bright green coat was standing there, at the top of the steps. A long brown skirt, tall, a lot of black hair. That moment, for some entirely strange reason, Daphne wanted to wave, to lean out the window and say "Step here please." The idea scared her but still, to her wonderment, she felt no shock. She had not seen Blackie for twenty years maybe; but now the memory of her face in childhood came to Daphne—such a pale child, more than normally serious with lovely hair, coarse and strong as an Indian's.

By then Black had come down two of her steps. Two more and she'd be in the yard, by the path.

Daphne said "Curt, don't say a word. She'll know who you are. Just unlock the car and be ready when I turn. You take the lead."

Curtis shut the door gently and moved to the car. As he bent to unlock the door, Blackie gave a wide slow wave, took the last two steps and started toward him.

Then Daphne was scared but also angry. Curt must get out of this, with no more hurt or shame on his head. So she opened her door to meet what came. Blackie was no more than twenty yards off, looking down but still moving.

Curtis looked back with a heavy scowl. "I'm serious, Mother. Go turn around and wait down there." He pointed to the white sycamore. And when his mother paused, he said again "*Go!* Go straight home now. If anything's wrong, I'll hitchhike in."

His power was so new that Daphne obeyed it. She went to the huge tree, backed around slowly; and though the woman had got down to Curtis and they were standing as still as horses, Daphne passed on by.

When the sound of her car had vanished, Leah said "You got to be Curtis."

"Yes ma'm, I—" He felt his face burn and pointed to where his mother had gone. "I guess I'm supposed to drive this home."

Leah said "Was it his idea, your father's?"

"No ma'm, she—" He pointed toward Daphne again.

Leah smiled a little and raised a hushing finger to her lips. "No need to call me *ma'm* now, Curtis. I may be pale but I live with the niggers."

He laughed, then flushed again—this was all wrong; he was falling all over himself like a child. Finally he said "If this car's yours, or anything in it, I'll hitch right back. It don't really matter." Not thinking, he had switched to the voice he used with Negroes.

Leah corrected him—"*Doesn't* matter"—but renewed her smile. "I been to school, Curtis; I did right well." She leaned to see inside the car. The back seat was littered with Kayes's farm papers, old catalogs, a pair of gray socks. "Not a thing of mine, nowhere in *sight.*" Her smile hung on. "You might be standing there, two or three days. This road is lonesome."

Curtis nodded. "I know it. My father and I, we hunt out here." They had not hunted for nearly two years.

Leah said "You know how much you look like him?" Her hand came up and touched her own face.

Curtis said "Exactly, before he changed."

"How much has he changed?" She asked sincerely, truly not knowing.

Somehow the boy felt stronger now, older and honest. He said "I didn't mean you and—all this." He pointed to the house. "I mean all the years I've known him, fourteen."

Leah said "I knew him longer. My grandmother cooked for your great-grandmother. I was in her kitchen when he was a boy."

Curtis said "I didn't know that." It was only the truth, though even as he said it, he knew he could barely hear himself think. Nobody had dealt with him like this, in his whole life till now—this clean dead-level eye-to-eye truth. He knew he was being rammed forward through time. Any second now, he would be a grown man, tall enough to do what was right. But though they both stood waiting for a long time, nothing, right or wrong, came to his mind.

At last Leah said "What if they say no and he comes back?

"Fine by me—"

"The car, I mean. What'll he have to drive, if you take the car?"

Curtis said "He can hitch into town and get it. You don't have a car?"

Leah looked around as though she might. The only other machine in view was a dead old cookstove, flung in a ditch. She turned back to Curtis. "I don't have good sense, much less a car." She wanted to laugh but a hoarse bark came. She wiped her lips slowly with the back of her hand.

So Curtis said "Did he live here?" He pointed uphill.

"Who?"

"Mr. Kayes Paschal, the man we mentioned."

Leah also looked behind, to the house, as if she had waked in another life and sought landmarks. And she spoke uphill, away from the boy. "He spent most nights for the past six months, ate a good many suppers, drank a whole world of coffee—"

"Hope the Army has coffee or he'll desert."

She said "They got it."

Curtis said "Don't think I came out here to be mean, but tell me one thing please—what was this *for*?"

At first Leah thought "He can't be a child." Then she knew nobody but a child could have aimed it, that dead-eye straight. She said "You trying to kill me, fast?"

"No, I'm hoping to find my father. See, I'm the one missed him all this time."

Leah's hand went out again—stop please now. Thank Jesus she'd spent no time around children. "I wish I could answer, son. Did we hurt you bad?"

"Bad. Yes. And I'm *his* son." He tried to ease it with a partial smile.

She took it full-face but had to wait. "Did me being colored make it worse on you?"

Curtis knew at once and shook his head firmly. "It was you being in this world, out here."

As calmly as if she asked for the time, Leah said "You want me to die right now?"

He said "No. Not now—years ago, before I was born."

"What about your mother?"

He said "What about her?" He had already noticed they hadn't mentioned her.

"You don't fault her for any of this?"

Curtis said "Not more than fifty percent."

Calm as she looked, this meeting had struck Leah harder than anything yet, anything her mind had bothered to store. She said "How would you be different now, if this hadn't been?" She also pointed back at Red's house.

He tried to think. But all he could find was "At least I wouldn't be praying my father would head out to war and be shot dead."

Her hand went up to her open mouth.

Curtis nodded.

"Say no." She took the steps forward and reached for his wrist. Then she shook it between them in the strong new light—the sky had cleared all through their talk. "Tell God right now you don't mean that."

Curtis said "I don't. I meant to hurt you."

Leah said "You did, man. Don't worry, you did." But he looked so much like her memory of Kayes—Kayes way back when—that she had to say "You hate me this much?"

Curtis had heard her call him *man*. He all but smiled. "I'd probably like you. I'm an outgoing fellow."

"But the way things happened put bad blood between us—" She read it as if it was printed plain on the hood of the car.

Curtis said "I guess." He did not know yet, but his face was sliding back in time. He looked like a child again, tired and hungry.

Leah said "You eat your breakfast yet?"

"No, I came out here too fast."

"I'll cook you some eggs."

He meant to say yes; he could learn so much. But now he was young, he said "My mother is waiting for me."

Leah said "If Kayes comes back, I'll tell him you drove it." She looked at him closely, the first time since they grappled so close. He looked even younger than he had at the start. "You sure you got a driver's license?"

Curtis said "No but that won't matter. All the young patrolmen are off killing Japs. These poor old fellows won't even see me."

Leah nodded and walked a long five steps on the uphill path. Then she turned and said "*I* see you, Curtis. I wish I'd seen you sooner than this."

He said "No you don't. I'd have ruined your time." He didn't know everything he meant. He did know he wanted to smile once more but his mouth refused.

Back in the house, Leah went to the mirror and faced herself. No change, same eyes, same clean tight skin. She thought "I'm going to pack my duds and walk out of here, *whoever* comes back. I didn't set up to be this harmful." But the thought alone hurt as much as any words said this whole long day, that had only just started. In the glass she could also see behind her the neat-made bed where her grandmother died and Red (gone crazy) and where she and Kayes had spent their nights.

In that empty space, above those pillows, they said things neither one had said elsewhere—Kayes promised her that. And where were they now? The words anyhow were gone past hearing, they had hurt as many people as they helped, she must get them out of her mind right now. Before she could turn away to pack, Leah faced herself a final moment. "Leave it all here, Black. Leave it and go."

And all through his peaceful ride back home, Curtis knew he had learned some large true thing that would lead him into a better life than he'd known till now—less mess, less meanness, fewer people draining his life for blood. He tried to name his hard new knowledge; he wanted to say it out loud in the car so he'd never forget it. And he dug to find it but got no further than the words "I must—"

He pounded the wheel with both clenched hands and rode for more than a mile, feeling bad. But then he noticed how the sky had opened. The sun was strong as he eased into town; and when he paused at the first stoplight, two country girls from his grade in school crossed the street before him—Willie and Flay. They were both already grown up front and had known, for months, things that still baffled him. So he knocked on the windshield and leaned his face well forward in the sun, with eyes half shut.

Both of them saw him, shrieked; then waved and skipped faster, though they looked back, time and again, and talked a clear blue streak till he turned left and moved away—*Curt Paschal's driving, like he's got good sense when we know he* ain't.

SIX

KAYES WALKED through the morning like a man still dreaming. When he entered the draft induction center, he found exactly the room he expected—a dim tall space, two-tone gray walls with benches and maybe a hundred men. Mostly boys, as he'd imagined, all smoking like chimneys and nervous as squirrels. The obvious cause for worry was a sergeant, built like a concrete bunker and seated on a low platform in a kind of pulpit. Everybody tried not to notice him, Kayes included. So Kayes stopped inside the door, leaned on the wall and searched all the faces. Some of the boys looked younger than Curtis and were digging at their crotches, trying to laugh. Only when he hunted a place to sit did he find a friend.

A deep voice called his first two names, "Wilton Kayes." An arm went up, a man half-stood; and Lord, it was Brutus Bickford from grade school.

Kayes stepped over to him. "Brutus, they caught us."

Brutus had grinned but now his face sobered. When Kayes was safely down beside him, Brutus said "They ain't catching *me*, I tell you." He fumbled in his watch pocket, drew out a capsule not much bigger than a grain of rice, revealed it to Kayes, checked to see that the sergeant was turned away and then gulped it.

Kayes said "What will that do?"

"You remember I had high blood pressure, don't you?"

High blood pressure in the third damned grade? Still Kayes said "Sure, I forgot for a minute." Wide as Brutus was, and dazed in the eyes, he looked like a calm rock bathed in the sun.

"I've already had what they call strokettes. A friend of mine claims this pill *guarantees* me freedom today."

Kayes thought *Well, death may amount to freedom—good luck, old son*. But he said "We'll know in an hour, I guess."

Brutus said "Kayes, Christ, when have I seen you?"

To his surprise, Kayes knew, to the day. "The morning your mama pulled you out of Miss Allen's class and left. The sixth grade, right after Easter Monday. Y'all moved up here, if memory serves."

Brutus took it for granted that his past was remembered. He merely nodded and said "That bastard, Calvin Pepper—Mama said they were married, her third or fourth husband; I still think they were just shacked up. Anyhow some scoundrel meaner than Cal took umbrage one Saturday night that summer and drilled Cal's pea-brain with one clean shot, smack-dab right *here*." Brutus tapped a huge finger between his blue eyes, then broke up laughing. "Her and me bought a case of Pepsis with his cash and two bus tickets to Carolina Beach."

"You still live there?"

"Oh no. She may; I come on back up here and been working. I got a young wife, and she's got kids of her own to feed, so I'm a plasterer and good at it too—let me lay you some walls." Then he locked an unblinking stare on Kayes. "Where you been, Bo?"

Kayes suddenly knew he would tell the truth, and it felt like a fruitful island discovered after months at sea. "I been living in the country with a Negro woman named Leah Birch, Red Birch's niece. You remember old Red, mean as a snake?"

Brutus said "I've known very few niggers, Kayes. We couldn't afford em and now I don't care."

Kayes took it peacefully, telling himself *That's a novel approach. In a million years, I'd have never guessed that.* There was nothing to say.

But after a wait, Brutus said "You love her?"

Here was a whole new level of surprise. It seemed as unlikely as an angel visit. And a need to tell the truth was still strong. So Kayes said "I doubt I know what love amounts to."

Brutus laughed. "Sure you do. You used to be smart."

Kayes suddenly saw a new piece of the afternoon when Brutus's mother took him away. It was right after lunch; and they were into rest time, hearing Miss Allen read *Penrod and Sam.* No warning at all, the hall door opened. And there stood a tall woman, dark purple dress, like a country girl with a big open face but confused in the eyes and with caked-on rouge. She didn't even speak to Miss Allen but looked round wildly and said "Where you *at?*" Brutus sat two seats from Kayes; and at that, he stood like a child agreeing to die at dawn. She said "Hey, boy. We're leaving *out.*" By then Miss Allen had summoned her wits and was asking questions. But all the woman would say was "No, he's mine and we're going."

When Brutus had got his jacket from the cloak room—his books were still inside his desk—he went to his mother but looked back at Kayes. And when Kayes half-waved, Brutus had to pretend he couldn't see. His eyes flinched hard but then firmed up and never blinked, from then till the time she turned him and vanished. Kayes had thought before that the worst thing would be to have your father come to school drunk and call your name. But to have your mother come like this, a raucous gypsy—it shocked

Kayes, even now, to see it. So he said to this big man beside him, "I hope I do." In the midst of the words, Kayes wondered what in the world they meant.

"You still married to the Mitchell girl?"

How would Brutus know that? "Legally, yes."

Brutus laughed again, not mocking but in sympathy. "That's what matters, ain't it?—that thin piece of paper. They can slice you with that worse than any bullwhip."

Kayes tried to smile and skate on through it. "They've got you over miles of barrels, all right." He wondered how many wives Brutus had left, but he knew not to ask. The sergeant had picked up a clipboard and was standing.

Brutus said "You're praying he takes *you,* I bet." By then his face was a new shade of red; the pill was working.

The sergeant said "Alphabetize yourselves." The alphabet was strung round the walls on dingy cards. A lot of the boys were baffled by the order, and Kayes was trying to smile at that.

Brutus spotted the B and pointed to it, but he said to Kayes "I never saw much wrong with niggers that money wouldn't fix. How dark is she, Bo?"

Kayes said "Light as me."

Brutus said "Then you're waist-deep in cow pies, ain't you?" But he didn't explain and before Kayes could ask, he whispered "Look, I'm not feeling so good. If I stroke out here, tell the doc what happened and send my regrets."

Kayes said "Be glad to."

Brutus laughed and went.

Half an hour later when Kayes got upstairs, naked as a newt in a line of men in similar trouble, huddled there in a corner was a ring of doctors around a cot. As Kayes worked through a set of chores for medics—kneeling, bending, exposing his ass and throat and coughing—he came near enough to see the cot. Brutus was laid out naked too, pink as a shrimp with a blood-pressure sleeve on and two doctors, each one holding a wrist. Brutus's eyes were shut and Kayes wondered if he had killed himself with that one pill. He figured the doctors didn't know names, so he said "Brutus" firmly.

Brutus looked up and found Kayes near. Hot as he was, for a long moment Brutus tried to look solemn. But then he checked on the doctors—they were busy—so he winked at Kayes.

Kayes lifted a finger and smiled. But through the rest of the next half hour, in other rooms, he went on seeing Brutus two ways—the boy leaving school and the clown on the cot, swollen with blood, gambling with death. And when he had done all the shameful stunts they forced on his body and another sergeant had looked down a list and said "So Paschal, you're found fit to serve," Kayes walked away with a stinging surge of raw grief in his eyes and mind. Over and over, he told himself what he thought was the truth. With all the pain he had on his own—the people he had crushed and a war to face—this sadness now was for no one or nothing but Brutus Bickford years ago, a twelve-year-old boy run like a wind-up doll by a whore.

SEVEN

TWENTY MINUTES LATER, dressed and calm, Kayes got his turn in a dark phone booth. He paid for the first call, to Riley's house. Riley would hardly be home yet; and though his wife had let Kayes know she despised his face, he could tell her at least that now he was boarding a bus to Fort Jackson and basic training. That should satisfy her so much she might unbend enough to say his name, which had not crossed her lips since the night he left home.

But Riley answered on the second ring with a slow "Riley Paschal."

Kayes seized up again but cleared his throat. "Sir, this is Dog-Soldier Paschal, reporting."

Riley said "Oh God—"

"They're herding us onto a bus any minute now, for South Carolina. I passed, flying colors, which is all I know. I'll write you from down there, soon as I can."

Riley said "Kay, *call* me, night or day. And call collect; that'll make it go faster." He needed a long pause. "You bearing up?"

"I plan to live."

Riley said "Don't say it."

"Why?"

"Just don't make claims. This is one show run by others now."

Kayes chuckled. "I recently got that impression."

"What can I send you? You're bound to need something."

Kayes said "I've got my shaving kit. They throw in the clothes at camp, I guess."

"Sure, you'll have a full khaki wardrobe, down to the handkerchiefs. I just meant—what?—snacks, playing cards, writing paper, a Bible with one of those bulletproof covers."

Kayes said "Could you ship me a live new brain?"

"Beg your pardon?"

"A head, in good working order. I could bolt it right on."

Riley said "Got a headache?"

The joke had failed. Kayes paused to say it right. "You remember I asked for one more favor."

"I do indeed."

"Will you please do it soon?"

Riley said "You think she'll still be there?"

"I guarantee it."

"Then what do I say? I don't want to tell her too much, good or bad." Riley might have been contemplating trade with the stars; he was that far out of his element.

But Kayes stayed calm. "Just tell her the news—I'm gone; I've already told her the rest. Then see if she wants you to drive her somewhere, in reason, today. She'd never use my car; and you scared me a little there, mentioning trouble. I guess I was fool enough not to expect it. You know Red's got those peculiar nieces on the Alston farm, the ones with orange hair. They'd take Leah in, for a few days at least. She'll run it from there."

Riley said "Red's house is Black's now, don't forget. I can't make her leave. Far as we're concerned, she can stay on there till the roof falls in or she's dead—one."

Kayes said "That may be any day now." He knew he was suddenly past understanding himself.

"You want her to stay?" Riley spoke with the cool authority of a good secretary, taking dictation.

Kayes had never asked his brother's advice in this before. But the desolation of an airless phone booth forced him on. "What if I say yes, keep her there till I'm back; set her up in style?"

Riley knew at once. "I'd say you were cruel."

Kayes suddenly saw why he hadn't asked sooner—Riley would never volunteer a judgment; but ask him and you got it, full blast, both barrels in the mouth. "Bud, is *cruel* all I've been up to now?"

Riley said "I prize you too much, Kay, to answer that. I think you did what you wanted to. I know you watched where you put your feet. You saw who you crushed. And I doubt you pressed anybody too weak to bear your weight."

Kayes said "Curtis."

Riley said "Well, Curt—" and he paused too.

Kayes knew he could not take up the slack yet. And in that instant, the smell of boys' feet and the scurf of this old phone's mouthpiece hit his empty gut. He swallowed hard at a gob that rose to his tongue and teeth.

Riley said "You and Daphne have swamped that boy. You owe him and me a careful war, Kay. Get your ass back here in one piece soon, and make him a father for a few more years."

Perfect, Kayes thought. *Thank Jesus for Riley.* But all he said was "Bud, my ass comes in halves like yours."

Riley said "I wore my ass off years ago, dragging after you."

Kayes said "I love you."

Riley said "*Ditto.*"

Kayes took ten seconds to crack the door, draw a deep breath and ask the next boy in line for two minutes. Then he dialed the operator and placed a call, collect to Curtis Paschal. The ring went on till he almost quit, though he couldn't imagine the maid at least wasn't home to answer.

Then it stopped, a long wait—Kayes thought it was dead—and Daphne spoke. When the operator asked for Curtis, she said "Curtis Paschal isn't here. I'll accept the charges if your party has a message."

Kayes had not heard Daphne speak in four months; and through that prologue, he could barely listen for the shock he felt in hearing a voice he had all but forgot, a voice he had once loved near to distraction—what?—two or three seconds ago in his life. Time felt that short; his whole sorry life felt five minutes long. So he said "Operator, I'll talk with the lady, if she accepts."

Daphne said "Surely" and the operator vanished.

"Daphne, it looks like I'm in the Army."

"I'm sorry, Kayes." She meant it, though she had not thought of the ways.

"Curt's gone, you say?"

"Right now," she said. "He's out at old Red's place, getting the car."

Blood flooded into Kayes's eyes and mind, but he knew to wait. Then he said "That can't have been Curt's idea."

"It was mine. Your son and I are your family, nobody else yet." Her voice was level, no glint of meanness, just the facts to-date.

Kayes said "But what if I'd got back tonight?"

"The car would have been yours the instant you asked."

He waited again.

So Daphne said "I'm sorry you're mad."

"Oh Jesus, I'm not. I'm standing here though, trying not to break."

Daphne said "I know. Think how I'd have felt if that girl drove your car up here and knocked on the door or left it in the yard."

Kayes said "She's a full-grown woman, Daph, with manners the equal of any I've known. Red raised her, remember, the same as me."

"Your manners—yes, well." Then she heard that they'd come, one more sad time, to the place where every speech was a blade they forced each other to walk, barefoot. "You want to leave some word for Curt?"

"Just the news—the government wants his dad for a while. I'll be in South Carolina by dark and will write him a letter as soon as they let me."

"I'll tell him, Kayes." She seemed to be writing the actual words. "Will you go overseas?"

"May well. This war is far from won."

"We'll both pray for you."

"Can you do that?"

Daphne thought, to be certain. "I haven't stopped yet. I married you—yesterday, it feels like now." Then she almost laughed. "It's hardly likely I'd cease to care."

"Can you say how much?" He amazed himself.

"No, not here, not down a phone wire."

Riley was right; he hadn't broke Daphne. So he honored her pride and said "I'll try to write to you, hear? I'm a rotten—no—I'm the youngest boy in this whole building, and that's a big claim. It's a poor damned excuse, but I swear it feels true." He knew nothing else.

She said "I'm so old, I knew *Elijah.*" And she thought "Where in God's name did that come from?" She found herself laughing.

Kayes joined in, glad for the first time in days.

But before he could say a decent goodbye, she was gone, hung up.

He spoke her name twice to the dead receiver, then hung up also, clamped his eyes to flush the pain and opened the booth. To the tall young Negro patiently waiting, he said "I wish you better luck, friend."

The solemn black face nodded but said "If I get it, be the first time *I* smelled luck."

Kayes wanted to stand, like a steer in the road, and bellow, *bellow*. Very likely nobody here would notice. But he looked for the bus door and soon found a sign for *Loading Dock*. Those wide red double doors had to be it. Three boys that looked a bare fifteen were pushing through, grinning. For a long moment, Kayes saw their skulls and how they looked in the graves they would find, no time from now.

EIGHT

BY FOUR that afternoon, Curtis and Cally his only real friend had shot three squirrels and a rabbit between them. They would head on in by dark, skin the catch and take it to the freezer-locker plant where they were storing the fall and winter meat for a stew to serve their grade at school on an early-spring picnic. But while the light was as good as this, they sat on a broad flat rock by the creek and watched the creatures they had spared for now.

Cally watched anyway; he suspected Curt was not seeing much. Beyond the water was a chattering flock of starlings that a full cyclone could hardly scatter, much less a rifle. They flung their bodies through the woods like handfuls of fat black seed; then walked around like important Negroes, casing the leaves.

Cally knew that today was touchy for Curt, and Curt had not met his eyes for hours, so he finally took the risk and spoke. "You see your pa off?"

Curtis nodded. "Yesterday."

"Will he let you know if they draft his ass?"

"No, Cal. He'll just vanish off like a ghost. He don't give a shit."

The voice was so hard, and the fury behind it, that Cally thought Curt meant all he said—he hated his father for living with a nigger and was glad to lose him. They'd said very little about this, through these past six months; but with Curt not caring now, maybe he could ask. Cal said "You ever get a look at that girl?"

"What girl?"

"Blackie, I guess they call her—you know."

Curtis faced around with eyes blank as washers. And he waited about a month to speak—it felt that long anyhow to both boys. "I spent a good part of this morning with her."

"*No.*"

Curtis swore in silence, with his hand up between them.

Cally had known Curt all his life. Even with a rifle beneath their hands, he knew he was safe. "You feel like telling?"

Curtis looked off again, back toward the starlings but still blank-eyed. Then he passed his left hand over all he saw. "I feel like wiping out everything but me." His right hand dug in the dead rabbit's fur, as if for gold.

Cally said "You'd wipe out *everything*—the WACs and nurses and General MacArthur?" He had always served as Curt's private jokester.

But Curt nodded fiercely.

"Present company included?"

Curtis stood up suddenly; the starlings lifted, then settled again. Cal's rifle was still at his feet on the rock. Throughout what came, Curt kept on hurling rocks at the birds, who hardly noticed. "I flat-out liked her. I saw the damned point."

"In him living with her? Quitting you and your mother to live with a nigger in a one-room shack?"

"Your mother didn't tell you that word was trash?"

Cally said "Sure but I figure she's earned it—that Blackie girl."

"She's old enough to be your mother."

"Thank Christ she ain't." When Curt said nothing, Cal tried again. "You're bound to know what people are saying."

"People are what I'm wiping out, when my time comes."

Cally said "*Halt*, when's that going to be?"

"Me and God only know."

"You think any white girls will go with you now—down the road, I mean, you know, dates and screwing?"

Curtis said "I screw my own right hand. It's free and it's safe, never hurt *nobody*."

"How about your friend God? He claims it's a sin."

Curtis said "Friend God has said He loves my ass, right down to the ground. I bet He forgives me."

"I won't stand by you on Judgment Day though; I might get singed."

"Cally, you were jacking off four times a day, when I thought dicks were plumbing fixtures."

"You know better now."

Curtis said "I know they've caused more trouble than Adolf Hitler and the Japanese Navy."

Cally said "Not mine. Mine's good to me."

"You wait." Curtis put both hands to his mouth and threw a long shout to the trees beyond them. It was not a word; but it seemed to have meaning, though no one bird paid the slightest notice. He took the cool bodies of all they'd killed and, one by one, pitched them gently toward the deepest pool of the creek below them. Then he bent for Cal's rifle and stood a long moment. He thought "Pray Jesus don't let him speak. I might go wild."

But Cally sat calm as the rock beneath them, still watching the pool where the squirrels had sunk. For some weird reason the rabbit's head was floating still.

When it finally sank, Curtis started back to a home he'd rather have died, here now, than see again.

Cally spoke out strong enough to carry. "I'm still what I've always been to you, hear?"

Curtis never looked back.

"That's my damned rifle."

Curt said "Come get it." But he thought "*Die,* fool" and kept on going, hoping he would see, sometime between this minute and the grave, one narrow path in the thicket ahead that darkened now with every step.

NINE

RILEY TURNED OFF the road just before five. He saw at once that the car was missing, and he naturally thought that Blackie was gone. But smoke was rising from the chimney still; and since the house might burn if the stove was lit, he got out and headed up the hill. Before he had gone six feet, up there the door opened; and Blackie was standing—it had to be her, right age and color, though Riley hadn't seen her since Red's funeral-day and then just a glimpse, when her eyes were down.

She watched him come another three steps; then she put a hand to her mouth, turned back and shut the door.

Riley saw a good stick beside the path and leaned to get it, in case of dogs. Since childhood Riley had dreaded dogs; and Red kept a rough old mongrel that could be here. Dogs hated strange skin-color worse than people did. But he got to the front steps with no mishap and stood to wait. Surely she would come to the window at least. When a quiet minute passed, he called out "Hey?" No answer, nothing. So he climbed the rickety steps and knocked. Absolute silence, a far-off crow, cars on the highway two miles west. He tried the china doorknob—open. And he entered slowly.

The room was dark but he stood on the sill and let his eyes open. Then sitting there on Red's old bed was a woman, fine hair and skin, with eyes big as saucers. He said "Is it Blackie? It's been a long time."

"Leah Birch," she said. "You called me Blackie when we used to play."

Riley covered the distance and held out his hand.

She stood and met it—her own palm was cold. Then she went past him and stood by the stove. "I know they took him."

Riley could hear she was sealing a fact, not asking for news. But he gave her a fair account of the trip to Raleigh that morning and Kayes's phone call—no mention of the will of course.

She heard him out, with hardly a move, both her hands flat down on the stove as if it was cool or she was iron. But even when Riley said that Kayes had asked him to drive her to her cousins' for safety, she never budged, shed a tear or spoke. Even as the stillness grew in the room, she stayed there upright frozen inside.

Riley saw Kayes's watch on her wrist. What else? How much more of his brother would walk out of here, if she left now? He didn't mean theft, just sad curiosity. Like others, he noticed when Kayes stopped wearing his wedding ring. Where was that for instance—in his shaving kit? What chance did it have when this all ended, Blackie up North and the war truly won? He told himself he was wasting time. And at last he spoke to Blackie again, "I'm as sorry as you." He had not said what he was sorry for—that Kayes was gone with four people hurt, that this here was ended or that Black must scuttle in the cold dusk now like a wanted thing. That far, Riley was truthful with himself and her—he did not know what he meant and might never.

Still no move from Blackie; was she drunk or doped? So he said

"Kayes is gone, to parts mysterious. That much we know. He and I talked about you as kind as we could. We think you may be in trouble here, if you try to stay on—all the mean old boys aren't dead yet, Leah. So I'll be glad to drive you on to your cousins' place or even the bus station now, while it's light. But listen, it's over. This time here at least."

Of all wild things, she broke out smiling; and her lips came open but still no words. She pointed to the left of Riley, toward the bed.

He looked behind him and there on the floor was a cardboard suitcase, a green umbrella, a bright green coat and a mannish hat. "Good. I'll take these down to the car. But first let's see if the stove is safe."

"Safe. I looked."

Why had that broke her loose? Whyever, Riley knew he must trust her. If the place burned down, and the brush all round it, he must not doubt her now. He saw into Leah's clenched mind that far. He took up the suitcase and said "I guess you'll wear that hat." Then he thought of the dog. "Red's old dog—is he still alive?"

"He was way too old, and nobody round here to take care of him. I killed him, this morning. Buried out back." She pointed through the wall.

"Killed him? How?"

"Red's pistol. One shot." She reached up and tapped the crown of her skull.

"Red never had a gun."

Leah nodded. "*Did*. Your grandmother gave it to her, week before your grandma died."

"Where is it now, Black?"

"In your hand. In that suitcase."

"Is it loaded still?"

She nodded. "Five shots."

"Can I open the bag and take out the bullets? You keep them on you, just not in the gun."

"I'll do it." She stayed there but held out her hand.

So Riley stepped over and gave her the suitcase.

She took it with both hands and looked hard at him. "Riley, please go on down and wait. I won't keep you."

At first he thought she wanted the privacy to open her things; so he stepped out and was halfway down before he thought "Oh God, this is it." He walked on slower, awaiting the shot. If it came, he knew the sheriff would believe him—no risk for him. But for everybody's sake, he hoped she'd live. The sight of her hair came now to his eyes, in beautiful waves. He actually spoke, "No, Black. Go easy."

By the time he reached the car, there had been no sound. So he stood on the far side there and waited. The light was leaking away fast now, and a chill was rising. By then he was thinking it might be fate—he believed more nearly in fate than God, some blind hand liable to thrust in the dark. And nothing behind him, in all his life, told Riley who to blame. He thought they had each done the natural thing, every soul involved. Nobody had set out to strew blood and pain. Nobody was wrong but he knew who lost—everybody in sight, Black and Curtis the most. What was taking so long? He thought "I'll call her name again." It would break whatever spell they were under, that barred them apart while each one waited for life or death. With both hands up to his mouth, Riley called out "Leah?" twice.

And at once she was there in the door, climbing down. Even this late, the green coat looked like spring on the way. The hat was far on the back of her head, and it made her look tall as the nearest pine. She had left the umbrella but clutched the suitcase.

Whatever he believed, Riley said "Thank *you.*" Then he went to help her, the little he could.

When he met her halfway down the path, she held out the bag; and when he took it, his hand brushed hers. To himself Riley said "It was simple as that"—he meant the tie between her and Kayes. What else was it for but two human skins, together awhile? It was not a mean or scornful thought; it was really what he guessed had been here. Now it was over. In all his years, Riley had touched no woman but his homely wife. And though his mind, even now, could drift in warm spring weather, no one yet had drawn him toward her—God knew, none here. This pitiful soul with no home to take her and skin that was four strikes against her, wherever. Again he thought "Just let the pain fade." He mostly found that was all you could hope for.

They reached the car. Riley opened the trunk and put in her suitcase. It didn't weigh six pounds; was this all she owned? Surely she had things stored up North. He knew he had a twenty-dollar bill; he'd give her that much.

By the time he got to the driver's door, Leah had seated herself in back, the usual seat for Negro women bound home from work.

Riley almost asked her to sit up front, no harm in it now. But when he looked in the rearview mirror, he thought he could see that her eyes were closed. He cranked the engine and looked again. By then the eyes were open but fixed; so he said in the gentlest voice he could manage "Which is it—the bus or your cousins' place?"

She waited. "Riley, I just don't—" She stopped, dug into a pocket of her coat and brought out a quarter. She cupped both hands to make a tumbler and shook the coin for a long ten seconds, saying "Heads is the bus." Then she opened her hands and looked. "Heads it is."

"The bus station then?"

"That'll be a first step." She still looked down, talking to the coin.

Riley said "To Wilmington, Delaware?"

"Or North Hell, Arkansas. I'll know when I get there." She suddenly laughed.

He tried to join her. "You sure you got the fare for that distance? I could help you a little."

Leah said "I'm richer than you know, Riley. I could buy me a ticket from here to the moon, if the notion struck me."

"Let it *strike*. Shoot fire!—that's a fine idea." He turned back, grinning at the change of tone.

And Leah nodded to him but said "Easy, child. We're all too sad. Let's show some respect."

Riley also nodded, then backed out slowly. By the time they stopped at the first crossroads, it was pitch-black night, that soon and final, the dark of the moon.

TEN

AT THAT same time a long way south, Kayes woke in a dim bus among boys, mostly asleep and dreaming. He checked the watch of the gaunt lad beside him and saw that somehow he had slept two hours. Then he checked his mind—no dreams he recalled, no blameful faces. But then the stifling pall of grief he had borne all day fell on him again. He shut his eyes and, for the first time, asked to know what he could do to heal some part of the lives he'd crushed—his wife and son and Leah Birch.

Curtis and Daphne at least stood together and shared the weight. But the sight in his mind of Leah alone hurt too bad to watch, even here far off. So he silently asked her face for pardon; no sound came. Why in God's name should it? He knew there was no least hope of pardon till Riley could write and say she was gone, was safe again working and fed somewhere up North where people, at worst, would just ignore her.

It could be a long wait. How could he last through it?—well, minute by minute like all the pain a grown man causes. How could *she*? Kayes tried to imagine her mind, a thing he had never attempted before. Even as a young boy, he thought he had understood his mother when she left them all. He knew he could read all Daphne's thoughts; it was part of why he had to leave—she ached too much every time he touched her.

But part of Leah had stayed shut to him, the part of her mind that planned for him. He was almost sure it had nothing to do with her color; he had known old Red like an easy book. (Among what Kayes could not know here was that, trusting him with her actual life, Leah was forced against her will to hide and damp her hope and dread.) So now he cleared his mind, leaned back again and asked for strength to wait in patience, for the grace to recognize and make all due amends as time cooled down. He sat for a long dry spell in the dark. But no help landed, no word, no clue but the moaning breath of the boy beside him.

In the orange shine of the aisle light, Kayes reached to his own feet, found his shaving kit and felt through it slowly, a blind beggar. Finally, under a damp washrag, he found the ring that Daphne gave him, before God and man, the day they were married fifteen years ago. He knew it would be wrong to wear it now, wrong to all concerned, a sorry joke. But vain as all his prayers had been, this empty circle might hold inside it his only chance of coming back whole from this new danger and starting over in decency.

He knew the notion was maybe childish, maybe wild as Brutus risking his life on a dynamite pill. Still he checked to see that no one watched. Then he brought the gold to his lips and slid it under his tongue. For all the last miles to this place, it stayed there, hard and bitter but hot. He hoped there would be a place at the camp, some vault or locker, to hide it.

But what Kayes knew—all he knew tonight—was a harder fact than a golden ring or even this night that hid the world (they might be parts of a riding dream). This much was true—he had spent from eight to twenty-four hours a day, these six months, beside a kind intelligent person who fit against his mind and body, and *chose* to fit, in every way a sane human being would pray to find this side of death. She was one real woman named Leah Birch—whatever her color or the size of her house—who had finally cared so deep and steady as to all but fill the gully cut in him by his beautiful mother when she heard his prayers one December night and kissed his cheek and then left him forever by morning. Now Lee was gone too. He had run them both off.

Who else on Earth will ever risk Kayes Paschal again?

ELEVEN

FIVE HOURS LATER, home from the picture show and asleep, Curtis told himself the night's first story, a dream to mend as much as he could in his own cut mind. *This boy and I are standing on a hill at the end of what looks like a big picnic—plates on all sides, chicken bones. All but us have gone on home, but we stand here and face the sunset. I tell him we ought to watch till it's gone, completely night. He says well no, then we'll never get down. But I can see he's not really scared; he just may not want to scramble in the dark. I think it's because he's older than me, more dignified. At least he's taller and his eyes blink less. I want his company so I fall in with him as he leaves too.*

He was right. Before we're halfway down, the light is too thin to see the rocks and gullies beneath us. I can't even see him clear ahead. Pretty soon I'm scared but I feel my way by listening to where he puts his feet. Before long though, even they fade off. I'm feeling my way with bleeding hands, from root to root on the steep dry ground. Finally I'm so deep gone in the dark, and losing blood, that I think "I'm going to yell. He's bound to come." But Lord,

I can't remember his name; so I do stop there in the miserable dirt and call my own name, more than once.

Then something pulls my messed-up hands. I can't even see them, but I feel the tug. And then there seems to be a new light, way above me. I'm not even sure which way up *is, but I take a chance. And yes, my friend—is he still my friend?—is flying there in a kind of fire that he seems to throw as he moves, like a falling star. But he rises. He rises in slow perfect circles—he knows the way or is climbing to find it—and after a while, I can barely see. I think he goes that far to catch the last daylight, and I try to wait.*

That's when the line really hurts my hands. My friend is moving now like a kite, and I've got the string. It's a thick plaited line and is almost gone, so I grab at it while I still have time. And recalling kites and how not to lose them, I reel him toward me turn by turn till, sure, he's back on the ground in reach. But his back is turned. By now I'm guessing it's Kayes somehow. Once he moves though, he's dark again and I can't know. Still I feel the line draw tight once more, and I guess he's tugging me on back down. Without even knowing his face or voice, I try to bet he's taking me home.

Even as the dream threaded Curt's mind and drew him on, in a whole cool room of his understanding, he saw he was dreaming, saw he was easing himself ahead with childish hope. Yet in that same room, he had watched Kayes soar and wished him luck. From the ground Curt even shouted his thanks to the arms that worked in pure dark now—or so he trusted. At the least, that sight of a useful father let Curt sleep till Sunday daylight, clear and dry with slow church bells, the first whole day of his grown man's life.

THE FORESEEABLE FUTURE

SUNDAY

6 MAY 1945

WHIT WAS TURNING her doorknob before he remembered and pulled his hand back. *She told us to knock.* The first time his daughter demanded privacy, he cringed to hear it. Her own room, a shut door guarding her secrets. It clearly meant he'd lost her for good. *Face it, Whit, and hope to get past it. Liss is leaving. A twelve-year-old child is more than half gone.* But Liss was more than half the reason Whit was here at all—in life, in the world. *She's leaving though.* Then he heard her laugh, one high note stuck in the air like a blade.

"You can *entrez,* Pa."

Her voice had generally come as a rescue and never more than now. Whit opened the door and took a step in. Dark as it was, it was her world at once. The mild smells of her skin and hair claimed the whole space. His hand automatically went toward the light switch.

She said "Don't, please. Sit here on the bed. Your eyes'll adjust."

Whit took the last steps and sat on the edge of her narrow mattress, hard as a soldier's. She was lying on her back, and her long legs marked the center line. They stayed quiet an easy while till his eyes widened. Then a few watts of glow from the bedside clock were all he needed to find her face. Elissa Wade, the good thing he'd done. He didn't say it but was quick even so to correct himself, *Her mother and I.* Finally he said "You know I'm leaving."

Liss waited so long he thought she was asleep. Then she laughed again. "Your business trip? Don't make it sound worse than the Chinese children."

Whit's mouth smiled, helpless. He wanted more than anything to lay his head right now on her knees, just in abject thanks for her life. But eight months ago, June had written him plainly that Liss was a woman—

I tried to tell her what to expect. But it's always a stunner. And it caught her in school, after lunch today. She did have the sense to go to her teacher and get some quick help. But once she came home at four o'clock and saw me waiting, she broke right down. I of course boohooed but now we're fine.

Reading that, Whit had made a vow to touch Liss only when others were present. So now he laughed at her Chinese children. "I guess I don't sound that thrilled to go. At least the weather's mild."

Liss said "Not in school. We sit in those hard desks and sweat like hogs."

"Sugar, hogs don't sweat, not on Uncle Tuck's farm. When do you finish?"

"June the eighth, six years from now."

She'd worked the oldest child's game of all, sliding the grownup out of his world and into hers. In early childhood she'd been unselfish as any grown saint. But only here lately Whit had caught her stopping at the front-hall mirror to watch her face. He said "Liss, anybody smart as you ought to study overtime five nights a week, just making her brain do somersaults." By then he could see the shape of her face, the great dark eyes and all that crown of thick black hair.

Her hand came up from the sheet in a crisp salute. "Aye, aye, Sergeant Wade. By Wednesday then I'll be a big genius."

"I'll be gone till Friday. You can wait till then." Liss had left her hand up near her brow. It was a simple habit but one she'd fallen into most nights of her life since she was a baby, her welcome to sleep. For whatever cause, to Whit tonight it seemed like an angel's parting wave—the absolute last glimpse he'd get of perfect beauty. In this world at least. He tried to say her entire name, "Elissa Anne Wa—" Then his voice quit on him.

He was not a weeper. In fact, not quite a year ago in a French cow-pasture with a hole the size of a fist in his chest, he begged for tears—anything to drain the agony—but no tears came. Now he waited for calm, and he asked himself *What in God's name is so wrong now?*

In the dark her left hand found his left fist. It opened to take her, and she said "I think you just need more time. Pa, I can lie here at twelve years old and remember bad dreams I had when I was three. Remember the night I saw the Devil, clear as you, walking toward me down a long red hall? It scares me right now." With a finger she made a cross in his palm. They were lifelong Protestants, who'd only seen Catholics cross themselves in movies. But for years they'd blessed each other that way. Then she said "Look. Count last week's blessings—we're all three healthy, old Hitler died, peace'll be blowing through any day now. Count that far anyhow and then you'll relax."

Whit tapped her lips one quick time for silence. "Don't jinx peace, Liss. It's taken too long, too many dead boys."

"And children. And women. But you know it's coming, don't you?"

Whit said "Darling, I fervently hope."

Again she crossed his folded hand, on the ropey back. "And then you'll be home."

Whit brought the blessing to his dry lips. "Thank you, doctor. In spite of myself, I may yet live." *I may* yet *live?* It came as a shock, just knowing he'd said it. They were hard words to lay on a child. But Liss had heard worse. Howling nightmares, in this same voice—inside this house in the past five months. He touched the cool back of his hand to her forehead, the way he'd felt her for fever years back. He could feel her nod. So he told himself *Now go to your own room, and pray you mean to live.*

He'd left Liss's door more than halfway open. So when June switched on the bathroom light, it fell into this room and over them both.

June was four steps away. "I'm headed in here to *try* to bathe these weary bones. But tired as I am, I may well drown. If I'm not out in under ten minutes, please dredge up the corpse and dress it decent."

Liss said "Sing, Ma. Then if we hear gargling, we'll know to rush in."

Whit said "It's a promise," and June shut the door. But all Whit saw in that quick moment was Tim Grant's face just under the surf, not a whole year ago. Dead for good on a beach in Normandy and smiling like a high-school yearbook picture. One of the nineteen yearbook boys Whit saw shot dead that same chill morning.

Liss said "How far you going this week?"

"Clear down to the coast—Nags Head, Manteo. Lot of claims down there from last month's storm." *No claim from Tim Grant.*

"Will you pay everybody?"

I know nineteen that'll never get a cent. But he said "Liss, I'm paid *not* to pay. Insurance adjustors get a hearty hand-clasp from the district manager for every penny we shave off your claim."

Liss said "I ain't lost nothing, Pa, not the last time I looked."

Whit knew he'd loved her far too much, from the day she was born; so he'd trained himself to rein in his thoughts. *Don't ever tell yourself she's perfect, don't ever think she'll stay past twenty, this child will leave.* But tonight he said what seemed the only truth, "Lady, all you've lost yet is fingernail clippings. God just keeps hanging the presents on you."

Liss laughed. "I knew I was tall, but I'm not a damned hat-rack."

The *damns* had thickened in her speech lately. Whit leaned forward and lightly clamped her lips.

She mumbled against him, "Mmm, mmm, *mmmm*."

So he wound up holding her longer than he meant to. Then he stood slowly. "Said your prayers?"

"Yes Pa, long since. And I said em *my* way."

"Lying here on your back, in the hot pitch dark?"

"Yes, Father dear."

"Liss, I've told you. Serious prayers are—"

" '—Said on your knees, on the hard oak floor, with a good bright light so you don't fall asleep.' "

Whit said "My sentiments, more or less exactly."

"Rest easy, Pa. You're safe another day. I've seen to that."

He was in the doorway with both hands overhead, hooked in the framing. Liss was the one who always knew him. He could wipe his face as blank as chalk, she'd always see the one scared cell. He said "How so? You hired me an escort?"

"God and I have a deal."

"Can you tell me?" Whit said. He recalled his own childhood so clearly that it always surprised him to find Liss thinking of him as she did. At her age, he could hardly see the adults, much less pray for them.

Liss thought it out carefully. "Prayers are the biggest secret I've got. So please don't ask. Just trust me again."

He said "You're all I trust on Earth." It had slipped past his guard; but when he said it again in his mind, it felt near enough to the truth to stand.

Liss laughed again. But this time her voice dipped so low that Whit barely heard her above the tub water. "Don't load me too heavy," she said. "I may break."

He said "You won't."

She said "Good *night*" and a wide yawn caught her.

Well before Whit had walked the distance to his and June's room, a picture of Liss as a grown woman struck him. All his visions, even the one he'd seen in France, were of people's faces. And here in the empty air of the hall, Liss stood, full-grown. She had already got to be taller than June with long deep hair, fine as the day that had just shut behind them, and green eyes welcome as the world's first leaves. Standing still, in the sound of June's bath, Whit met those green eyes and felt proud to hope they could look out steady, each day of her life, as they had today in innocence. He thought *That ought to be all you need, Whit, from this vale of woe.*

But five minutes later, he was in his pajamas and on his knees. As always he said the prayer he made for himself at sixteen, *I'm more than half blind in my heart so guide my steps. I want to do right by you and my loved ones and the people I hate, but I'm weak as a yearling without your hand. Through Jesus, Amen.* Even now—in one piece, half alive at home—his mind snagged on doubt like a dry wood splinter. *Is it all a damned trick? Does anything hear me?* Whit had always thought of God as a thing, and nothing he'd seen in France or since had really changed that.

But he pushed past doubt. *If it's all a trick, I'll know soon enough.* He'd had enough anesthesia to guess that the worst death could be, barring Hell and fire, was dreamless sleep. So next he took up—one by one, with their full names—June and Liss, his Uncle Tuck and a few old friends. He gave thanks again for coming home safe in body, if not mind or soul. Last he brought up the thing that was eating his heart in huge raw pieces but that he couldn't name.

I know it sounds childish but I'm still balked. You tried to bring me back from death and safe home here. But I can't obey, not yet in my mind. You bless me daily with a patient wife, a daughter I'd chew ground glass to save from the slightest harm and a fair-paid job. But I feel like the worst old broken window the wind blows through. Nothing tastes good to me but the sight of my child. And before I know it, she'll be gone from here. I still keep thinking I ought to have stayed. Stayed dead in France with my dead friends, all younger than me. Nothing needs me here. I could vanish this minute and do less harm than I do every day I hang on here and fail my kind, my decent kin. I may be asking for something to love, that needs *my love, in a good right way. But you tell me.*

Whit waited on the floor to hear June's name. No one alive had been kinder to him or shown more patience in his five months back here, dazed and numb. His mind drew up a clear picture of her face, and he studied it thankfully. No love though, no hand out toward her. She'd thrive without him and so would Liss. Whit still knew suicide was wrong. But equally plain, he knew the world was already choked on the walking wounded; and what else was he? A useless victim, dead but not buried. *What worthwhile thing, alive on Earth, is wanting and needing my life to last?* Again, no answer. So he asked for permission to go on out or for light to see by, a road to take. *Let that be soon,* he thought. *Amen.*

He could hear June and Liss saying their goodnights. So he stayed down kneeling another whole minute to wait for an answer, if an answer was planned. More than once he'd been answered, though never in words. But tonight silence spread round him like tar, that dark and dense. His God was like that, not something he could stash in his vest watch-pocket and feel tick against him. God was a thing from far outside that kept Its own counsel and came, when It came, like a cyclone by night.

When he'd taken that brutal hole in his chest, and the blood was pumping into cool French dirt, Whit somehow managed to say his old prayer before he blacked out. And while he was out, he saw God plain as a highway sign. God or one of God's troops, a tall young creature with tiger eyes—that brown and gold, by no means human. The wide lips opened on visible music which poured on forth like a better reward than Whit hoped to get. He'd thought *That's it. I'm dead. But at least it's Heaven.*

Whit was used to God's silence. More often than not, it was what he expected. So tonight he stood up, turned back the white chenille cover and entered his side of the ample bed. The women's voices were trailing off. Then June's voice lowered and all Whit could hear was the rain outside. He knew they were whispering; they did most nights. And though he knew they were dealing in secrets, he mostly didn't mind. They'd proved they loved him, for what that was worth. The busy murmur that reached him now even made him smile. Whatever he'd failed, in these blank months, he had managed this—a stout dry house where women could face the night with no dread.

Two minutes later when June came to join him, Whit was actually asleep. Since he never tried to read in bed, the lamp was on her side. She had already laid her robe on the chair and switched off the light before he woke. So he turned his head toward her but stayed quiet while she slipped in gently, a leaf into water. Their door to the hall, as always, was open. And the night light crept from there and showed June's profile two feet beyond him. Though his eyes were clear, she still looked as young as the first day he saw her. So he watched her carefully through nearly shut eyes. He knew she was saying her own prayers now. For an instant he wondered what she might be asking. What in the world could he mean to her now, after eighteen years, more than half his life? Or were her thoughts somewhere else completely? Who was she to him? What if she vanished now, just faded out as he lay here watching? He knew at least that it wouldn't kill him. And the thought didn't scare him.

Then he tried what he'd tried so many nights since coming home. He worked to recall what they'd been for each other, young and drawn together like birds. He could see clear scenes of his own young taste for June's young body. He could hear exact whole sentences of pleasure in June's voice, covered by night in his first old car with the windows fogged by both their breaths. But now they reeled past his eyes like scenes from another life, nobody he knew or could want to watch. *That boy and girl are nothing to you. You let them be. Don't foul their memory.* Here, in reach though, was the same good woman. And she'd proved her devotion by seamless acts of care and faith through the worst early days of his time back home.

The first night back, when he'd dreaded showing the purple scar through which he died, June shook her head with pity to see it. But far from turning away or shirking, she'd risen above him in this same bed and bent to press her warm lips against it. He remembered saying "They say it'll fade" and June saying "Whit, it changes *nothing*." Yet all these dead months later together, he'd never fully thanked her body with words or touch. He'd never truly managed to prove that—in spite of dying four thousand miles east in the fat green grass of a Norman field—he was live again in a house in Raleigh and wanted June Wade's body near, to use and thank.

June's face turned slowly toward Whit and went dark. She kept her distance but tried to send her mind out toward him. What she thought was how, in a hundred and fifty nights back here, their bodies had met maybe ten quick wordless times and with no real profit for her or him. Was there some way now, this one spring night, they could break down whatever thick glass kept them apart? And then could they know each other as what they'd once been, for love and rest? June thought all that but she strained not to move, not to shy him again. Now she was only a near dark presence, maybe a hand's breadth closer than usual. For a still minute they felt each other's odorless breath, just warmth and fog. Then past the level of consciousness, each caught the frail clean animal scent of the other's skin. And both minds suddenly moved together.

It scared Whit badly and the wound burned hot. More strongly though, and for unknown reasons, he wanted to find her by pure blind touch. His whole mind said *Let's try this slow and with no human word.*

But June said "You seemed sad all day."

All day? Years *of days. And scared, not sad.* But her voice was kind, so his hand patrolled the sheet between them till it honestly seemed she was not there. Then he found her lower knee. There he wedged his fingers between her legs and, balked by rayon, slid on up till he stopped where she was warmer than he'd guessed. At first Whit couldn't believe what he found. More than once in these five months, he'd rolled down on her and oared away toward the point of light out *there* in his mind, though he'd never reached it, not gladly at least. But now this instant, grown as he was, most cells of his mind went green as a boy's and said *Now. Take your luck.* Only one small lobe held back and wondered. *Why start a job you know you can't finish? Why tell her a lie?*

June caught his drift and whispered slowly "Liss is asleep and her door's shut tight." When he still balked, her hand took his. And with a swift bravery he barely remembered from their first days, she made him nearly as strong as she. That saw them through a long ten minutes to mutual ease.

Till the actual moment when his last thrust bloomed, Whit couldn't believe he'd reach the goal. He'd forgot the goal and its broad-winged sweetness. He'd even forgot that the goal was a *place.* But once he was there—that long high moment—and settled back slowly to Earth unharmed, he realized that his deepest hope of all had been met: they had done all this and not said a word. June had not pulled so much as *love* or *thanks* from him. But she'd helped him reach that beautiful place and the peaceful lowlands that sloped down from it.

And when she was there herself, a minute later, she had the keen grace not to pour speech on it.

Whit rolled left slowly and drew her with him, so they both lay facing and both still dark. Whit thought there might be some chance for him now. He'd died. One doctor had actually said it, "You outright died, Sergeant. Why'd you come on back?" And here this minute for the first time yet, he'd glimpsed the actual chance of life. He might yet want to live above ground. He might even be some good to his world.

June also thought *He's begun to come home, after two years gone in England and France—then all those sick beds—and these flat numb months back in sight, the two of us huddled up under this roof like courteous strangers. He's begun to find home.* She trusted herself enough to think that she was Whit's home, she and this house and the child they'd made. She even caught sight of the hope of contentment. But she still didn't speak. With her left thumb, she found his eyebrows and stroked them down like wings that had flown every mile he covered from Normandy here.

Whit wanted to thank her. But he wanted peace more, this

healing stillness that lapped him now. Everything that had hurt, since he left his mother's body, had come with noise. When tears came finally, they came in silence. But he brought June's hand down and let her know their warmth and meaning.

Even then, she only wiped them away—no word, no sound.

Whit knew she wanted him here with her always. She'd said it so often, it sometimes seemed like all he knew but the days of the week and his handmade prayer. Then he wrote a clear sentence inside his skull, *Do I want anything on Earth but sleep?* In his mind he had no more than stepped back to read it and hunt down the answer when black sleep took him.

At four in the morning, June woke as she often did. She checked Whit's breathing—deep asleep still. Then she switched on her lamp to read a soothing few pages in her book, *The Robe.* Whit was flat on his back with his face tilted her way. She leaned and actually touched her chin to his fine mouth, a feather touch. It seemed that he'd been smiling already, and she thought the smile widened. But no, thank God, he didn't wake. June doubted she'd caused it (it was in her nature to refuse the credit). But anyhow it firmed the hope she'd glimpsed five hours ago—*He's on his way at least, toward me.*

Whit though was dreaming his usual dream. It was one more version of the time that he'd spent bleeding in a pasture, his run toward death with every pulse of an eager heart, glad of the nearness of that much rest and gladder still when sufficient blood was finally gone and death could fill his empty skin with unimagined peace and rest.

MONDAY

7 MAY 1945

WHIT WOKE UP rested, with less than his usual dread of the road. By the time he was dressed and downstairs for breakfast, Liss and June were far into the day.

Running for school, Liss pecked a kiss on the crown of his hair as he sat over coffee.

Then as she paused with the front door open, she called back toward him her old farewell, "Bring me something expensive!"

He and June barely spoke as he ate his eggs. Just the easy familiar syllables of years, the start of each day. But while she was packing his roadside snacks, she said "I hope you won't mind, but you look like yourself for the first time in years."

Whit wanted to ask her to list the ways. But he only said "Poor you, watching that."

Then the early mist burned off the trees; and all through the first two hours on the road, June's simple claim warmed in his mind as one more sign that he truly might live and someway thrive, from whatever desert he'd roamed here lately.

So he settled his first claim in Zebulon and was five miles short of Rocky Mount at ten-thirty when hunger struck him, and he looked for a place to stop awhile. Whit had worked this stretch of the road for years. And now he was sure that, in two more bends, an ideal place would lie on his right—a wide level shoulder and a poplar grove.

It was there, though the trees were oaks and seemed taller; and the old emptiness was also changed. Across the road on his left, somebody had hauled in a pale blue trailer with black smoke curling, on this warm a day, and three identical yellow dogs posted like monuments between it and him. *Monuments to what?* he actually wondered, but he smiled to himself and stopped anyhow.

The dogs didn't flinch.

So slowly Whit opened his door, got out and stood there to test them.

They registered him with twitching noses and consulted each other with earnest looks but nobody barked.

So Whit hiked off through the trees to pee. Peeing outdoors had been a real pleasure, all his life. Not for show to any passing human but just for the sense of doing something right, returning a loan of minerals to the Earth and showing a secret part of himself the look of the sun. He buttoned up neatly, glanced slowly behind him, saw his path was clear and returned to the car.

He reached in back for June's box of snacks. She parceled them out into five lunch bags, each one marked with the name of the day and neatly stapled. For the hell of it, Whit took the one that said "Wednesday" and sat on the left-front fender to eat. A bag of salted peanuts, three dried figs and a knotty green apple. Damn, he'd forgot to buy a Coke and was set for dry rations. But he dived in anyhow and choked it all down .

The dogs watched every bite, still checking each other for confirmation that a sizable event was due any instant.

Whit thought *Sorry, boys, nothing's happening here but a pitiful ghost exercising his jaws in front of a trailer ugly as Pittsburgh* (which he'd never seen). He didn't speak though, just brushed his hands and stood to leave.

A strong voice said "Son, you got to be choking. How about some cool water?"

Whit searched and had almost concluded that one dog could talk. Then he saw a man's face in the open porthole beside the trailer door. How long had it been there, grinning that wide? "Man, you scared me."

The face disintegrated into laughter. Then it finally said "I'm about as damned scary as a hot corn pudding."

Whit said "Haven't got a corn pudding *ready*, have you?"

The face said "No, just water like I told you."

Whit walked to the center of the two-lane road. The dog tails wagged in time like pendulums, and the smallest dog began to quiver with urgency. It came over Whit in a sickening wave that something was wrong, something here that would harm him. He looked to the grinning face again, grinned back at it and stated his fear in the odd way it came. "You're not a German spy, by any chance?"

A high long laugh, as safe as your mother's. "I was, till last month when they started losing. Till then, they kept me in high old style—big dinners, rock candy, all the beer I could drink. But once they saw peace barreling down, they dropped me flat, from a Stuka bomber at a high damned height."

Whit said "Trailer and all?"

"Trailer and dogs and my business sign." A fat hand appeared and pointed down.

Whit had missed the sign, small as it was. But propped by the cinderblock steps to the door was a miserable sign—*Mother Marie, Her Healing Words*. "Where's Mother?" he said.

"You don't *look* blind. She's grinning at you, boy." The smile on the face spread wider still.

Whit stepped forward to the edge of the yard. "These dogs aren't likely to kill, you don't think?"

"Hell no, more liable to kiss you to death. Come on in here." The face withdrew and the narrow door opened. A short stout middle-aged woman with bobbed tan hair stood smiling in a cotton house dress, figured but faded. Her face was not exactly ugly, but it had the kind of blank space between the eyes that can make any face hard to watch.

To Whit she looked more like a lady wrestler than a spiritual healer. But it all seemed worth a five-minute look, so he stepped on into the midst of her yard.

No kisses from the dogs. Not one of them moved any more than his head. They were all three male with black eyes hard as iron buttons.

She said "Call me Juanita."

"Why not Marie?"

"That's my spiritual name," she said and laughed even longer. As before, the laugh separated from her body and rose yards over her head—a strong bird cry, not ominous exactly but wild and free and about as spiritual as a band-saw spinning.

Up under the trailer, Whit thought he could see what looked like a long folded banner and a set of those round stools that animals pose on in circus acts—elephants and lions. He grinned at Juanita. "You work in a show?"

"Oh no," she said. "Just out of my home here. I'm *from* back up that last dirt road you passed—Juanita Branch, grew up around here, spent a few years down in Myrtle Beach misbehaving myself but finally got homesick and paid a sailor thirty-five dollars to haul my trailer back home six months ago. I'd had my bait of high society, at Myrtle and all. Now I love this *peace*. Course, none of my kin will recognize me. I dressed this body good as I could and went to church just yesterday morning—wore a straw hat, man. I looked all round till I saw what's bound to be my kid brother, Brent—can't be *two* men with eyebrows that long. And once I smiled, Brent knew it was me and started to wave. But then that wall-eyed Prickett girl he married saw me too and jerked the shirt half off of him. Brent and I both got a little laugh out of that. But all of a sudden, maybe five minutes later, that wife stood up and got Brent out of there and *gone* in his truck while my eyes were shut, just trying to pray. I'd thought that if anybody up here wanted me, I'd try to live quiet on my savings awhile and not show off. But after that treatment from my own blood kin, I guess I'm free to set up business by the public road and be anybody I damn well please. Mother Marie was my working name when I first went south. So I put that old sign out this morning, not an hour ago. Maybe I heard you coming from afar."

"My car's right loud."

Juanita laughed and shook her head. "I seldom heal cars."

Whit said "But you could?"

She nodded. "Not on Mondays."

Whit's pre-war taste for fun boiled up. *Lead her on a little. See how far she'll go.* But how could you fool with a face that homely? He took a good shut-eyed dose of the sun and finally said "What are healing words? Give me just a short sample." And to his surprise, that seemed to be the signal.

The question had no more than left Whit's lips when a dog broke pose and came to within a short lunge of his leg. It still didn't growl but cocked its big head to study him better.

Juanita ignored it. "Drink your water first, man. I didn't call you over here to take your money. I saw you choking that dry lunch down." With an uncanny lightness she turned, vanished and—before Whit could count—was back and down the steps beside him with a tin cup brimming water so cold it hurt every tooth by name as it passed.

It hadn't reached his stomach before he thought *That could be pure arsenic or lead. I'm sunk.* He gave Juanita the cup and said "Best water I've had since the day I died."

"Course it is. I bless it every day." She upended the cup, high over the near dog's head.

The dog looked up at it, waiting as calmly as if this happened several times a week.

Then she let the last drop roll down toward him.

He caught it like a fly, with a snap of his teeth, then seemed pacified and moved back off.

Whit said "You put some kind of spell on it?"

She frowned and then laughed. "Oh no, I'm a Baptist. I just ask God to bless every jug I take from the spring—when I remember that is, most days."

That sounded more like it. Whit finally smiled. "Can I buy a few words?" He thought it would anyhow be a good way to see how she lived, what she had in the trailer.

She put up a finger in the sign for *Wait*. Then she stepped round the trailer and came back with two old-time beach chairs—wood frames, canvas slings. She handed Whit his and set up her own, right there in the dirt.

The sun was way too fine to refuse. So he followed her lead and sat nearby.

The dogs all came a few steps closer and sprawled to watch. Again they monitored Whit with consultations among themselves that had their own eloquence, stronger than speech.

Whit said "This dog team here—they work with you, do they?"

Juanita said "Yes."

Then Whit noticed they were all aimed at him like spokes of a wheel, with him as the axle. But they had the smiles of normal hot dogs now, panting a little. He rolled his own head back and faced the sun. When he looked down, dazzled, he turned to Juanita.

She undid her two top buttons on a diamond of skin, white as cottonmouth gums. There was not much else to notice but small breasts. Rare on so well-set-up a woman and oddly reassuring to her clients—a stout woman, undersized in the chest, is serious business. She finally looked at Whit dead-level and said "First thing is, I don't *charge* money. You tell me your pains. I tell you whatever thoughts I get—and thoughts come at me fast, out of the blue. If you get inspired and begin to look glad, I stop right there. If not, I'm liable to start telling lies, depending on how my pocketbook feels. But you're somebody that's bound to start me. I knew it before you finished those peanuts. I said 'Anybody that can eat dry peanuts is loved by the Lord.' So if I say anything that feels right, feels like it might help you or those you love, you're welcome to thank me as you see fit—cash money or check, right now or years later. I've got cashier's checks stacked up, this minute, from boys I rescued five years back—eighty-odd dollars' worth."

Whit said "Good."

"See, I trust you, man. You might be a felon with a blade up your sleeve. But the way you drank that poison I gave you, makes me know you're honest."

"I thought it was poison," Whit said. "How strong?" He intended to smile but when he tried, it felt thin and pasty and quickly died.

Juanita waited, not batting an eye. Then she laughed so long the dogs looked embarrassed. "Let your heart start beating, man. H_2O is all you drunk."

Whit smiled. "I got badly wounded in France, eleven months ago, the Normandy invasion, first day around noon. My chest got torn into by some great punch that opened enough veins to bleed me dead. Then two medics found me and somehow brought me more than half back. Not all the way though, Juanita, *see*?" The best he could, Whit blanked all feeling from his eyes and face and showed Juanita, not the actual scar but his true appearance.

She studied it slowly, then nodded. "Shell shock."

"That was World War I."

"They're mostly the same, the wars I've seen." She spoke as matter-of-factly as if she'd seen all the wars since Greece hit Troy. "I don't mean to say you didn't get hurt. I can read eyes, man, and yours got *hurt*. But you're looking better—look good to *me*. Need a pound or two to fill out your clothes."

Whit said "No, I died."

Juanita took time to reconsider. Her pale blue eyes worked slowly from his shoes on up to his face. Then she smiled. "As dead folks go, you eat a big lot of snacks. I hear these sulfa drugs are saving boys daily. If only we'd had em ten years ago, my husband would be here. Ruptured appendix—turned him green as a garter snake and nothing I could do, much less the doctor."

Whit said "I'm trying to tell you what happened. I was running through a pasture with five black cows, headed for the finest barn I've seen, with flint-stone walls and a red tile roof. My squad was in there, all but me and Phil Dewar, when some kind of great light bloomed in my face. A mortar round, shell fire, shrapnel, whatever. I stayed conscious long enough to look down and know I was gone for good. I also noticed Phil Dewar was hit, but both of his eyes were open on me. He was dead, still looking at me for help. By then though so much of my blood was gone, I went on and—honest to Christ—I died."

She nodded. "Don't doubt it. But how did you know?"

"I saw a vision of God as a boy or a tall young angel. I could see him talk music."

"*Had* to be dead." Juanita was telling it straight to the dogs, and they consumed it with fixed attention. For all the surprise her eyes betrayed, she might have heard such tales at least daily. Then she faced Whit again and beamed a new grin—she had what looked like fifty gold teeth and deep dimples. They took years off her, though not many pounds.

For the first time yet, Whit thought she was a woman. And he checked to see how he felt about it. There was that broad blank space between her eyes, and she was past forty and bigger than him. For all his feeling no pull to touch her, he wasn't repelled. But she might have been an old school-friend turned up on a bus. He said "My wife and daughter say I'm doing better."

"What do you say, man?"

"My name's Whitley Wade, call me Whit—I'm not sure. I'm thirty-four years old, a lovely family I'd die to save, my same old job but with better prospects—" He stopped and whistled through his teeth at a dog.

"That's Don," she said. "Don't lead *him* on." Don was standing up and Juanita addressed him, "Sit back down, son. I'll tell you what next." Then she laid both hands out before her like pink dinner-plates in the generous light. She settled them slowly on her ample thighs. They looked like normal stout-lady hands, flushed and stuffed. One white-metal ring with a blue glass stone. "These hands built the pyramids—"

She's cracked after all. Whit eyed Don again.

Don was eyeing him with the fevered intensity of creatures ready to burst into song or tear out your throat.

Juanita said "You think we're crazy."

Whit said "I think *I* am."

"Tell me how." Her eyes were shut but the good effects of her smile survived.

So Whit shut his eyes and again faced the sky. The sun was cloudless and soon bore in through his lids. One more time, he was back at the moment his chest caved in. But to calm himself this time, he thought *Tell her the whole thing. If she tells the world, nobody'll believe her.* So he said "I hurt in every cell of my body. It has not stopped one conscious instant since June of last year. All the nerves from my waist up were ripped to shreds. If I'm truly alive, then when can it stop?" His eyes were still shut. And though he went on feeling the pain, his memory didn't bring back the sight of whatever creature had come to receive him at death's calm door.

In a level normal human voice, Juanita said "Nobody said *live* didn't mean hot pain. Since four years old, I've had eight surgeries to scrape dead bone here out of my leg—osteomyelitis. Twice they couldn't use ether because of my heart; I had rheumatic fever as a child. Take a minute and guess how good that felt." Nothing in her voice was asking for pity. "Did your brain get damaged or any of your backbone?"

Whit said "Not actual physical damage. What hurts is my soul."

"That *will* give you fits. Are you saved?" she said.

He said "Pretty surely. I'd rather drink lye than talk about it, but I accepted Christ when I was thirteen."

"And you know he loves you?"

Whit said "I do"—his eyes were still shut. And he braced for an oncoming missionary spiel. If it came, he would thank her and fight his way out through whatever trouble the dogs threw at him.

But Juanita kept up a long breathing silence. Then with a first little yip in her voice, as if she might have waked herself up, she said "Whitley Wade, you are now alive. Any day you'll realize that you have been healed."

It opened his eyes at least. He sat up and searched her face for more news. Nothing, blank as rice. He said "It just happened?"

"Ne' mind about when."

He said "You don't touch me?"

She said "I'd have touched you, if I'd seen a need."

"So you just prayed for me?"

By then Juanita had said her say. It turned out she had a deep pocket in her dress. She reached in, pulled out a long white rubber bone and flung it an easy twenty yards into thick underbrush. All three dogs lit out silently to find it and soon disappeared. She said "I just deviled me a dozen fresh eggs. You want to eat some, with hot cornbread and cold buttermilk?"

Whit said "Hold on. Is that all I get? I don't feel changed. I want Mother Marie. What would she tell me now?"

Juanita was still faced off toward the dogs. "She'd say you've been on a long hard trip, and it's been over now for some little while. You slept past the end. Lots of people do that, when they've died like you and been sent back. But you opened your eyes thirty seconds ago. You're back, that's all."

"So how do I act?"

"You already know. Any yellow dog knows."

"I might want to find me some willing woman and plow up the ground with just her face." Then sudden shame flushed him; where the hell had that come from? He had meant to speak of a hot urge to love, and it came out that mean.

But Juanita grinned. "There's plenty women yonder in Rocky Mount, ready. Just walk down back of the depot, man—they're cheaper than me and *my* help lasts. But you don't want any such thing now, on a day fine as this; and you damned well know it. You're kinder than me."

By now he could laugh. "Who told you that?"

"The cast of your eyes and my powers, so to speak."

Whit smiled. "You got em. Why hide down here in the backsticks though? Folks all over both Carolinas are sad and don't know why. You could do great good and make a cool killing."

He knew he was feeling two opposite ways—half grateful, half mocking.

Juanita said "When this war's over, I may move on. I'm old enough to remember 1918. Everybody said peace would solve all problems. God knows, I never saw folks any meaner, sadder or wilder than what came next."

"And it's coming again, any day—world peace." He said it smiling but it actually hurt, as if he'd somehow be exempted when the armistice came and must fight on alone.

"I'm not so sure. Those Germans can *fight*." She spoke with what seemed first-hand knowledge.

Whit said "I can surely drink to that. But Hitler's dead—what?—a few days now. No two dozen Germans are crazy enough to fight, now he's gone."

Juanita paused and her face was dead-earnest. "Hitler's *dead*? Old Satan himself? You got powers too?"

Whit laughed. "Got a radio. Don't say you don't."

"Far from it," she said. "Why you think I'm grinning so much of the day?"

It might have been instants; it might have been weeks, but somehow Whit phased out about then. Either that or he'd suffered more harm than he knew. Maybe the water was drugged after all. Or maybe Juanita had worked a change or was somehow a sacred thing herself and converted to light as they sat there speaking of deviled eggs, dogs and Adolf Hitler. Whit thought he was conscious. He knew he was sober, no pills or liquor for four months now. But what his mind confessed to seeing in extra-slow motion was a Nash County woman—maybe five foot three, a hundred eighty pounds—dissolve into some substance brighter than daylight and then condense in the space between them and hang for a while like a flame to touch or a cup to hold and raise to your lips.

Whit thought of the flash he'd seen in France. But this one was brighter. It lacked a roar and caused no pain. For once he listened hard for sound, a syllable telling him what to do—fall forward in worship to spare his eyes or open his mouth and let his throat pour out the true song he felt growing in him or try to stand and head for his car and get the hell on into Rocky Mount and pray it was still there, serving chopped barbecue and fried cornbread.

He didn't know it yet, but his eyes were open. And finally his right hand seemed free to move. It jerked straight up and stroked his chin, testing to see if he'd grown a beard or had anything as human as hair singed out of his hide in the shining change. What he felt was the normal noonday stubble, a low-grade abrasive. And there, the same two yards beyond him, was Juanita. She was still short and chunky as a stump, not grinning exactly but plainly not scared.

And she said "I've done everything I know."

Whit laughed and thought *I hope you have.*

Then she stood in place and yelled up her dogs. It took a few calls.

But in time they answered from what seemed miles and canyons away—first Don, then Walker, then Ann Marie (though plainly a male). She faced round to Whit. "I better get in now. I sunstroke easy." She took a few steps, then turned and said "What I really got to do is, listen to my programs. 'Ma Perkins' starts in five more minutes."

Whit said "I thought you weren't wired for sound."

She smiled. "Sugar, did I say that? Either way you're lucky. I've sunk whole ships of virgin boys, with my imagination. Sweet Mother Marie's been known to speak with forkèd tongue." She waggled a pink tongue long as a rug.

"How much you want me to trust you then?"

"Oh all I said directly to you was gospel truth."

"And the miracle? That wasn't just hocus-pocus?"

She hunted his face like one of her dogs. Then she laughed again deeply. And before she could speak, she had to wipe her streaming eyes. "Seeing's believing. I do what I do. But you read the message. Look at yourself in your car mirror yonder." She took her beach chair and folded it neatly.

So Whit stood up, not as easy as he'd planned; he swayed a moment. Then he folded his chair.

"Sure you don't want some of these fine cold eggs and Juanita's tea?"

Whit said "I'm already late in my day."

She nodded. "You were. But now you're on stride." She held out her hand and accepted his chair. "Going home tonight?"

"No ma'm, not till Friday. I live in Raleigh."

"And you got a wife and daughter—twelve, I believe you said?"

"Did I? Yes ma'm." He didn't remember giving Liss's age.

"You call em tonight and say what happened."

Whit looked way past her to the line of pines, the nearest woods. Somebody's dogs, surely hers, were belling their glad way onward. Then he found Juanita's eyes again. "You tell me."

"I told you. You're healed. You were, the instant you drank that water. It was nothing on Earth but pure cold water from a clean old spring up the road, half a mile. But you trusted a stranger so ugly she's stopped all progress for miles. She might have been crazy and killed you dead. She might have sicked three yellow dogs at your throat and bled you dry—they've killed before to save my skin—but they spared your ass. God healed you for that and a good deal else."

Whit could finally laugh to greet the claim. "You sure about that?"

Juanita soared off in her own high glee, then eventually said "A guarantee'll cost you *money*."

He reached for his billfold.

Her right hand came up, bigger this time. "Oh no, Mr. Wade,

I was pulling your leg. I'm *sure*, you bet. A week from now, you drop me a postcard—Juanita Branch, Route 1, Spring Hope. Hell, postage *due* and just say 'Nita, you done it again.' I'll file it yonder in my tin box with all my eight hundred more testimonies."

Whit smiled. "Amen." He still held the billfold. *Give her five dollars? Crazy as she was, that seemed sacrilegious.*

Juanita caught his drift and, when he looked up, she shook her head and winked. Then she propped both chairs against the trailer and moved toward her steps. She climbed them slowly, opened her screen and hauled her weight up the last hard inches. Only then did she turn.

Whit kissed his fingers and didn't quite wave but held them toward her.

She grinned the best yet. "I planned not to tell you; but man, I can't stop. You're the finest thing I've seen on Earth since the Luray Caverns when I was nine."

Suddenly all three dogs were at him, kindly as children. They even led him back to his car like the school patrol and stood in the perilous midst of the road till Whit lost the sight in his rearview mirror. For all he knew, they also turned into angels of light, the instant he vanished round that last curve, and bore Juanita and the entire trailer to their next appointment with destiny. Anyhow he was aimed at Melton's Barbecue—hot pork, coleslaw and sweet iced tea. Then a long afternoon of settling claims. Other people's claims on other people's money.

Whatever had happened and would happen next, Whit knew he was feeling readier still. The whole past year had been a chain of deaths, deaths pounded in his mind like rivets from a gun, that merciless and deep. His own old life had ended in France. Nineteen men he'd personally watched meet death head-on were still buried there. And once back home he blundered daily into parts of a past he couldn't remember how to use. Mainly June and Liss. He asked again *What in God's own name can Whit Wade mean to women that strong?* What was he but a relic, hung in space somewhere, with half his blood gone? Last night at home though and here this morning in the open country with either a lunatic, a spirit or both, he'd started suspecting he really had risen from actual death and might be good for something yet.

By late afternoon he had worked his way through all the day's claims with little trouble. He suspected he was giving too much away, but the company had yet to rein him in, so he went on making most customers happy. One elderly lady, Amantha Carr, in the woods near Bruce had tried to rob him by claiming full value on a horse that died mysteriously. She said it had "won her hundreds of dollars from as far north as Fredericksburg and was still glad to race and pay my bills right on to the grave." In her dark low house, there were numerous pictures of her dead husband on it, a roan named Sohrab, and a wall full of ribbons. But something in her feverish eyes raised Whit's suspicions. With concealed amusement he thought he could smell her secret hot delight in deceit.

He called on her vet for a second opinion; and the vet said outright, "Old Rab hadn't walked a mile in five years, died of pure old age. Watch out if you cross Miss Amantha though. She could pack you and me in one pillowcase, haul us to Raleigh by dark tonight and sue our hides off." So Whit had honored the outrageous claim, adjusting her estimate to salve the home office. Old as she was, she talked too grand a line to deny. And she looked as if, despite her spark, the grave she mentioned was near at hand.

As Whit turned to leave her, she said "Mr. Wade, you resemble my father." And when he thanked her for the compliment, she said "You sure it was praise? Maybe so. He was also a sport. What I mean is, you take a joke very stylishly."

He was finished there by five o'clock and planned to push on to Plymouth by dark. The hotel there served excellent waffles and sausage hot as Mexico. He wasn't that tired and his first appointment tomorrow was late. So he cranked the car, made the first two turns and realized he was headed home. Not to Raleigh—June and Liss or his dead mother's house, full of strangers now—but to one of his boyhood homes nearby, on the Pamlico River, three miles from Bath. This late in the day, it was all but certain Uncle Tuck would be there.

A half hour later when he pulled into the drive, Whit thought he'd been wrong. No sight of either Tuck's car or the pickup. He'd leave a note then and head on to Plymouth. Whit got out a notepad and licked his pencil, then heard a door slam. A bent old man had come out and stood on the edge of the porch, facing a little to the left of Whit's car. He wore a white dress-shirt buttoned at the neck and starched khaki trousers. Tuck was seldom clean till just before supper, so who the hell was this and could he be blind?

Then one of the man's short arms came up and beckoned twice, though he still looked askew.

Whit climbed out and stood. The man held his ground, not coming to meet him. Then he knew it was Tuck. Lord, when had he seen him? Nearly two years ago. He walked toward the porch on crushed oyster shells he had helped bring here, twenty years past.

"Who is it?" Tuck said. His voice hadn't aged, deep as a well.

"Your favorite nephew." By then Whit was only ten yards away; he waited there.

Tuck had finally homed in on the sound and was facing Whit. But he said "I still can't see your damned face. And I ain't about to name a favorite."

"You've just got one, your only sister's only boy."

The old eyes shut for a long thought, then looked again. "I thought you were dead."

Whit came on forward to the foot of the porch steps. "I was, old friend, but Hell refused me." He gave a short laugh. "I looked you up, hoping you can say why they barred me out."

Tuck searched Whit's face for something familiar. With no trace of a smile, he said "Get gone. You're too much like her."

Whit smiled. "Like Mother?"

Tuck nodded. "My Anna." Like a long-legged colt, he lurched to a rocker. Then he sat and faced the road.

Whit said "Can I join you?"

Tuck said "Help yourself."

So Whit came on and sat two chairs away from Tuck. Whit had grown up in Raleigh, his parents' home. But this house had been a big part of his childhood, his mother's birthplace. And when his father died young, this old man had been more nearly a stand-in than anyone else. After the hours on the road, Whit's mind was still in a limbo of motion. So he kept the chair still and watched the dirt road in silence awhile.

Then a tall straight Negro girl walked by in a summer dress. She moved through Whit's eyes as firm as any Egyptian painting in King Tut's tomb in her resolution not to look their way. Whit didn't think it but he felt the result—maybe she knew that, posed in profile, she stood her only chance of lasting in somebody's memory at least. She was that fine to see. Every line of her young skin spoke in the folds of thin blue cloth, much lighter than the sky. One of the earliest losses of Whit's year had been the ache that flows from such sights, the body's surge to rush and share the goodness.

She was almost gone when Tuck spoke finally. "You're not speaking to her?"

"Wish I knew her. No sir."

"You know her indeed. Fact was, years back, I thought you knew her in the Bible way."

Whit said "I'm lost. Who you think she is?"

Tuck faced Whit then and, for the first time, bloomed a smile as broad as if he welcomed this visitor seated beside him. "That, young sir, is your friend Martha."

Not only blind but gone in the head. The girl was rounding the final bend. Whit watched till she vanished. *No way on Earth.* He looked to Tuck. "You mean Martha's child?"

"No, I mean what the words said—Martha, Martha Burton. You were all but hot on her, no time ago."

The feel of Martha came up, fast and vivid. Though he'd almost always known her by night, the recollections were bright and warm. Her matt-black skin, always lightly dusted, and the coral slash. The first woman he managed to know and as fine as any, that whole last summer working down here. "Tuck, that was a young girl, twenty at the most."

Tuck's smile deepened. The index finger of his left hand reached out and pressed in hard between Whit's eyes. "Ought to have got you some free eyeglasses before you let the Army discharge you. Nobody on Earth's that mean and proud but Martha Burton. She saw us, saw *you*—just too mean to speak. She's been back down here some little while. Knows me some days, some days not."

Whit worked to think when he'd seen her last. When he came down here to bury his mother years ago, she had been at the cemetery, standing way back. He had left June's side and walked the distance to speak to Martha, and she'd held her ground. He thanked her for being there. She said "Whit, I'm thanking her—Miss Anna liked me. You go on back." She looked ash gray and swollen then, from liquor or dope. The girl who just now passed was burning youth like phosphorus light. Whit had never argued with Tuck in his life, so he wouldn't try now. But he did say "I thought Martha checked out for parts far north, before the war."

Tuck nodded. "Did. Come back last winter, said her titties were froze. I told her she'd come to the thawing place."

Whit laughed. "Meaning you?"

Tuck faced him again with a genuine frown. "Meaning Beaufort County, our temperate clime."

"Beg pardon. I forgot your sanctity." In youth apparently Tuck had burnt a path through the local girls, of various shades. Then he swore off at thirty for no known cause and never married.

Now Tuck was deep in another long look at the road. Finally he tapped Whit again, on the back of his wrist. "You and the war didn't see eye to eye?"

"I wrote you my news."

"You did. Many thanks." Tuck's eyes looked over and stayed on Whit. "You guess you'll make it?"

What had gone bad here? Whit had no knowledge of harming Tuck. He had come down to see him before he enlisted. He had written him every month that passed. From boot camp, England, the English infirmary and the three slow months in a Maryland hospital, staring at life and mostly refusing. And in his answers, once Whit was wounded at least, Tuck had even gone past the usual news of weather and crops and tried to say Whit's life mattered to him. The letter Whit remembered said "Try to live, Whitley, and get back down here to rest on the porch. Too many empty rocking chairs already. I'm a selfish bastard—you go and *I'm* gone. No two ways about it, Your uncle, Tucker Boyd."

So what held Tuck now, walled off like this and picking at sores? The two years had stooped his back and shoulders. The liver spots on the backs of his hands had almost merged. Only his eyes were as bright as before, and they could hardly see. He was—what?—past seventy. *Well, strike for the heart.* That was Tuck's old way. Whit said "You holding some I.O.U. I forgot to pay?"

Tuck jerked away and faced the road. "I live by the Bible in that one respect—I forgive my debts every seven years."

Whit knew he hadn't owed Tuck a red cent in years, but he said "I'm relieved. I couldn't stand losing a friend old as you."

Tuck didn't waver to look his way. And though he didn't move so much as an eyelash, his mind was plainly flying from here.

But Whit kept watching and, to his amazement, he thought he could see those blue eyes fill. If Tucker Boyd had ever shed tears, Whit hadn't been present.

But no water spilled and finally Tuck said "You fooled me, slamming in here like this. I never was strong as you wanted to think, you nor your mother. Anna always said she leaned on me. Christ knows, she died and I nearly *choked.* I went to my room and stretched out *under* the goddamned bed, on the freezing floor, and howled one whole long winter night." His hand fumbled up and unbuttoned the collar. But he kept his eyes intent on the road, though nothing had passed worth watching since Martha.

This pitiful world of people all thinking they prop *each other, when everybody's separately hung by the neck, touching nobody nowhere.* Whit watched the thought cut through his own mind and then felt the shock. He shivered slightly. That was the way he'd thought in England, at the pit of his trouble. To redeem himself he quietly said "I was down here, Tuck, and lonesome to see you." Then he heard the hollow echo. If he'd truly missed Tuck, he'd have been here five months ago.

Tuck must have thought the same. He still didn't turn.

"You want me to leave?"

"I didn't say that."

Whit tried a short laugh. "Look at me then. Say what you see." He had not thought it through; the words fell out.

But Tuck obeyed. He slowly turned and gave Whit's face a thorough search. Then he said "I see what's left of a boy I thought right much of years ago."

"It's that bad, is it?"

Tuck kept looking. Then he nodded firmly and wiped a long

brown hand on the air, as if cleaning glass. "It's all mostly gone, the boy I knew."

All the women were saying otherwise. In the past few hours, hadn't Liss and June and big weird Nita said Whit was finally breathing again? But Tuck's was the oldest trustworthy voice, and it shook the strength Whit had worked to gain.

"You're finally grown."

Whit said "Hold on. Which one is it, Tuck? You say I'm *gone*, then say I'm *grown*. I don't know whether to cry or clap, shit or go blind—like you used to say."

"It's both, like I said. I knew you, see, when you were still down near the calf of my leg and staring at me. That boy's all gone. I don't know the man."

Yesterday and all this morning, Whit's eyes had finally seemed to be clearing. The actual air in front of his face had opened as he moved and let him through when, for months, his mind had sealed him upright in a tube where even his arms couldn't reach his face to shade his eyes or feed his mouth. For two days he'd almost dared to think he was back and glad. And now, Lord God, he'd walked into this with eyes wide open. If he hadn't got drunk too fast on hope, he'd have told himself to wait a few more days and plan this right. He was due back down here late next month. He should have held back and written to Tuck or called him and asked permission to come. Then Tuck would have had time to say a flat no or to sort his feelings and get his face set for company .

As the only live male younger than Tuck in all the family—and worse, as one of the two things Tuck had loved, in a world where nothing else earned his praise but trees—Whit had left here and sent home nothing but heartbreak, *If this is home and where else is?* Rocking here, with the broad warm river a hundred years off, near this old man who taught him so much, Whit chose it once again for home. And he'd waited so long, he said it out loud now to the road, "You said you don't know the man I am. That makes two of us, Tuck. I live all day with a stranger's mind. I brought him down here for you to name" (his mother had always said Tuck named him, when his father declined).

Tuck seemed not to hear. Then he turned so quickly it felt like a lash. But his eyes had eased. "—Named Whitley Wade."

Whit said "*Here,* sir."

Tuck said "At ease." He had spent eight months in something worse than the Normandy invasion—gassed in the trenches, 1918.

At the same moment both men rocked their chairs. Whit at least heard the unison creak and wanted to laugh. But there to his right was Martha again, retracing her steps in the dusty road. Wherever she'd gone for so many years, the place hadn't tamed her. Her head was high as a circus pony's. Whit touched Tuck's arm, then stood up, walked to his car and waited by the bumper.

This time Martha saw him from yards away and focused on him till she came nearly opposite without slowing down.

She plainly wasn't drunk so Whit assumed she didn't recognize him. "Evening, Martha."

That stopped her cold. She turned full toward him and took her time. Her face was solemn but in no way angry, in full possession of herself at last. And at five yards distance, she looked even finer, shining in the light. She said "Hot enough for you?"

It had been a mild day. But to keep her talking, Whit nodded and said "I feel right faint."

"Don't faint on such a happy day." A smile took her mouth; she surrendered and let it glorify her face. She still had skin white women would die for.

"You know me?"

Martha said "Do now."

Whit made little motions to primp his hair. "How you think I look?"

"I just now told you—looking too sad for this happy day."

Whit needed to hear her say his name. But he looked to the sky—cloudless, deep blue. "I'm always grateful, any day the sun shines."

Martha waited, then stepped on nearer to Whit. But she looked toward Tuck and raised her strong voice, "Mr. Tuck, go turn your old radio on."

Tuck cupped his ear too late and stood to join them.

At close range Whit could see her age. Not in sags or wrinkles but a woman's strong bones and, when she was silent, exhausted eyes. He said "What happened on the radio?"

Martha frowned, disbelieving. "Nothing but peace. Half the damned war's over."

Whit said "Who told you?"

She gave in finally to brimming gladness. "Every talking fool on the radio." She pointed behind her toward Morton's Store. "Germany quit, child—unconditional."

By then Tuck was with them. Martha's face was so bright, Whit let her tell him. "Mr. Tuck, the German war is *finished*—this minute, on the radio."

With all the good news of the past two weeks, Whit was stunned, far worse than he planned to be. At once he saw Tim Grant again, dead in the water but trying to see the enemy still. To clear his mind Whit looked up at Tuck. "Your radio working?"

Tuck was also amazed and at first pointed mutely back at the house.

Martha said "Your radio in the kitchen."

Tuck nodded and started an explanation of how the other one broke last month and couldn't be fixed, though any fool can fix radios if—

Whit stopped him gently. "Come on, Martha. Let's see if

you're right." In the shock of her news, Whit no longer saw anything here now but thronging faces of young dead men demanding a life they'd never know. He almost hoped she'd misunderstood. *Let it run on for good till we're all gone under.*

Martha said "I'm right or the man in the radio ought to be shot."

The three of them went toward the house, single file.

And Martha was right. Though victory had not been officially declared, the last of the German armies had surrendered. The next thing would be a proclamation by Truman and Churchill, expected tomorrow. And then the Allies could turn on Japan, those teeming millions on their own sacred ground.

The two men had sat at the kitchen table to hear the words. Martha had sat a little way off, in a green straight chair. When the news moved on into local events—the plight of tobacco in the current drought—Tuck cupped his ear for news more pertinent even than surrender. But Whit had to stand, pale, short-winded and not feeling yet or knowing what to feel. The only words his mind would send were still the names of boys, stalled for good that day last June.

Martha knew Whit of old and read his drift. She also stood and, once the tobacco news was past, she said "Mr. Tuck, what you got for your supper?"

Tuck's answer at least was ready to hand, "Sardines and crackers, not a damned thing else."

Martha frowned. "Great God, you killing yourself by the *minute*. I told you to let me buy you some groceries or come on in here and work for you some." When Tuck only smiled she turned to Whit, "He just too stingy to spend money, Whit. I don't know who he's expecting to feed him—crows in the sky? Won't pay me even five dollars a week to come in here and cook for him, sweep these cobwebs down." Her eyes made a sweeping tour of the ceiling, "Christ A-mighty, you *breeding* spiders."

Tuck laughed. "You got it—I plan to sell webbing. Martha, I'm *saving*."

"For who, me and Whit? We'll be *long* gone, be strumming our harps in the pearly streets when you get there."

Tuck turned to Whit. "Take her to Raleigh. She's city folks now, too smart for down here."

Martha said "Shoot, Raleigh's nothing but a pitiful try at—" Before she rounded off her point, she scanned the counter and the open cupboard shelf. "Mr. Tuck, you got ten dozen fresh eggs and half of that ham I baked you last week." Her eyes were plainly hatching a plan when she turned to Whit. "He don't eat nothing, just turning to air. Forgetting he's got a heart to stoke."

Whit loved the sight of her rising to life, in her old tracks here. He said "Please feed him."

She first shook her head, then picked a speck off Whit's red tie. "Where you aiming now?"

"Plymouth, I thought, but it's getting late."

"*Plymouth?* You head out of here this late for Plymouth, you'll spend your night with the swamp alligators."

"Maybe old Tuck here'll lend me a bed."

Tuck considered a moment, then nodded gravely.

Martha said "Mr. Tuck, we got us a crowd. You want me to cook?"

Tuck's eyes were baffled and he looked to Whit.

But Whit hesitated to choose.

So Martha raised her voice a notch and tapped her words on the air with a finger. "How bout I fix up a big hot feed? Whit come all this way back from the grave, least we can do is feed his poor face."

Tuck at last understood. "Best news yet, Martha. See what you can find. Whit, you still eat, don't you?"

Whit suddenly thought he knew for certain. Even his old home was drawing him in. He felt the actual rush of waters as his mind seized hold on this new line thrown toward him in the room. The waters were clear of all but him, no familiar dead eyes. He said to Martha "You're an answer to prayer."

Martha's face crouched back. Then she laughed a low note. "Oh Lord, Mr. Tuck, Whit's talking religion; and it ain't even *night!*"

The two men's laughter mixed with hers, and all three looked to the same tall window. Even with the longer days of spring, they had let night seize the house and them in it.

TUESDAY

8 MAY 1945

THOUGH WHIT SLEPT in the bed he used as a boy, assailed by dreams of women and falling, he slept Monday night without waking once. And when he heard Tuck get up at dawn, he let himself take another hour unconscious. Then he shaved, drank a pint of Tuck's strong coffee, promised to see him for longer next trip and was underway by seven-thirty to work a long day.

The first client he disappointed was the father of two sons, both still in Europe. But the man was so elated by news of victory that he shook Whit's hand.

And even the final slighted client could hardly tear himself from the radio long enough to ask "What part did you play in this mess?"—implying that Whit had been some brand of coward or weakling.

Whit smiled, rubbed his scar and said "I contributed two quarts of blood and some pulverized bone-meal to a French cow-pasture."

A half hour later, driving east with the low sun behind him, the words still rang like a fitting end to his first whole day of freedom and safety in more than two years. It was also the first day yet when his chest wound gave no pain that demanded notice. He had rounded a curve in the narrow road, just past Scuppernong, when he realized that fact—no pain today. He reached up to touch it; and the instant he found the hard ridges and holes of the scar, he heard a sharp crack in the empty air.

His immediate thought was *Some kind of gunfire,* and he got as far as thinking he was safe when the space around him began to roll. His right-front tire had suddenly blown. *Jesus, I'm rolling way too fast.* In the next few instants, he did his best to wrestle the steering wheel back to the left, but his hands were dry, and the wheel continued to slew from his grip. He said out loud "This time I caused it." Then he clenched to brace himself in the seat.

The next four seconds went on a long time—the roll, the surprising lack of noise, the failure of gravity as Whit rose slowly and struck his head, then was flung back onto the passenger side. He knew the taste of his own blood. So *Blood* was his first thought when motion stopped, blood in his mouth. He looked in the mirror but saw nothing too bad—a bit top lip and a small skinned patch, up toward his hairline.

It was only then that Whit realized he was back upright. The car had gone down a steep-sloped shoulder, spun a whole revolution and was on four wheels at the edge of a field of young tobacco with the engine running. He tried his door and found that, though it gave a fierce creak, it would actually open. So he climbed out, stretched his arms and felt them, then stooped and bent his knees to check. Everything seemed to work. Even his eyes—his vision seemed clear.

But the land was so flat that, at first, he thought he could see straight over the next forty miles to the Outer Banks and the ocean beyond and the dark rocks of Britain—The Lizard, Land's End. He thought he could taste the thick wet air of English days. But that couldn't be. That could not be. Then he checked the blown tire. It was one June had bought while he was away, wartime synthetic rubber and worthless.

He had a spare; and for some uncharacteristic reason, he had checked the pressure on Sunday afternoon. He had changed a hundred tires in his life, so this job shouldn't take fifteen minutes. But a soft plowed field would eat up the jack. He needed to get back onto firm ground, the hardpacked roadside. And he'd opened the door to climb back in and drive the few yards when he heard strong voices yelling his name, his actual name in this strange field. *Whitley, Whitley.* Then for the first time, he saw the house—a low white house in a small oak grove, with old outbuildings. And because he was stunned, his next thought was *Don't let me see a white horse now. Then I'll* know *I'm dead.*

But the voices came on, saying his name. And at closer range they seemed to come from two boys, loping toward him through the rows. Sometimes their short bodies merged into one, but that might be when they walked single file and one got hid. At closer range they really were boys—maybe ten and twelve, both in overalls and shirts so white they dazzled like morning snow. They were frowning deeply but the older boy wore the calm assurance of children prematurely forced to be grown. Whit thought *Your dad's in Europe or Asia. You're the boss man here.* And though he felt his lips make a smile, Whit didn't speak. They apparently knew him; let them take over.

The young boy was first. "You do that for fun?"

The older boy said "Vance, shut your trap." Then he met Whit's eyes. His own were so light blue they seemed nearly white. He said "You don't look all that broke."

Whit said "No, money's the least of my worries."

"Broke bones, I meant."

Whit laughed. "Oh no. I'm magic, see. Been dead once and raised; they don't take you twice."

They paid no attention whatever to that but circled the car, assessing damage. Like all country boys they revered machines and understood them. They didn't seem worried about their tobacco—maybe thirty plants ruined. He'd offer to pay them the market value. *But they know my name. Did I stop here before?* He said "Is this your dad's tobacco?"

The young boy said "It's his" and pointed.

The older said "*Vance*, goddammit, go home."

Vance said "Aye aye, sir" but didn't budge.

So the older boy turned to Whit. "Just be glad you're here."

Whit said "My company will pay for what's lost."

The older boy said "My name is Tray."

"Like Old Dog Tray?"

"My name is Traynham Burns." His face was nowhere near playing games.

Whit said "You know me."

Both boys shook their heads. And Tray said "No sir, we were heading to supper and heard your tire."

"But you called my name."

Vance looked to Tray, then dissolved in laughter.

Tray said "Mister, you're hearing things. You're bound to be hurt."

You're bound to be right. But Whit said "May be. I was hurt in France." He pointed northwest. Then he thought of the boys in front of him now. "Your dad in the Army?"

"No sir, our father died two years back." But Tray's huge eyes were still stroking the car. He said "Will she run?"

"She was running fine. I just turned the motor off when I got out to look." *Their father died two years ago. Must have been in the war, maybe while I was gone. I must have settled some hail claim for him. It'll come to me soon. But* Whitley*—how did they know my first name?*

Tray said "If you let me and Vance drive her out, we'll change your tire if you got a good spare. If you don't, we can't do nothing but boo-hoo."

Whit said "I bet you haven't cried lately."

Tray's face was firm as a well-braced table.

Vance said "He cries every time they play that 'Anchors Aweigh' on the radio."

Tray said "Go to Hell." Then laughing, he grabbed Vance's head and scrubbed his knuckles in the quarter-inch stubble.

Vance laughed even louder—"Aye aye, *sir.*" Then he dropped in the dirt and came up brandishing a crushed tobacco plant.

But Whit had nodded and Tray was already opening the door to start the car.

A half hour later the tire was changed, Whit had heard a lot from Vance—family news and names—and Tray had refused to take so much as a dollar for his help, though he said he'd appreciate whatever sum Whit thought was fair for the damaged plants.

Whit had his adjustor's tables in mind; but he said "Tray, you're the expert here."

Tray slowly surveyed the damaged rows, counting with his lips. Then Vance said "Fifty dollars, maybe forty."

Whit said "Goddammit, Vance, get home to Mama."

Vance crossed his eyes but held his ground. He had the big powerful feet of a man.

Tray looked back to Whit. "Fifty dollars sound fair?"

Whit said "Try sixty."

For the first time, Tray committed a smile. He had a man's gigantic teeth in a boy's small jaw, and they made him look younger than he had till now.

Whit wrote down the details of name and address, then extended his hand in thanks.

Vance bounded forward and shook it hard.

But when Whit turned to Tray, Tray's face was dark with a furious blush.

Whit said "Something wrong?"

Tray said "No sir, just hate to see you go. I like that car."

It was nothing but a '39 Hudson that June had pampered while Whit was away, and now he'd given it the scare of its life. Whit said "You ever get your license, let me know. I might hire you on to drive me some. I hate these lonesome trips I take." It was loosely said, to ease his departure. But as each word left Whit's mind and tongue, he felt his body get that much lighter. And the last thing he saw for a while was both boys' faces, wide with surprise. *I'm leaving again.*

Sometime later he came to himself and was in a car, moving. By the tan upholstery, the car was his. But a boy was seated behind the wheel and appeared to be driving. To left and right the land looked familiar. Flat black fields with young tobacco, low shady white houses, Negro shacks. Then he knew the boy but only by his full name (he couldn't think Tray). He said "Traynham Burns, you know my name."

It had not been a question; but Tray said "No sir, never seen you till now."

Whit said "You were calling my name back yonder." He pointed behind him. "Back there in the field, when you and your brother—"

Tray said "No sir, you were hearing things. We were saying 'Don't move,' like they teach you in school, not to break something worse if it's already broke."

Whit shut his eyes a moment, hoping to rest. But he needed to know. He looked out again and said "Son, what in the world's going on?"

Tray said "You fell out cold by the road. Me and Vance picked you up, and I'm hauling you in—the car runs fine."

Whit's head had to stay on the soft seatback, but he said "In to where?"

"To Plymouth, Dr. Samms' place. Only clinic worth a toot between here and Greenville." Again Tray spoke with a grown man's assurance. Then he swallowed hard, "Don't blame me now but can I just ask—you ever have fits?"

Whit thought, then laughed. "Like running fits, some old dog tearing around the yard?"

Tray had blushed again. He was facing the road. "No sir, I saw an epileptic fit once, in a church in Plymouth; and it near bout scared me out of my seat."

Whit said "What happened?"

"Some poor old lady, on the bench just beyond me, stood bolt upright in the the midst of the sermon. She sang a long high note that kept on rising till next thing she wound up down in the aisle, grinding her tongue and the blood pouring out."

Whit said "I didn't carry on like that?"

Tray said "Oh no sir but you did say 'No,' a long string of No's."

"Under what circumstances?"

"As you fell, back yonder. You were looking at me, and then you said 'No,' about five or six times. After that, you were *gone*. I thought maybe I'd made some big mistake."

Whit said "Not you; you're doing grand, Tray. I must have been speaking to somebody else. I've had a lot of bad dreams, the past few months."

"Dr. Samms can take care of that," Tray said.

Whit smiled and thought it was best to watch the road. He realized again, whatever had happened, that his chest felt safe. In fact it didn't feel there at all. But he didn't try to touch it. He felt round his eyes, checked his hands, then looked to Tray and said "Am I bleeding?"

"Nowhere I can see. I'm guessing you got a lick on your head and need to be still."

Whit had to admit it did feel right—lying back on the seat, letting this young man do all the work. *Man?*—Whit suddenly recalled Traynham's youth. He also thought *Go slow here now. Don't scare anybody.* And he finally said "How old are you, son?"

"Fourteen."

Whit said "No you're not" before he remembered that to underestimate a child's age is a real offense.

But Tray smiled slightly. "I'll be fourteen, seventeen months from now."

Whit said "Many highway patrolmen down here?"

"They all know me," Tray said. "I help em."

Whit wondered how but trailed off peacefully and didn't look up till Tray had stopped by a red brick building with wide swinging doors.

"You stay right here and I'll get you some help." Tray slid out and through the wide doors so fast, he was all but a streak.

The moment Tray vanished, Whit thought *I may well have ruined myself here, one more time.* At last his left hand came up again and probed the scar. Even through cloth it was hot to the touch as if again his blood was draining off unseen.

The next time he looked, he was in a dim room. And a woman in starched white was taking his pulse. White shoes and stockings, white dress and hat. He said "I thought hostilities ceased."

The nurse kept counting but somebody laughed.

Traynham stood up from a dark easy chair and said "You did it again, looks like."

By now Whit's mouth was sporting a thermometer, so his eyebrows mimed "What do you mean?"

"—Rolled right over and landed on your feet. You were one

loose goose when Vance and me caught you. But they say you're going to be fine some day."

When the nurse freed his mouth, Whit said "Is he right?"

She was maybe pushing sixty, a round sad face. You'd have thought you could trust her. But she said "Dr. Samms will be here directly. You let him tell you."

However it hurt, Whit actually craned his head up to check. Both legs were still there. Two long straight ridges at least, under cover.

The nurse turned to Tray. "Son, aren't you a Burns from Scuppernong?"

He said "Yes ma'm. How did you know that?"

"I nursed your father when he was in here. That was—what?—last year?"

"Two years in June."

"Is he doing all right?"

"Oh no'm, he died—in here, next door. You forgot he died?"

Her face delayed in showing its feeling—pity or surprise. But she finally said "Then how in the world will you get home? It's a dark lot of miles. This man can't drive you."

Tray told her "Doctor said I can stay with my uncle, right here tonight and long as it takes."

The nurse faced Whit and, once she turned, Tray shot him a wink. "Is this child your nephew?"

"Yes ma'm, can't you tell? He's got my eyes."

The nurse said "Sir, your eyes are exceptionally brown."

Whit said "Lord, I *must* be hurt. They were blue this morning. One thing's the same though—I love him like a son." He thought *And I almost do, this soon, tonight.*

She knew they were lying. But she liked their eyes and contented herself with a parting shot. "He's the spit image of you, but he ought not to drive. And buy him some shoes. It's way too early for barefoot boys."

Before she managed to shut the door, Whit said "He saved my life, sweet lady. He can drive me anywhere his heart desires, barefoot or shod."

She pretended not to hear. But she rigged a noncommittal smile and shut the door.

Once she was thoroughly gone, Tray said "*Tallahassee.*"

Whit said "Beg your pardon?"

"Florida—you said I could drive you anywhere my heart desires. I've always wanted to see Tallahassee."

Whit said "Someday, it's a legal promise. Did you call my wife up and say I'm safe?

Tray said "Uncle Whit, you didn't tell me that."

"Maybe not. But remind me to tell you next time I'm awake." And again he was gone, safe in the thought of this honest guard here, brave beyond his years and as plainly hungry for a grown man's notice as Whit had been, till now, for hope.

An hour later Dr. Samms walked in. He was the main white doctor in Plymouth, and the whole clinic belonged to him. He was well over six feet tall and white-haired. The air and the walls divided for him, as he went; he was that forthright. Inside Whit's room, he nodded toward Tray, "You all right, son?" The young face scratched once at his memory—had he seen this child in surgery?—but he couldn't place Tray (he'd stood in the room next to this, this near him, and helped his father die). He stepped to the bed and took Whit's wrist. "Mr. Wade, I'm Dr. Samms. Look here and speak to me."

Whit floated up from wherever he'd drifted. "Tell me what to say."

"Try this—'I'm a lucky damned fool to be here.' My assistant says you rolled your car over and struck your head a good hard blow."

Whit raised his right hand. "Swear to God, that's it."

The doctor laughed. "I'm not the Law. You're entirely sober and your X rays show you're a lucky fellow. No hemorrhage or fractures, apparently no concussion."

Whit said "Many thanks."

Dr. Samms pointed to Tray in the corner.

Tray took it as a summons and hurried over.

So the doctor laid a long hand on his shoulder. Then he said to Whit "Thank this boy here. You'd likely be dead in the road but for him."

For his own reason Whit raised both hands, in a double oath. On his left was the wide gold wedding band; on his right, another small gold ring set with a bloodstone. He took that off and held it toward the doctor. "Give that to my friend."

The doctor said "Who?"

"My savior there." He pointed again to Traynham, who now looked large and wise.

Tray said "No sir, that ring's all yours. I'm *enjoying* this."

Whit said "I need to thank you somehow."

Tray said "We know I saved your life. But I don't wear jewels."

Whit said "Sell it then; take the money and run."

Dr. Samms looked around and winked at Tray. Then he said to Whit, "You're still a little bushed and we're not crowded. Rest right here tonight. I'll see you at sunup and maybe you can go."

Whit said "No danger?"

"Not visible, no." He paused and looked through the chart in his hand. "You had a service wound. Any problems with that?"

Whit said "Maybe you'd better look at it too." He raised the loose hospital gown.

Dr. Samms stepped forward to see the scar.

Traynham joined him, as though he had full right to be there.

The doctor's fingers were thin and smooth; so as they felt the ridges and valleys, they raised no pain. When he finished he pulled the gown down a little but then thought better and did a strange thing. He looked to Tray. "You're not scared, are you?"

Tray said "No sir. Not much anyhow."

So the doctor reached out, took Tray's strong right hand, raised Whit's gown again and let the boy also touch the wound—"Gentle now."

Whit said "I was hit, about noon on D Day."

Tray said "By a German?"

Whit smiled. "Well, not by my family."

So Tray laughed once. And his testing hand felt the same as the doctor's, that light and knowing.

When the boy had finished, Dr. Samms said "Son, never pick up a gun unless you're starving, you or some of your kin."

Tray looked amazed. "Never?"

"Unless somebody you love is hungry."

Whit understood how odd that was, coming from a man in deep farm country. But he heard himself say "Absolutely."

And Tray nodded. "Yes sir."

Whit said to the doctor "Look all right to you?"

"Good as it can, this soon in the game. Twenty, thirty years from now, you'll have a nice souvenir to show your grandchildren."

Tray laughed again.

And the doctor told Whit "You've had two close calls now, too close together. My best guess is, this latest scrape just needs a night's rest." He looked to Tray. "Son, you look young for this; but you did a fine job."

Tray said "Shoot, I can drive in my sleep."

Something in the boy's face was nagging at Dr. Samms's mind still, *I know that boy and he's seen too much.* So he asked Tray whether he'd called his mother.

Tray said "She knows. I'm gone more than not."

In a voice that mimicked W. C. Fields, the doctor said "Ain't it what boys are *for*—to break Mama's heart?" Before he was finished he'd passed through the door.

And by the time the glow from his white coat had died in the air, Whit was asleep.

In spite of two visits from the late-night nurse, he slept in what was more like a trance than human rest. But in all the scraps and tatters of dream, he knew this night was especially good—a further cure. So he let it take him and plunge down with him as far as it must. Not till almost five in the morning did anything reach him. And then it was only a whispering voice, *Uncle Whit, it's me. It's not even day*. When his eyes opened, the room was pitch dark.

It was Tray by the bed, holding Whit's right arm.

At first Whit couldn't begin to place him—Whit called him "Fitz," a boy from Kansas he'd known in England before they embarked. But Tray held ground, and finally Whit knew it was only the child that had saved his life. By then his eyes had opened enough to see by the street light filtered through blinds. The boy's lean face still showed peach fuzz in the bluish shine—*Twelve years old*. Whit tried to think of himself at thirteen. But all that came was a memorized picture from his boyhood Bible-story book—Jesus at twelve in the Holy Temple, astounding the scholars in their floor-length beards. Finally he reached his left hand across and covered Tray's. "Why did your dad die?"

"From lightning, one late July day. Him and me were walking the rows, topping off suckers and singing songs—he had a big voice and sounded better than most white men. Then before we knew it, a storm rolled on us. Just rain at first but rain so hard it hurt your skin. Dad said to meet him at the Mabry oak. That's a big old oak that's on our land now but used to belong to a mean bunch of Mabrys. Lightning crossed my mind when he said it—he'd already taught me lightning prevention, and trees were half of what he said to shun. But I didn't hear thunder, so I came to meet him. Course I got there first, but he was close after. And we enjoyed it. We kept on singing old war songs and hymns. Dad had just started on 'Take My Hand'—I think they call it—when out of the rain came one streak of lightning down that tree. My ears were gone for more than a week, and a great strip of bark tore down like paper. I knew I was dead—no question about it—and it shut my eyes. But whenever they opened, I saw my arms. They were no worse than wet. I saw my own two muddy feet and my dad flung out twenty feet from me, like a beat-up doll." By the end of the story, Tray had wandered away. At least his hand was gone from Whit's, though his voice seemed near.

Whit said "You mind me asking about it?"

Tray said "No sir. You're the first one that did."

"Was he somebody you liked?"

Tray waited, then laughed. "Couldn't you tell? I said he was my father."

"A whole lot of boys I knew in the Army hated their fathers worse than the Germans."

Like most white children who worked with blacks, Tray could speak flawless black when the need arose. Now he said "Shame *on* em. Who they coming home to, now this mess is over?"

"They've all got billfolds full of girls' pictures. No shortage of girls waiting for them, I guess."

Tray grunted "Hunnh."

"Girls haven't caught your interest yet?"

Tray tried another "Hunnh." But he followed it fast, "Here lately round home, girls have been changing fast."

Whit said "How's that?"

"All of a sudden they're on my trail like ducks on June bugs. Won't even let me eat a baloney sandwich in peace. Got to try to rub their bosoms on me."

"*Bosoms?* What grade are you in?"

Tray said "The seventh."

"Bosoms that soon?"

Tray said "Nothing much, understand—nubby bee stings."

Whit said "Oh God, that's it. Here it comes. Get ready."

Tray said "Comes what?"

"Hot love. Get your comb and brush, some sweet hair tonic; get your razor and blades."

Tray tried to whisper but it came out clearly. "You speaking of screwing?"

Whit laughed till his bruised skull creaked at the seams. "I hadn't got all the way there yet, no."

Tray said "I heard about that, far back."

Whit said "Then I can go on to sleep. Clearly you know your way through the ropes."

Tray said "Ropes? I heard it was straps." Dark as he was, his voice was smiling.

"Straps *can* be a puzzler."

Tray said "I keep me a good sharp knife."

"Whoa now!"

"I'm gentle. Or I pray to be by then, down the road."

Whit said "I believe you." A long wait stretched till Whit concluded the boy had dropped off.

Then Tray said "One old boy lives up the road from me—Elton Felts, going on sixteen. He won't tell much but he says some of it is hard on your health."

Whit said "Just see what it's done to me." But then he said "No, there have been boys and girls that got damaged. Keep yourself gentle though, like you said. You'll be fine."

Tray sounded nearer. "Elton says it near drives him crazy."

"It won't," Whit said, though he knew, strictly speaking, that was false assurance. He was tired again but then he recalled he'd meant to check on one more thing. "Tray, sit up here on the edge of the bed."

From wherever he was, Tray came up slowly and hopped like a spaniel to a spot near the footboard.

Dim as it was, Whit knew he'd lost track of a number of things in the past few hours. This man here with him, for instance, was a boy that had left home hours ago with a stranger on V-E Day. He said "Traynham, what does your poor mother think?"

Tray said "About what?"

"You leaving home hours ago like you did."

"She's used to me making my own arrangements. Anyhow, Vance helped me load you up. You remember Vance? He told her the news."

"You hope he did. Tomorrow's a schoolday."

Tray said "Don't worry. Vance loves bad news. And school?—I've run out of stuff to learn. The doctor told you to rest all night, so give us a little obedience please."

In the dark Whit smiled with more satisfaction than he could recall. His mind was brimmed with strong ideas, all circling fast as lights in a sign that he couldn't read. Maybe they'd given him some kind of shot to soothe him down. It had backfired on him. He couldn't take drugs. Drugs flew him too high, left him too ready to think and talk. But none of his ideas came in words, just streaks of light and shreds of music that finally seemed to translate for Whit the stream of silence from the mouth of God or the angel he'd seen as he died in France. Whatever or why, it all wove together to bring him again in sight of happiness—he'd been a happy boy. Tray Burns was a worthy friend to tell, so finally he said "I got struck too, my own brand of lightning."

"You said it was a German."

Whit said "A German shell or shrapnel, pretty surely. Something mean at least. They say there's enough steel under my skin to build you a car when you hit sixteen—just a two-door roadster with a rumble seat, nothing big or expensive."

Tray leaned far over, toward the covered wound, as if the shrapnel were magnetized and drawing him in. But then he pulled back. "It did look rough, I'll grant you that. But it's all over now. This war took the best part of my life—hell, since I was eight. Now it's all but over. And Mama says everybody, me and you both, has got to learn to get by without it. I enjoyed it though, at night on the radio. I already miss it."

Whit knew his mind was bound to be bruised, but wasn't this one more sign sent toward him? Four women—Liss, June, Juanita, Martha—and now this country boy had said he was strong. He reached his arm out to turn on the light and see if Tray was actually present, not a substitute spirit consisting of goodness and invisible light. But just enough horse sense survived to stop him. Still he did say "Why on Earth are you here?"

"You want me to leave?" Tray said and seemed to move. "I'll leave this minute."

"It's one of the very last things I want. If we get lucky I can drive you safe back home in the morning and go my way." Whit had thought Tray was still at the foot of the bed, but a dry warm hand pressed over his lips then.

"You're still not resting. Hush up and sleep." The voice seemed deeper than Whit remembered but the hand withdrew.

Whit said "Say your prayers."

Tray said "Aye aye, sir," echoing Liss whom he'd never known. Still it made him think of Vance his brother who said it a lot to make Tray mad. Except for being in different grades, this was the longest Tray had been apart from Vance. And it bothered him now, how much he missed a child that lived to pester him. He tried to see Vance but couldn't quite manage, not his thin narrow face or his beaming eyes. But he heard Vance's voice exactly, so he held onto that. Then he said to Whit "Say you've got a big family?"

"A wife and one daughter."

"No boys at all?"

Whit said "Not yet. You want to adopt me?"

Tray said "I've been thinking through it all night."

And Whit started wondering if he'd raised this boy's hopes higher than was good.

But Tray laughed. "Wouldn't Mother and Vance fall out in a fit if I brought you home and said you'd hired on to help us out?" The thought plainly cheered him, but his low earnest tone said Traynham Burns knew what was a dream and what was true.

Everything in the room went quiet till dawn. Even the death of the man next door—a soldier home on a three-day pass and hoping to hitchhike back to Bragg but hit by a truck—made no more noise than the moon on the roof. And through all the stillness, Whit's mind (that had been so stunned for months) began to loosen and take its own ease. All the news he'd learned this week—from his family, Juanita, Tuck and Martha, from the end of half this paralyzing war that had gripped him so long, and here tonight from a manly boy—they all were aimed at prying his shut heart open to life. Life as risky as any French field and at least as strange, though he knew the common language here. In his room in a crossroads clinic far from home, Whit Wade asleep was famished for life.

And just before day, not in a dream but in what seemed a hopeful one-sentence prayer, Whit said three times *If they let me live, I'll find me a son.* Even drugged as he was, he knew June had a big say in that. But he also knew that the hope came now as a form of thanks to one kind human, near at hand, whose name he had lost. In sleep, Whit hunted to find it—Traynham Burns—but he found only words like *lean* and *abandoned*. He consoled himself by knowing he'd find it when daylight broke in and struck all faces.

WEDNESDAY

9 MAY 1945

THAT HUNGER grew through the whole next morning, as Whit left Traynham on the road near his home and worked a few claims between Scuppernong and the Atlantic Ocean. On the western side of the Alligator ferry, he lunched on June's next dry snack—two peanut bars, a hard green apple, a lemon ball and a piece of paper intricately folded to the size of a quarter that eventually said "*The eternal God is thy refuge, and underneath are the everlasting arms.*"

It was in June's hand; and below she'd added

I'm not crazy yet, just thought you'd want a little spiritual food in the midst of your long week. It's from somewhere in the Bible, though not sure where—I've known it all my life. Can't promise my arms are everlasting. *But Fate permitting, they'll be here open to you on Friday.*

Her father had been a criminal lawyer, and her mother was one of the first woman pediatricians in the state, so June wasn't given to religious outbursts. She had to be serious, saying that much.

It unnerved Whit. Did he seem that frail, to need easy mottoes to prop him through five days of light driving? He even felt anger. He was the earnest believer in the family. Not a month ago, June had finally admitted, without telling Liss, that her own faith came and went like the weather. When Whit was struggling, in three hospitals, to get his mind settled in this new body, his strongest prop was intermittent faith in a lasting soul. But kind as she'd been, June's presence at hard times could blow a strong wind of doubt on his flame. Now before he worked up a foaming grudge, the ferry hove up slowly into view. Whit folded her message tight again and put it in his watch-pocket—*everlasting arms*. Today at least he believed they existed and were waiting somewhere, unknown but findable. He also guessed they would outlast him and his loyal wife.

On the half-hour trip, Whit stood on deck in steady sunlight and gave his face to the stiff west wind. He had waited all week for the smell of salt, wondering if he'd dread it. Would it bring too strong a taste of last summer—the stench of the English Channel in darkness, a relay of scared boys doing their best to vomit in silence over the side of a landing craft as stable as a rubber soapdish in a gale? But this wind was dense, not with dread but the depth of rotting swamps behind him. Whit would need to wait for the second ferry, over Albemarle Sound, for the taste of brine. Meanwhile the pendulum sway of the broad boat gradually calmed him. So the second ferry—Manns Harbor to Manteo, a much bigger boat—was an actual pleasure. And the still-hid ocean (the western edge of that water he'd crossed, eleven months past, in certainty of death) was now a destination, not a fear.

When he landed on Roanoke Island and drove through the huddle of Manteo north to Nags Head, one of the first things

Whit noticed was the sign outside an Episcopal church—*Thanksgiving for Victory, Tonight at 6:00.* Similar signs at other churches had marked his way since Monday night, and Whit hadn't felt drawn to any one service. By five-thirty he'd finished his beachfront claims, all valid, and was headed down to find the hotel.

When he passed the church again, a few cars had gathered. And a tall young woman with splendid dark hair was climbing the steps. Whit slowed to a crawl and said aloud "Do you mean me to go?" The usual silence threatened to follow, and Whit was almost about to think *One more time, Bo, you're on your own.* But then the car, of its own will, hit a bar of sand, made a sharp left turn and stopped on the grass. Whit checked his looks in the rearview mirror. He smoothed his hair and then sat back a moment to think this through.

You asked a question and here's your answer. You're going in there with the best intentions, to do what the sign says—give thanks for peace. The sign said *victory* but Whit thought *peace.* His war had been with the Germans in Europe, so he was at peace now or praying to be. *The black-haired woman is not your business. Get that through your skull.* His skull and brain had worked all day, with no sign of harm, though at dawn Dr. Samms had said to go easy.

Whit was raised a Methodist but had always enjoyed the Episcopal church on the few occasions he worshiped there. What he liked was not so much the candles, vestments and bowing and scraping that seduced some others but the spooky mist in their sanctuaries. There was a thin warm fog he could taste in Episcopal churches and none other but Catholic, though he'd seen few of them. The moment he entered the dim space now, he caught it, first breath. Invisible but cleanly rank and somehow kin, in Whit's mind at least, to the Holy Ghost, the secret breath of God's present spirit as it waits to strike with help or pain. The one word *thanks* slipped from Whit in a murmur, and he sat near the back on the hardest pew he'd yet encountered in a lifetime of pews. All the other people knelt as they entered and said silent prayers. But despite his nightly practice at home, Whit stayed in his seat. This was public ground, he despised display and he'd already said his heartfelt thanks.

All through the next slow forty minutes, he said it many times more, just the one word. A warm kind of service went on around him (except for the hymns—he'd almost forgot Episcopal hymns, not a tune in the book). And the people did seem to be here sincerely, not showing off new hats or white linen suits, not craning around to check the roll and award demerits. He had already seen two strong-faced women with gold-star pins on black lapels, meaning dead sons or husbands.

And all around them, attending the stars, Whit started again to see the dead he knew from one day's battle. Men and boys he trained with, real and respectful in the church here around him as in any crap game at Fort-damned-Jackson or drinking warm beer in a pub near Dover. None of them faced him with blame or fear. But again they clustered with well-meaning calm and brotherly respect, saying just four words—*We bought you this.* It was only the truth and, no way left in all his life could he half repay them.

The sight, and the slow transaction at the altar, held Whit so close he forgot the woman he saw outside. He was watching the past file by him. As real as the sound of surf nearby but calmer now—no blood, no cries. And only toward the end of the service did his eyes drift rightward and catch the woman's face again, the great dark fall of her lustrous hair. In the series of sick wards Whit occupied, he often struggled at night for reasons to live, awake, through one more day. And tonight as he saw this woman, he thought *I wish I'd known this, just this picture.*

Even as a child he cared a good deal for beautiful sights—mostly trees and the arrowheads he found, a rare deer or bird. He saved them up as other boys save baseball cards or agate marbles to tide them over. And when he was old enough to save the sight and smell of beautiful women, it was not always as a goad for sex, sights to rub his body against, but as frank reminders of the world's amazing tendency to please. And here this woman was, well worth saving from tonight forever as a charm against hard times to come.

Her profile was toward him; and the window behind her was a risen Christ, stepping out of the tomb. Christ's hips were hardly covered with rags; his palms were outward, displaying their ruin. His side was bleeding and his lips were very nearly smiling. It came as a shock to Whit—that threat of a smile, the first he'd seen in a hundred pictures of this ferocious moment. The man looked glad. *Glad? What working man ever laid down to sleep and* wanted *to rise?*

For the first time this week, the bitter dregs of Whit's long war rushed up in his throat. And even the luck of the past four days or this young woman with Christ behind her, even the end of his actual fight and these slow prayers of thanks and praise could not turn the poison that burned his mouth and flooded his mind. *Whit Wade was not the man to raise. Who signed their license to haul me back? Not me, not Whit. Whit Wade tried to leave.*

In the fresh hot slap of the old pain, he looked toward the woman and laid a sudden bet on her, on the line of her face. *If she turns this way in the next ten seconds, I'll fight to take this offered life and use it.* But she stared on forward at the lighted altar, as if something more was happening there, something huge at stake that Whit couldn't see in the glow of starched white linen and silver. When he counted *ten* that hope expired, and he had to force his body to stay.

Well before these thoughts relented, the last prayer ended. And the organ moaned its windy path into one last hymn, "Unending

Pomps of Prayer and Praise." Whit stood with the others, though his lips refused to sing any word but the deep *Amen.* The rector spoke a benediction—"May the partial peace of this glad night soon spread and join the world in its arms"—and then the woman was free to turn. Everybody was leaving and more than one person nodded to Whit as a welcome stranger. He nodded back, thinking only how short they all were. An island people, bred short for speed in their war with the sea.

But the woman he watched sat a few seconds more. Then she knelt again and bowed her head. Though he knew how strange it was for him, Whit stood in the pew and kept his eyes on her. Since boyhood he'd had the occasional power to read others' thoughts. Now he tried to burn his eyes into her shut head. And for an instant he thought he'd succeeded. He saw another face, a young man's face. The eyes were dark brown, open and blank. Then he got a name, *Fleming,* but no other clue. Then he got the feeling the man was dead. A dead naval officer—her husband or brother? She was praying to join him. Whit suddenly saw that he and she were the only two left, and he moved toward the aisle.

She rose from the kneeler and came out behind him. And by the time Whit reached the door and was speaking to the rector, she was close at his back.

Whit had introduced himself as Whitley Wade from Raleigh. So to his surprise, the rector said "Beck, this is Mr. Wade. He's from your hometown—Rebecca Barksdale, Whitley Wade." For the first time in ten years, Whit felt the actual stun of beauty. She stood almost as tall as he, and he was a shade under six foot one. And though her hair was black, she had dark blue eyes and the richest whitest skin he remembered. Without seeming strange, it seemed deep as pile.

She said "Oh *Whit*—" with a slow broad smile, then extended a gloved hand as if she knew him.

He shook her hand gently. "I know you, don't I?" It seemed impossible but he suddenly thought he had always known her. She seemed as familiar as his memory of daybreak. Was he out of his mind someway, from last night?

She said "You *could* but I seriously doubt it."

Even more, Whit thought he was wading a dream, not standing on the steps of a green shingle church near Manteo. He even put his hand out again, for a second meeting.

But she said "Beck, Rebecca—on Breeze Road, Whit." The splendid face was trying to smile, but a trace of fear narrowed her eyes.

Breeze Road was two blocks up from his mother's. He'd left the neighborhood for college sixteen years ago; then his mother had died. Was this some neighborhood child, years younger (she looked maybe thirty)? He said "The brick house at the top on the right, with the tangled roses?"

Her smile renewed itself. "Exactly."

Whit was more baffled still. But since he felt crowded by the peering rector, he wanted to get her alone and ask a long list of questions. He said "Can I give you a ride somewhere?"

Beck said "As a matter of fact, I'd be grateful. All the excitement today—I'm weary." She looked less weary than a rested child.

They thanked the rector and shut themselves in the car before they spoke again. Beck said "Don't worry; I know you don't remember. I'm four years younger and was just a lanky brat when you left home. My mother was your drawing teacher though, in grade school."

"But that was Mrs. Jayne."

Beck nodded. "I used to be Rebecca Jayne. I married Donald Barksdale."

Whit cranked the car and backed toward the road. Don was two or three years younger than Whit, but they'd swum together on the high-school team. *Don Barksdale—God seldom made a dumber soul. But Lord, he could swim like a show-class porpoise. And all the vacant space in his head was packed with trust and laughter.* Whit glanced at her left hand, a thin gold ring. Had he heard any news of Don lately? Hadn't Don joined the Navy after school? "Where's Don now?" he said.

As they rode toward town, Beck faced the land side, dunes and oats. "Don was killed last June, just south of Rome." Her face had stayed level.

Whit said "Which day?" and knew she was going to say the sixth.

"The third or fourth—the original telegram said the third, but the letter from his captain said the fourth." Beck faced round to Whit and managed another hedged smile. "What a strange first question—I mean, you knowing Don well as you did. Don Barksdale died; can you say you're sorry?"

"Oh God," Whit said, "I could watch Donnie Barksdale swim all week; he was that good at it. Remember how high he rode in the water? I was always scared he might just lift on up completely and take full wing and vanish from sight."

Beck said "Exactly." But again she turned away. "Excuse me. I didn't mean to blame you."

He wanted more than anything to touch her wrist. But he only said "What I meant was just this—for practical purposes, I died myself, two or three days later, on the sixth."

"You were in the Normandy invasion?"

Whit nodded and drove a half mile in deepening silence. They were passing houses with weak porch lights. They even passed a porch where a girl maybe twenty was sitting on the front steps gazing out, with the stars and stripes draped from waist to foot. But even with this fine woman beside him, all Whit saw was the grass of the pasture where he met death. Nothing else he'd known was that bright green or that cool and deep. After the angel ended his song, the next-to-last thought Whit had before death was *Remember this color. You'll need it one day.* Then he had thought *No more days left.* But now, in the car, he was seeing that same green, deep in his head and rich as ever. *As good a place as any to stop. Stay there.*

Beck still didn't face him, but after ten seconds she said "That light up yonder? I get out there."

Whit laughed. "*Whoa* now."

"What?"

"You live at that light?"

Beck said "I work there." Finally she faced him. "I live back behind it."

"The White Star Inn—you the master chef?"

"Don't I wish," Beck said. "I'm the day desk-clerk."

Whit was still laughing.

She smiled. "That's a thoroughly respectable job. That light you see is very *white*, Buster."

Whit reined himself in. "To be sure, I'm sorry. What I mean is, I almost stayed there myself. But at the last minute, I decided on the Spar."

Beck said "You'll like it. It's nicer than us. Of course it costs twice as much."

Whit slowed and signaled to pull to the right. Then he puffed his voice comically, "Us expense-account bosses travel first-class."

Beck said "When was your last trip to Manteo?"

"Nineteen thirty-eight—we brought our daughter down to see *The Lost Colony.*"

"I feared as much. See, the pageant's canceled till the whole war's over. And if you're expecting first-class quarters, you're in the wrong town."

"Wrong state, wrong country." Whit stopped the car just short of a shell-lined walk to the inn. "How did you land this far from home?"

Beck waited. "Desperation—once Don was gone, I couldn't stay in Raleigh. Long before I learned he'd landed in Italy, I somehow knew he wouldn't come back. He and I had lived in our own little place off White Oak Road. But once he was gone, I moved in with Mother. You may not know but her eyesight's failing. And I let my pity drive me too far."

"Pity for what?"

"Her going blind, bumping into things. But mainly for me—the pity, I mean. They never said so outright in words; still nobody understood why I loved Don. But God, I *did* and when that awful telegram came, my world just pole-axed over on the ground. In less than two weeks, I begged Mother's pardon and ran down here."

"Why here?"

It made Beck find a reason at last. She smiled again, broad as when they'd met at the church. "Couldn't get any closer to Rome, I guess—why else? Lord knows, it's some sort of jumping-off place, full of people too crazy to live landlocked."

Whit said "I may need to move on down."

Beck said "You look sane."

"So more than one woman has told me this week, and I'm grateful to all, but I think you're wrong." Whit knew it wasn't the right thing for now, but something made him blare his eyes and snarl through his teeth.

It came so suddenly that Beck's hand went to the door handle, and her body leaned forward.

Whit finally touched her, a hand on her arm—the white patch of skin between her glove and the sleeve. "I'm safe as Mahatma Gandhi's kid brother."

Beck's right leg was already out of the car. But she looked around, checked his face and waited. "Thanks for the ride, hear? I hope you rest well."

He said "You had your supper yet?"

"I don't eat supper." But she smiled and waited.

"Then watch me eat. I'm famous on two whole continents for eating."

She frowned at the prospect—he was lean as a tree—but finally she laughed.

"No really, please join me. I'll go check myself in and meet you here at eight."

Beck said "Our dining room closes at eight."

"We'll find a place."

"Whit, you truly don't know this town. It's still out of season; it's bolted shut."

"Then we'll drive west till something's open."

Whit gave no sign of coming round to help her, so Beck got herself out and leaned back in. Young as she was, she moved with a slowness that signaled pain. When she got her balance outside, she turned and leaned back in. "We might well drive till dawn for something open. But I'll be here in the lobby at eight, if you're still hungry."

Before he thought of how it might sound, Whit suddenly said "I'm married. Did I say so?"

Beck leaned farther in and her face was earnest. "Maybe I smiled too much, back at church—you were such a surprise. But understand; I'm married too, in my mind at least. My home is gone but if I'd set out to wreck other peoples', I'd be a sick fool to set up shop on an island with more sand crabs than people."

Whit smiled. "Beg pardon. I was telling myself. Family men need to do that, you know?"

"I didn't, no sir. Are you that kind of man?"

Whit said "Lady, I'm no kind of man. You are facing a boy that very likely died the same week as Don."

"Don't joke about that."

He knew it was the second time he'd done it this week. But he raised his right hand, a solemn oath. *No joke, believe me.*

Beck waited, then withdrew and stood upright. "If I see you later, you can say what you've sworn to."

Before Whit could speak, she somehow vanished. And she'd made so real a place for herself, there beside him, that the hole she left in the evening air was also a scar.

Whit had lain down to rest for ten minutes. But the weight of the day sank him lower than he guessed, well below dreams, to a place where his mind ate sleep like a food. Yet his built-in alarm eventually woke him. He sat upright and checked his watch—two minutes past eight. He rushed through a shower, dressed in clean clothes and got to the White Star a quarter hour late. The brown lobby was empty, so he rang the desk bell. It was maybe two minutes before a school boy appeared from the office and said "Well, *welcome.*" He had a freight-elevator Adam's apple that lurched as a helpless smile went on spreading.

Whit returned the greeting. "Is Beck in there?" He pointed to the office.

"Beg your pardon, sir?"

"Rebecca Barksdale—I'm here to meet her."

The boy flushed scarlet. "Oh I thought you were somebody looking for a room." He throttled back to a confidential whisper. "I've been here a week and have yet to rent a room. We're real overstocked." He was maybe fourteen and his voice was also seeking its level; there were sudden drops and peaks.

"Sorry to disappoint you. Mrs. Barksdale though?"

The boy extended a long pale hand—"I'm Paul Basnight"—but he still ignored the question.

So when Whit had shaken the hand and grinned, he headed for a chair to wait out the mystery.

That shook Paul out of whatever late-spring torpor he suffered. He studied Whit's face awhile and then said "You must be who she gave up on. She was in here, seems like, an hour ago, all decked out and nice. But it looked like she got mad and left through the back." Paul nodded vaguely toward the farthest wall.

"You know where she went?"

"Home, I guess."

Whit said "Where's that?"

"If you don't know, I better not tell you. She's very particular about information."

"Can you get her on the phone?"

Paul's head shook hard. "Oh no you don't. Mrs. Barksdale *boils* desk boys for supper."

Though the need to find her only increased, Whit still took pleasure in the slow exchange, like watching a dancer in clear thick oil. He said "Son, don't tell me—I bet I can guess. You're from the *old* lost colony, aren't you?"

"No sir, I can't memorize two lines."

Whit said "Not the pageant—the original settlers, from Sir Walter Raleigh."

Paul's stunned eyes wallowed. "You mean the real one, 1585?"

"You seem that kind of relaxed and easy, your old-timey ways. You seem historic." Whit knew he was teasing a slow-witted boy. But he also scented the same heady air he breathed at Juanita's and with Tray in the clinic. It smelled like a hint that average people—in trailers and at desks—were as ready as he for the slightest clue that a life of days, in this world here, could end up finally with a true meaning, not just the black grave.

By then Paul thought he'd met his first looney, but his good manners held. He said "Oh no indeed, I'm a modern boy."

Whit said "Ah good. Then I know what to do." He came all the way back, took out his wallet, found three dollar bills and palmed them to Paul. "Now where does she live, and how do I find it?"

Paul pointed again. "Go out the back now and climb the rise. It's the only hill between here and Raleigh. She's got her a shed up there, maybe three rooms. She painted it dark gray all on her own, but of course you won't see that at night. And I bet she's gone; she was *hot* upset."

Whit smiled. "Me too. But listen, let's bet. If she's not there I'll stop back by here and double your tip. You could change a ten-dollar bill then, couldn't you?"

Paul said "Absolutely." His smiles were exhausted and, as Whit turned to leave, Paul said "Known her long?"

"Most of her life."

"Someday when she's gone then, stop back in here and tell me her secret."

Whit said "What do you mean?"

Paul shook his head. "If you don't know, I doubt I believe you've known her long." Then he hid again in a whisper. "Manteo's no big city, I grant you, and people get wild this close to water. But not one person in town's got *her* number."

Whit was tempted but, for once, knew better than to press. He said "Paul, women, in general, don't have a secret no more than you, me or the dog. But they've got a lot at stake in making you think they're the Sphinx herself."

Paul said "I thought the Sphinx was a man."

Whit was leaving already. "See what I told you? She's *hoodooed* you."

Paul's eyes were as troubled as if that was food for thought, long years to come.

And once the door was shut behind him, Whit begged again *Don't leave me out in this night alone, but oh don't let me shirk my duty.*

*

The shed was a low shingled cottage, and Paul was right—it looked more black than gray in the dark. Dim lights were on but the shades were pulled, so Whit had no choice but to knock on the door.

Finally a strong voice said "Who is it?"

It didn't sound all that much like a woman. But Whit said "Whitley Wade, running late."

The voice said "Why?"

"Why *late* or why *here*?"

"Both," it said.

"I tried to take a cat nap and I overslept. I'm hunting an old friend from Breeze Road, Raleigh."

The door opened halfway and Beck stood tall in oil-lamp light. "I was never your friend."

At least Whit thought it was Beck, by her outline. But the hair was different, pinned up someway. And the whole side facing him was dark. For one long moment, he was twenty years younger—a scared boy. And he thought *Haul ass while you're in one piece. This is turning too weird.*

"You got cold feet."

Whit actually shook himself. "No, I told you the truth. I just overslept."

Beck's hand came out and hooked the screen door. "It's too late now."

"It's not. I checked. Some cafe called 'Sheriff's' is open. I phoned and the man said "I'll shuck oysters, buddy, long as you eat em.' "

Beck said "You'd really go there?"

Whit said "Why not? It's advertised."

"On every *Wanted* poster in America."

"Ma'm?"

"It's a robbers' den, a cutthroat heaven."

Whit said "Then I can test my nerve."

Beck took a moment, then said "All right, give me one long minute." She turned away.

"Can I wait inside?"

"No sir, you can't."

So Whit stood in the cool dark, half thrilled to be there, still so sunk in the recent surrender and being all these miles from home again that he thought no more of June and Liss than of any ruined boy he'd known in the war. He even threw his head far back and studied the sky, the zillion stars. As always he thought A *crying damned shame—all that up there and I never learned their names*. Oh he knew the two Dippers and even the Bear, but not the name of any lone star. At the same instant a single star seemed to flare out reddish.

Whit fixed on it and, for some reason, named it for a nurse he knew in England—*Redmayne*. Nobody known to Whit above ground was tougher than she. So he fixed on the star. *Redmayne, watch my steps tonight. I'm walking in thin air. Don't leave me blind.* Nothing till then had made him feel guilty—to be with a woman here, dark and somehow poised for more, if the woman appeared. He quickly turned his face to the ground, his feet half buried in sand and grass. *Watch the Earth, old son. You live down here and nothing you've done here yet means harm. Keep it that way.*

Inside, somebody threw a switch and a powerful bulb lit up by the door. Its sudden burn scalded Whit's eyes and mind. But then a woman was also there, in a black dress with long white collar-points. Though her hair was up, it was plainly Beck. Of all the evident bounty of his trip—Juanita's healing, Tuck's calm welcome, Martha's face untouched by years, then peace in Europe and Traynham Burns's trust—of all the unearned good and hope that had ambushed him these past four days, the two eyes meeting his own eyes now were the finest promise. He smiled and bowed and said "I'll never forget you now."

Beck stopped in her tracks, searched his smile and found the thing she'd needed most since the day Don left—courteous notice and a kind man's will to admit the pleasure her presence could bring. She swallowed the *thanks* she longed to say and turned back quickly to lock her door.

Whit had shocked himself with his declaration. So separate, with a good deal of night between them, they walked round the side of the inn to the car.

Two hours later they were nearing the last of a roast oyster feast. Sheriff himself—a near-albino, red-haired four-footer—stood at their table and mutely opened every shell with the patient care few human beings invest in work. As the meal lengthened, Whit and Beck eyed each other with what they thought were concealed comic glances referring to their host—his size, his patience and graveyard demeanor.

So when they called quits, they were more than flummoxed that Sheriff bowed deeply and said "Don't get me wrong—you ate like you meant it, and I'm glad you did, but I hope you don't have no baby born afflicted like me."

At first they were speechless. And then Whit scrambled to explain how they meant no harm and hadn't meant him. They were just elated to find each other after long years apart and were laughing at that.

Sheriff thought about it and finally rigged a complex grin that made his face collapse on the mouth like a dying apple. But as he bowed a final time, he said "Don't never forget I warned you. Don't have no baby now, else you'll be sorry."

Any other place or time, they'd have thought he was crazy and excused themselves. But here tonight—so close to an ocean that, days ago, had been prowled over by Navy subs—they felt as destructive as eyeless giants. Sheriff was gone though, no way to reclaim him. They sat in silence and tasted their guilt.

Before the warning, they had ordered pie. A black woman brought it in now from the kitchen, handsome wedges of coconut pie so gold it almost weighed her down. And when Whit faced the woman and asked if Sheriff had gone on home, she said "Mr. Sherf hid back in yonder by the cookstove, crying like a baby."

Beck said "Oh no. We never meant to hurt him."

The woman said "Don't pay him no mind. He live on nerve pills, syrup and snuff. His nerves a heap worse off than mine. He brittle as this pie crust." She took up a clean fork and raised a bite of the pie to Beck's lips, "Here, see if I'm lying."

Beck took it in. The crust was so buttery it literally melted. Then she said "You're telling the God's own truth."

The woman nodded, righteous. "Tilda, my name. Next time you in here, ax for my pie—cooking chocolate tomorrow, lemon on Friday. And *forget* Mr. Sherf. He back in yonder like I said, eating rolls."

Whit said "No no, you said he was crying."

"Doing both," Tilda said and wheeled her bulk with the grace of a troop ship beyond them in the night, bound from Norfolk against the Gulf Stream for Panama and then northwest toward bristling Japan—ignoring subs, all monsters of the deep and the hopeful fragile bodies aboard her.

Whit watched Tilda go and felt it like that, not in words to be sure. But he saw an actual ship in his mind, and he thought of boys no stronger than he being shifted across more than half the world to offer their necks a second time to a blind axe already thick with blood.

*

When they'd eaten every crumb of the pie and finished their third bottles of beer, they could speak again (they'd mainly been silenced by Sheriff and Tilda and the cutthroat faces around them in booths). Beck smiled and said "It tasted fine but don't you suspect it might have been poisoned?"

Whit said "No question" and they both fell forward in abandoned laughter; their heads touched gently. Beck drew back first and looked toward the ceiling. Deep in the booth like that, and dark, her pale skin shone against the black hair. If Whit had understood radiation, he might have thought a nuclear core concealed in her spine was spending itself in lavish haste to glorify Beck. For all the two years of Army sex-talk—where no five minutes went without mention of women cut down to nothing but skin—Whit had hardly watched another woman. Not that June's body still crowded his head; he'd just had far more pressing needs, like plain survival or the knowledge of whether survival was worth the steps he'd have to take to live.

Here for the first time in—what? three years?—was an actual woman so fine he could not believe her. Yet his body was telling him, this hot instant, she was way too real for any dream. It craved all of her. So he tried to cool down, though he still watched her eyes. *Rebecca Barksdale, you are too fine. Let me watch you from here, with both of us safe.* Clear as it sounded in his mind, Whit said it over three slow times like a gift she'd never know he gave. For the first time in longer than he could remember, he was in one place—and happy there—not strewn through a field or longing for somewhere calm and dark.

A black-haired man in the opposite booth was also staring hard at Beck. His eyes had the strength and the locked intent of a hunting cat's.

And when Beck lowered her gaze again, she turned toward those fixed confident eyes.

The man's hair lay on his brow like rat tails, matted and lank.

When he understood he'd drawn Beck's look, he reached up, pulled his left eye out and winked the empty lid. He held the huge glass-eye out toward her on the palm of his hand, the size of an egg. Then he brought it to his mouth and made a hard gulp, as if to swallow it.

Beck formed a round O with her thumb and forefinger, the *Righto* sign, and called over to him "You can say *that* again." He hadn't said a word, and she meant nothing really. She was only showing how relaxed she was—the first easy evening since Don left home, her own first chance to sit again and not feel stripped of a strong limb without which she'd never stand again or walk.

The one-eyed man caught her drift and grinned.

But Whit was calmed also and obeyed Beck's call to "say that again." With both hands up like a band conductor, he almost whispered "Now one more time—I died and came back." When the words were out, he couldn't think why or how they pertained. But by then everybody was well underway on the harsh cold beer that was sometimes scarce in the wartime countryside but plentiful at Sheriff's.

Beck had heard him. She frowned in puzzlement. Then her hand reached out. On their table was a burning candle in a bowl. Beck pulled it toward her and held a finger over the flame. In a moment she flinched. Then she said to Whit "You try that now."

"Try to burn myself? Your eyes have done that."

"Just do what I did."

So Whit bore the flame as long as he could, then drew back his finger and blew on it hard. "You plan to explain your purpose, O Priestess?"

Beck still watched the flame. "I hoped you'd get it, just watching us both. But since you don't—" She poured a few grains of salt in her palm and licked it up. "I think I meant this. Whit, I've got no idea how you feel—about me or Don's death or your own pain or your wife and daughter up the road in Raleigh. But then you don't know a thing about me. I could have plans for murdering you at the stroke of midnight."

She reached behind her and took out the combs that held her hair. It fell down free and she paid it no mind, not even a touch, though she knew it doubled the force of her words. "Did you ever think this?—I can't even tell you what a word like *burn* really means to me, and you can't tell me. We can just watch each other's hand get burned and flinch from the fire, and then we guess that the word *burn* must mean the same to us two at least." Her eyes went to Whit. "That's all we can know."

Whit said "I couldn't have said it like that. But lady, I don't plan to fight you on it. Sounds right to me. I may even be the main authority, in this room anyhow, on what you said. I flat-out died, in a real time and place, not a whole year ago. Two medics and a boatload of doctors brought me back. They absolutely brought me back from death, sure as you bring a sack of corn meal home from the grocery store."

Beck nodded and moved her right hand slowly across the wood toward his flat hand, stopping two inches short of touch. "And you can't know what I'm feeling now, can you?"

Whit pushed his hand a half inch closer. For most of a year, since the hard dread seized him, he hadn't been near any flesh as charged as her hand here. And here was a woman who claimed she knew him and had managed to grow into this fine shape without his having one memory of her. He said "No ma'm, you're a closed book still. But I see your hand has moved this close."

"And yours toward me." Beck sat back suddenly, both hands out of sight.

Whit said "I'm guessing we better leave now."

Beck looked down and her voice half sang. "—To separate cabins in the ship of life." But she didn't quite laugh. And when she looked up, her beauty had grown a whole two notches.

Whit knew better than to speak of that. He knew he was facing a risk as great as he'd taken in France. He stood and reached for his wallet to pay.

Twenty minutes later they'd left their shoes in the car and were walking against a stiff south wind, as near to the shifting line of the surf as moonlight would let them. They were separate still and, because of the wind and crashing water, they were silent again, only pointing now and then toward something—a glowing log or a ghostly crab. In limitless space, Whit's head had cleared. And the magnetism he felt in Beck had simplified and moved farther off. Ten yards ago he'd thought he might try to hold her hand.

But where they were now, in cooler wind, he thought he felt no need to touch her. He wanted only to be beside her, in sight and reach, if she ever needed help or protection. With all his devoted thanks to June, Whit knew he could walk out any day and not harm her life. June was stronger than he, though she wouldn't know it till he finally vanished. And Liss already was bearing the weight of first womanhood with a limber grace that proved how little she leaned on a father, even one she liked.

He thought it was time to say what he meant. Still barely touching Beck's loosened hair, he leaned to her ear and said "Let's go find us a dry place to sit." There seemed to be a low dune on their right. Before they were there, Whit thought *Have I hurt anybody yet? When this night's over, will anybody living be hurt by this?* He told himself he couldn't know what *this* would be. He said to himself *Remember you're back alive, Whit Wade. And two good women are waiting for you in the place that's home.*

They sat at the top of the twenty-foot dune for maybe five minutes before Beck laughed and pointed out toward the restless water, with its parallel bands of silver moonlight. "Excuse me for laughing—no question about it, this is as fine a sight as I've seen for a good many weeks. But it looks so much like a Hawaiian vaudeville show I saw at the State Theater when I was a girl."

Whit remembered too. "I must have seen it the same week as you, with Ginger Rogers in *Kitty Foyle*. Steel guitars and gold grass-skirts. I've wondered ever since how they made that moon. It looked as real as this one here."

"Who says this is real?"

Whit said "Don't you?"

"I can't even start believing *we're* here."

"Feel your hands," Whit said. "You feel sand, don't you?"

Beck tried it. "Yes sir."

"And I do too so we must be here."

Beck waited awhile. "We may well be."

"What's against it, in your mind?"

"—Me wanting to be here, someday with you." She still wouldn't face him, but she strengthened her voice to carry the distance. "When you lived there in your mother's house on Beechridge Road, I memorized your daily schedules. I knew when you got on your bicycle to take your piano lesson, I knew when you went down to Byrd Street to play basketball. Most of all, I knew exactly when you left for school in the morning. And I'd leave home two or three minutes behind you and catch the same bus. I could usually guess the shirt you'd wear and whether you'd choose your gray coat-sweater or your letter jacket."

Whit said "I never saw you." It didn't sound cruel.

"I knew you didn't. I'd have died if you caught me."

"How much older was I?"

Beck said "*Was*? It was three years' difference, back then anyhow. I guess it still is."

"Truly?"

"Three years and four months, your April to my August."

Whit said "In daylight you look a lot younger."

Beck thought, then laughed. "And at night I look about a hundred and ten?"

"I didn't mean that."

Beck said "I know. And I don't feel it, not now at least."

Whit leaned back on both elbows and again watched the stars. Moonlight blanked the weakest shiners, but the powerful stars were gleaming harder to make whatever point they intended (he thought they weren't pointless). "When I was a boy I read somewhere that if you go to the bottom of a well and look up—even at high noon—you'll see stars, bright as ever in the sky. Can that be true?"

Beck said "Very likely. I believe things a whole lot stranger."

"Want to give me a sample?"

"No, you've got the floor. Say more about your well."

Whit said "On the sole condition you live in a well, you've got you a sky full of stars, day and night. I always meant to ask a well-digger, but I never met one. Still looking though." Another long upward gaze and he said "What's the strangest thing you believe, here and now?"

"You mean, on the order of grown men dying and coming to life?" There was no hint of laughter.

Whit said "Nothing strange about that—a plain fact. Happens every week or so in a war. You meet all kinds of boys, walking round dead or thinking they are."

Beck said "I believe Don's watching me still."

Whit's first thought was *Don never did anything else but watch. He spoke so little you'd get to thinking he was some different creature, watching to see if you'd stand or run. Then he'd hit the water and swim a lap, and soon you'd remember he was more of a dolphin than a landlocked boy.* When he looked at her then, Beck seemed as alone as a thing could be, a well-made pillar stood up in a dry field with nothing but wind to know she was there. He said "You believe Don's watching you—you hope it or what?"

Beck said "It's a real fact, real as your death. I've seen Don three times—never head-on, just there at the corner of my eye as I turn. He always vanishes before I can focus and really see him."

"You truly believe it?"

Beck said "You believe this is sand on your skin. You believe you and I are meeting like this after riding the bus to school together some few hundred mornings, then spending most of our lives apart. We know the Germans lost the war, not two days ago. The radio told us. Sure—Don Barksdale still watches me."

"What does that say about your future life?"

Beck said "Wish I knew. I can't very well do much but wait. For the first few months, it seemed so utterly welcome and right. The first night he came was five or six days after I got the wire. I was still at Mother's. We'd finished supper and listened to the news—I feel some need to follow the war. Then after the ten o'clock report, Mother asked me to read her something. I chose an old book she's had since school, *A Hundred Best-Loved Poems*. She asked for Bryant's 'Thanatopsis,' and I got right to the famous close. I'd memorized it as a junior in school." She began to say the last few lines and got as far as "approach thy grave" when her memory slipped.

Whit took the line from her and attempted the end,

> "As one who wraps the drapery of his couch
> About him and lies down to pleasant dreams."

Beck took it back, seamless. "Don was there, a little behind my right elbow."

"You sure it was him?"

She waited a good while. "I am. Sure. It was his good smile."

"But you didn't see his face?"

"I already said I didn't." Again she waited. "He stood there naked—it was warm last June, in Raleigh anyhow. He'd never been any kind of nudist at home. But I do recall thinking 'Thank God, Mother's blind.' Then I thought I certainly ought to be scared. But what I felt was, shook to the marrow of every bone in my body, head to foot. Still I never broke step. I finished the poem."

It sounded right. Whit chose to believe her, having seen with his own eyes last June a creature if anything stranger than Don. "Did you tell your mother?"

Beck didn't seem to hear. "He stayed for the end. And just when I thought I'd have to look back—or he'd step forward—Mother said 'Beck, set those roses on the porch. I won't sleep a wink; they smell too fine.' Mary Dorton had brought us a big bowl of dahlias that morning. It was not them though."

"When did you think how strange it was?"

Beck said "Not till just now—here, telling you."

"But he's been back again?" Whit said.

"Every few months, when I least expect."

"You still haven't seen his actual face. Has he said a word?"

Beck said "No." Then of all things she laughed a single note. "He's put his clothes on, every time since."

Whit said "And you didn't come out here, to escape?"

"Whit, Don and I came out here for a week, right after our wedding." She leaned slowly over and tucked her head between her bent knees as if she never intended to rise.

Whit was determined to ask no more. Now was surely time to leave.

But then Beck sat upright, turned toward him and sounded as natural as a voice on the street. "It's worried me lately."

"How?"

Again she sounded sane as a child. "Two big ways. I can't help wondering if it means Don's punished—the fact that he can't seem to rest at night but must trail after me (he comes at night). And then what you said awhile ago—can I have anything but his and my life? Is there anything I can do to help him rest?"

"Or drive him off."

Beck said "You know you never meant that."

"I may," Whit said.

Her voice hardened through every word. "Then maybe you need to hurt somebody to prove you've made it back yourself and have got human powers."

"Do I look that much like a killer?" Whit said.

He had drawn back fast since they climbed the dune, and she couldn't think why. But Beck could see the line of his face. Like no other man she'd known in her life, Whit Wade had kept his original light, the coal of heat back deep in his mind that his eyes still watched, which conferred the dignity—even in laughter—that made him a thing to study and tend. How could she know that, here and now, Whit felt his own version of the same about her? She finally said "I don't know how many boys you killed, but I think you do whatever it takes to work your will."

Whit was shocked. "Great Jesus, Beck. I hated this war till it drove me wild before it killed me."

"I meant here and now."

Whit sat upright and waited a long time. Then he stood and loped down the dune to the near cool edge of the feeble surf. His mind had boiled that suddenly. And even now he had no real thoughts, only the groans and cries of anger. Slowly the cold water numbed his feet. Finally he saw three legible sentences, spelled out before him. *You're not out here, bird-dogging this widow, fine as she looks. You're a grown man, trying to learn to last. Climb back up there and drive her home.*

When he turned to go, she was standing behind him—so white

in the dark that, for one cold instant, he thought she was surely an actual spirit, armed with death. But once he knew her, he showed her his hands, as white as hers and as empty. He didn't mean to draw her toward him and she understood. He said "Beck, I'm nobody strong enough to watch, much less try to help. Let's get you back in your own warm house."

"I came down here to say I'm sorry."

Whit said "For what? If you said something wrong, I was too tired to hear you." He walked on past her, back up the dune to get his shoes. Then he knew he'd left his shoes in the car. From there, he could no longer see her at all. But he called out "Beck, can you meet me at the car?"

Some voice made a long string of high sounds that were more like bird calls in jungle movies than human meanings.

And when Whit was still ten yards from the car, he could see somebody in the driver's seat. He almost turned back to wait it out. But he forced himself on till he leaned down close and saw through the windshield that Beck was the driver, at the wheel anyhow. He opened her door and said "Slide over."

She said "Your feet are wet and sandy. I'll gladly drive."

"You scared of me?"

"No, I just thought I'd make your life easy."

Whit looked down for his feet; and the best he could see, they were gone for good. From mid-thigh down, there was nothing but dark. He broke out laughing and said "Move, woman. Let a legless ghost get you home, if he can. He needs that chance."

Beck thought and chose to let him try.

The dashboard clock said ten to one. Whit and Beck sat as separate in the car as they'd been all evening, and every house they passed enforced their natural silence. No more than five windows showed any light. Beck understood that, if anybody stirred in the darkened rooms, they were still obeying the wartime blackout (Germans had sunk more than one ship in sight of this beach). So despite the surrender, night seemed what it was in Whit's childhood—a time to be watchful of everything. And the heart of town, all dozen buildings, was the ruin of a humble race of creatures who'd paused here awhile on a search for refuge. The huddle of roofs and dry wood walls was insubstantial and might well vanish behind you as you moved.

Soon Beck said "Turn left up there," then "Take the second right and stop at the possums."

Whit asked no questions but obeyed exactly, and soon his headlights trapped three possums in blinding glare by a mound of strewn trash. He hadn't seen a possum for maybe three years. And the pale fur and shining eyes made them seem like visitors from another world where hunger was the only thought or feeling.

Beck said "If they weren't as helpless as babes, I'd poison them all."

Whit realized she'd brought him, a new way, to her back door. The trash was spilled from her garbage can.

Beck said "If you leave your lights on a minute, I'll run them off and pick up the trash."

Knowing how personal a trash pile can be, Whit at first obeyed. But when Beck had squatted to scrounge through the junk, he switched off the engine and went to help. She didn't say a word; and all through the job, he felt the hidden eyes of possums press their rage against his eyes. When he picked up the last tuna can and stood, he realized Beck was on her knees, cupping her face in her hands, eyes covered. Whit shared one trait with every other man—he'd had a mother. And whatever the cause, the sight of any woman in pain was always his own unforgivable fault. He bent low enough to take Beck's arm and offer to raise her.

She said "Please, no. You go on to bed."

He went back to the car, turned off the headlights and waited beside her.

She rose and was almost totally dark. "I asked you to leave." Yet she stayed in place, facing Whit.

"I won't sleep till you say what's wrong."

Beck got herself up and moved toward the house. More than halfway there, she turned and said "Please come on in."

She was out of coffee, and by then anyhow they both were cold, so she brewed big mugs of chicken bouillon. Whit had never drunk it, and its oily saltiness warmed him quickly. Whatever thought had overcome Beck was under control, so they went to the boxy living room and sat on creaky wicker chairs. Since the numerous pictures must have come with the house, Whit didn't take them as clues to Beck's mind—a set of hefty girls outdoors in various sports, with different costumes for every game but identical grins. Whit waved at the wall and said "Your family?"

"Wish they were. Aren't they cheerful? Must have spent more than half their days changing clothes—they look so snazzy."

"They'd look better stripped." It slid from Whit like steam from a kettle; and he actually blushed, a rare event.

Beck laughed for the first time in more than two hours. That riled her chair, and it cracked like blazing underbrush. When she calmed again, her eyes were as new as some other woman's, rested and blameless. She said "Can I say it?"

"Say anything you please." At the beach Beck had said Don's presence thrilled her. Nothing harmless had thrilled Whit's mind since Liss was born. But now as he waited for Beck to speak, he felt his skull take the growing pressure of simple joy after years of pain.

Beck stood up, went to an oil lamp and carefully lit it. She turned off the overhead light and stood, outlined by that warm shine. Then facing Whit she laid it out with her hand, word by word. "I know we both want to leave this room and get dark again."

Whit wanted to laugh but kept it in. It was that fine to hear; he'd come this far. A woman this grand, familiar with death and with none of June's duty, could want the live present fact of Whit Wade. Old as he was, and after two years in the fighting Army, he'd still never known a woman this frank. In its wildness it went against the beauty of her face and the way he'd met her on the steps of church. *But I asked for a sign, and then I saw her. That drew me in.* He took their meeting as one more hint that, together now, they were meant to press forward. But his eyes went back to the girls on the wall, young and untouched. Then his mind saw Liss, younger even and with far more hope than anything here, if the ground stayed beneath her. He silently said *Don't make me choose.*

Because he hadn't stood, Beck sat again and took up her cup. She blew on the broth and stirred it slowly. Finally she looked up and said "I told you how I feel about Don, him being nearby. He's not here now. You got anybody here that I can't see?"

He thought of Liss Wade again, just her name. No picture of her face, saying yes or no. He made himself think June's name too. Then he nodded his head, "I do. Yes I do."

Beck smiled. "I doubt this is marriage we're discussing—'I *do*' or 'I *don't*.' "

Whit said "All right, I'm a Sunday-school simpleton; but in my mind it would come to that. I made June Wade a promise, years back. And I've kept it till now. If Don Barksdale was alive out there in the yard this minute, you wouldn't be in here, saying this much."

Beck waited. "I might."

"You wouldn't and you know it."

That struck like a lash. Beck's eyes half-shut and she swallowed hard. "You never knew I was breathing on Earth till sundown tonight. Who gave you the right to read strangers' minds?"

Whit said "Beck, there's no cause to get mad. You're as fine a woman as I've ever seen. I just meant—"

Her voice seemed calm but the sense was hard. "No, tell me. Who gave you the right to sit here and say what I think or feel?"

Whit said "Nobody, no higher power." He tried to laugh. "I've just got two good working eyes. I can see you clear as my own right hand—your eyes and hair and the way you move. They tell me you're far too fine and good to crash into other people's lives and start cutting."

Beck thought a long time. "It wouldn't be that—two people out here on an island one night, one hour alone and never again. It wouldn't be *against* anybody, Whit."

The fact that she said his name then shook him. But he held back and said "Who would it be for?"

She had scared herself. If she'd shaken Whit Wade, she'd thrust her own self way past any limit she'd known till now. And suddenly she felt her mind lift off and into the sky to where she could see herself very clearly—her eyes and hair and a good deal else. Alone and lonesome, not only now but from here till the end. So she came back and checked Whit's face again, *yes*. She said the plain truth, "It would be for me."

Whit started a laugh, then stopped and waited. As he watched her now, still as the room, he suddenly felt much older than she. Not ancient and feeble but worn and wary. When he finally spoke, it was nearly a whisper. "I'm a *person*, look—just one aging boy, tired and true. Nothing to ease your pain, now or ever."

Someway Beck found the patience to watch him. The lamplight had helped him too, his grin. But slowly she began to see him that way, as what he claimed—a tired person, in an actual room. And she felt as if a strong brand of mercy were settling in the air now, well before day. In her mind for years she'd treasured this face. Tonight she'd found it again, still fine, while she had eyes to see it and the strength to speak her meaning.

But now as Beck watched, something from outside—the light, the hour?—slowly blurred Whit's face and hands till at last she could see time wearing him down, even here in this room, this one long night. The young taut struts of his face and neck softened slowly. The laughing mind that had been so quick to seize its wants and eat them entirely was bruised and yielding. He said he had died. But he'd been brought back, maybe luckier than Don or maybe not.

She glanced to her wrist. What time could it be? Was this taking hours or minutes of time? She'd left her watch on the kitchen counter. Whit anyhow looked as patient as she. He still hadn't yawned or shut his eyes. And finally she knew a helpful thing. Whitley Wade was one more thing she'd loved, that was leaving. At such a moment, she firmly believed, most creatures would have sprung to take their needs. So plain and easy to take, here now. But she and Whit had said a calm no. She thought a whole sentence, *Rebecca Barksdale's got to live with herself.*

Through it all, as if to threaten his breath, Whit felt a tide that crested and spilled; then turned and shrank. He couldn't know what fate had done for Beck here now and for his life to come. But the calm he felt, and saw in her, left him gladder still to have found Beck in this present beauty, before age broke her. He knew he'd shown how he felt that strength and had nearly paid its entire need.

The thing outside—a source of mercy that chose to spare them or blind cold chance—had brought them here to a barren island and face to face at a time of thanks for peace and rest. In something as hard to resist as the moon, and this near the ocean, they'd showed each other their own best lights—their faces and minds—and they'd mightily yearned to join and shudder in each other's arms. In declining to meet, each understood that they'd lost and won on a sizable scale. What they couldn't know, and the sad waste was, they'd never meet again.

THURSDAY

10 MAY 1945

WHEN HE FINISHED BREAKFAST, Whit shut his eyes and leaned back to take the clear sun that fell in through the window behind him. He'd slept really well, though not long enough. But he felt still more of the wires in his mind slacken a little. *Life may be offering terms I can take.* Even in the favorable signs of the week, he hadn't stretched to think that far; and it struck him as risky. He squeezed his eyelids tight and thought *Get home safe. Then see what comes.*

In high school his favorite subject was Latin, and he'd made a report on Roman sacrifice. That knowledge of a billion doomed cattle in procession, combined with all he'd read of the bloody Old Testament, had made Whit wish that Christians had kept some real blood in the church. Then a man could rise on a morning like this and ask a preacher to anoint his forehead, say, or wrists with a thumbprint of blood. It would guard him through the hours and miles till he threaded his way safe to June and Liss. As it was, he felt young again and unshielded.

He reached to his plate for a last crumb of toast, chewed it slowly and leaned into the warmth again. In his mind he actually spoke to the sun, *Lead me home safe. Let me be safe for them, let them be whole and glad to see me—they've waited too long.*

"Don't pass out yet, Bo. Day's barely started." The waitress had come up without a sound.

Bo was a name Whit had always liked but never been called. He said "Oh never, I'm wide awake. Just thanking the sun."

She said "Sun's never done a thing for me, not with this red hair." She tapped a finger on her high right cheekbone. "They cored out a dark skin cancer last month." She debated laughing but wrote out his check. "I may yet live."

Whit had already noticed the scar, a real crater. He said "Looks promising to me."

"Promising to *kill* me—you a skin specialist?" Early as it was, her eyes seemed to hint at another meaning.

"Wish I could help you. No, I've got one myself." He touched his upper chest through the jacket. "A German hole you could put your fist in, or could last June."

She frowned accordingly and whispered to spare the other guests. "God *damn.* I wondered what you were doing out here on the edge of the world, this loose, eating oysters all night."

Whit said "Were you at Sheriff's?"

"No, honey, I got a reputation to keep, not to mention respecting what's left of my life."

"Then how do you know what I had for supper?"

"—And who had it with you. And where y'all went when you finished your pie. This ain't Texas, Bo, the wide open spaces—just an island too small for secret business."

Whit said "No secrets. I was good as gold, all night."

She said "I'm glad. From what I hear, that old friend of yours is a sketch to behold but a tiger to cross. What *I* think is, everybody's got to sit still and be good till this war's over."

"I heard it was over." It wasn't a joke; he felt as much.

She took a step back and studied his face. "Then why is my precious baby farflung?"

"I was teasing," Whit said. "You know where he is?"

"Okinawa, last month. Haven't heard a peep since Easter Sunday—he wired me a flower. You think I'm a fool to be scared still?"

Whit said "No, it's serious business but you might do better to keep up your prayers."

"Prayers? If I pray any harder, Bo, I'll starve to death. It's all I can do now—to stop praying long enough and eat me a bite. I haven't had a square meal in eighteen months, not since he boarded that bus out of here. Just aspirins and Pepsis." She was six feet tall, not one fat cell.

Whit laughed. "It's doing both of you good. You keep right on. He's probably having the time of his life."

She said "Many women on Okinawa?"

Whit said "Not a one," not knowing of course.

"That's *some* good news."

"You mean you don't want a fat grandbaby with tilted eyes?"

She said "I don't want nothing on Earth but him in one piece." By then she was clearing Whit's place, so she leaned in closer and lowered her voice. "Understand, I don't even want him scratched. But every three days I write him a letter. I say 'Del, catch you a terrible case of athlete's foot. Get your butt *home*.' You think that would work?"

"It didn't for me. I had to blow this hole in my chest."

"Thought the Germans helped you some."

Whit nodded. "They actually fired the shell. I arranged to meet it."

She said "But you're home and happy."

Whit smiled. "Not yet."

"Then some starved sucker absorbed three eggs with sausage and toast while you were sunbathing."

Whit said "My appetite's catching up with me." And suddenly for the first time since Monday, he thought of June's voice and wanted to hear it. A perfectly normal young woman's voice, that had never stopped calmly haling him in. His watch said quarter past eight. With any luck he could climb to his room here, place a call home, catch Liss as she headed out for school, then speak to June.

Two rings and Liss answered, a breathless "Hello."

"You're bound to be tardy." He'd lowered his voice.

A puzzled silence, then she said "I know."

"This is the Truancy Office of the Raleigh Public Schools. We're looking for Elissa Anne Wade."

A shorter wait. "This is her—*she*."

"Your grammar's improving. You studying at home?"

"Wait—Pa? You rat!"

Whit laughed. "If I'm a rat, what does that make you?"

"I feel like one. But I really didn't know you."

"Wait till you see me. I'm a big surprise."

Liss said "You're not sick? You coming home early?"

"I'm fine, darling. Run on to school. I'll see you tomorrow. Let me speak to your ma." For a long moment Whit thought she'd left with no goodbye. That was no way to start a day.

Then she said "I wish you didn't have to travel. I miss you too much."

"I don't want to travel, but you need to eat. Thank you though." Thanks didn't pay for the smallest trace of the joy that rose in his mind. This child had said the best thing yet.

Liss called out "Ma—" Then she said "Pa, you be careful on the road."

"You be right *there,* tomorrow evening." *She'll say "I will" and I'll say "You will if God says so."*

But Liss was gone, a clean hole in the air.

How can this happen? I was doing so fine. Whit thought he could hear the front door slam.

Then June said "Hey. I was out in the yard."

"Something wrong?"

"Calm down. It's garbage day, remember?"

"And you and Liss are both all right?"

"Fine, Whit—nothing out of the ordinary. Went to church Wednesday night."

He said "Me too."

"Does it feel strange to you, all this much peace?"

Whit said "It'll feel a lot stranger when the Japs quit. I've spent a fair many hours since Monday, counting the faces of boys I knew that are gone for good. That's been hard as ever. But no, I feel a lot like *me*. You think you can stand it?"

"Stand what—you? I told Whit Wade I'd be here when he came, if I lived that long."

"Can you hang on then till sundown tomorrow?"

June also heard the firm beat of Whit's best voice, but she'd lost it before and was too gun-shy to speak of it now. She said "I thought I almost knew you, here last Sunday night."

He said "Almost. But I'm stronger still."

"Don't risk a thing. Be careful, boy."

Whit hung on her *boy*. Through all their courting, they had played blood games. They spent whole secret nights together as brother and sister, mother and son, father and daughter. Now he saw that—all these months he was back from France, strong as June had been—she'd never once tried to play mother to his wounded son. So he said "Look, girl—you do the same." Before the words were gone from the air, he knew they were right. For the first time lately, he wanted June present.

She said "I'll go sit down this minute, in the softest chair. You take little safe back roads, drive slow."

"I barely passed ten cars between you and here."

"You sound far off as Russia," June said.

Whit said "Just Manteo—it almost is."

"And where tonight?"

"Greenville at least."

June said "Wherever, these arms await."

Whit thought of *the everlasting arms,* her Bible text in his Wednesday snack. He said "Everlasting."

She laughed. "Even June can't promise that."

Whit said "I bet on it, all the same."

As he started twenty minutes later, he thought of stopping by the White Star to see if Beck had weathered the dawn. But his car declined to make the turn. Once the ferry pulled out, he took a long look toward where he guessed Beck's house would be. And he felt his way through what he recalled of their strange long evening. It already felt like a deep-sea dive in dark green water through tons of weight. The thing he wanted to know was, had he cheated the trust she showed him? He'd met June early and kept faith with her, so he hadn't known a great lot of women. But three at least had done the hard thing. Sooner or later they described, in words, the shape of what he meant to them—his mother, June and Beck. One of his easy joys in Liss still flowed from the fact that she'd never drawn that scary shape between them on the ground. He never quite knew where she stood in her mind, and it kept him toeing a hopeful mark.

By the time his wheels were back on land, his own mind cleared. And he worked a full day of small claims in Ponzer, Pantego and Beckwith. He'd worked with the company for years before the war. It saddened his mother when he quit Wake Forest after three years of honorable grades. But at twenty-one the thought of a joint life—with June, in the world—had flushed him out and into jobs that landed him here, a traveling man. Even today he felt no regret.

Like the lion's share of the human race, Whit craved no work more rewarding than this. He managed to help well over half his clients, and he'd yet to hear anything but thanks from the company. He knew he had no special gift to feed and tend and pass to mankind. He survived on honest, time-killing work that tired him enough to keep him from mischief and hating himself. And he'd have no regret, when he died for the last time, of leaving nothing but Liss behind him. Elissa Wade was as hopeful a legacy, in Whit's mind now, as any warehouse of marble statues or shelf of books. And so a Thursday divided in pieces among eight people with claims for money was a day well-spent, if the weather was fair and if he could honestly please, say, five of the eight with nothing worse than money. If he also got a peaceful evening and six hours' sleep, then life was good for one more notch on whatever stick they notched Whit's days.

When he wrote the final voucher in Beckwith, it was nearly dusk. He'd told June he hoped to make Greenville by night; that was forty miles on. But now he was suddenly tired and sad at the thought of a lonely supper and night in a college town. No real choice though—he had a big claim to deal with tomorrow, a fraternity fire. The whole top story of an old house gutted, but not one drunk boy lost or singed. So he'd gone five miles in gathering dark when he had a quick memory.

June had called him *boy* more than once this morning. Had his own fresh start stirred her hope of having a son? She was thirty-three, only one year older than Whit's mother when she bore him after two stillbirths. Was Liss's womanhood also signaling June to try again? And could he stand to wait again through the maybe three years till a squalling baby was a reasonable child?

Of the men he knew, at home and in service, Whit was rare in admitting he wanted a girl child the first time out. And then Liss had proved such a steady pleasure, he and June had rested their luck in her till now. *Son,* a son—was that a thing he'd know how to use, this late in the day, after this much fear? Maybe not, not yet. *Be sure you stand an even chance of ending up a* father *to anybody you start, this far along.*

He might, this very morning now, have a son—what?—sixteen years old. The thought came on him that calmly as he drove. The summer his father died in Raleigh, Whit turned seventeen and was rough to handle. So his mother sent him down here for Tuck to tame. He worked in the fields, brought in tobacco, helped cure it in the log barns and grew a hand higher. Martha was no more than two years older and worked in the kitchen with her grandmother Boot. By early that August, Whit and Martha were "the best of friends," as Martha said when they met alone by the river at night.

It was all she asked, "Ain't we the best of friends, Whit?" And the way she felt to his searching hands, all over his skin—sunlight or moon—those words were nothing but the lovely truth, to him that early. He said them enough times so that, even now all these years later, Whit could hear his young voice on the river breeze, paying Martha her due and taking her thanks.

He'd left in late August for Raleigh and school. And it wasn't till Easter, when he came back down, that Tuck said offhand "Your friend's gone, Whit. Boot sent her to Newport News last month—Martha and a belly five sizes too big on that young a girl." And she stayed in Virginia for several years. Tuck said he heard she had a boy and kept him awhile, then left him up there with some people that liked him. She pushed on as far as Delaware; and for all Whit knew, had been there ever since except for quick visits. With the sole exception of his mother's funeral, this past Monday was his first sight of Martha since that last night by the moving river, thanking her again with both their wild smells joined on his hands.

Working through that took another five miles. And just as the sky went totally dark, he knew he wanted to do two things. The first thing was, he'd never told Martha his strangest thought in that whole glad summer. Every time they touched, he'd come home and lie on his cot a long hour, thinking she was finer than all the rest. A *wondrous creature,* known *to me.* Could he tell her that now? And second, was he the cause of her baby? And was it a son? Was it still alive; did it know his name?

The road behind and ahead was level and dark, completely empty of all but Whit and his present needs. He slowly pulled to the sandy shoulder, bowed his head to the wheel and thought *Let her be there. Let me tell her all she meant. Let me leave with the truth. And let that be some news I can bear.* He looked behind in his rearview mirror, then turned a wide circle and headed for Martha.

He'd driven her home after supper Monday night, so he knew where to find her. Her old house—Boot's—had caved in round the chimney years back. And Boot had thrown up a new place beside it with help from Tuck, three square rooms with lights and plumbing. On Monday night Whit had let Martha out at the edge of the road and not gone in. He also forgot to ask about Boot—was Boot alive or dead? Lord, she'd be a good ninety or worse.

He stopped on the edge of the road again and looked toward the house. The front-room window showed merciless glare from a ceiling light, so he waited awhile to see if any human would pass. Nobody, nothing. In a few more minutes, the slot of glare became an endless view of his future. *You'll sit here, son, and watch that glare till your errand's done.* The chance that he'd detoured here for nothing made his needs all the stronger. He'd knock on the door. And if nobody answered, he'd wait here however long it took.

The danger of anybody knowing his car and telling Tuck was next to none. When the fourth minute passed, he thought *Suppose I find Martha. Suppose she says yes, we've got a child in Richmond or here in the back room, changing his shoes—"Here he comes right now." A healthy tan smart son or daughter or a jailbird felon with a gouged-up mind. What good does it do? This is* crazy, *Whit. You no sooner start back living in the world, and then you poison everything you touch. Get home to Raleigh. Sit still and be glad.*

He was climbing Martha's steps before he recalled how much she loved dogs. Was some big dog in the shadow now, sizing him up? He knocked softly twice. Unbroken silence. A stronger knock and a longer wait. Then he heard footsteps. They stopped behind the door, and then a voice said "I'm asleep. What is it?"

"Whit Wade from Raleigh, hunting Martha Burton."

A considerable wait, then the door cracked open.

The head was so old, Whit thought it was Boot and almost called her name.

But the door opened wider, and Martha stood there in a man's old bathrobe. Her face was still unstrung from sleep, and maybe she'd washed her hair since Monday or the straightening grease was wearing off, but someway now it was all much grayer than he remembered.

She finally said "Whit, what in the world is wrong?"

He smiled. "Nothing. I was passing by and wanted to see you."

Martha covered her mouth—her false teeth were out. "You seen me then. Don't I look fine?"

Whit took a step back and mimed slow inspection. "Good as always, I'm proud to say."

She opened the screen door. "Step on in. But hold your breath. I was spraying the kitchen with one of these new bug bombs they got. Boot must have *bought* these cockroaches, child, from the mail-order place. I thought I'd seen bad roaches up North, but these down here are speedy and mean. They'll rear right up on their hind legs and fight you."

There was a poisonous smell from the spray, but the lighted room was neat as a clinic. All the furniture, old as the Ark, was pushed to the walls. Everything stood at strict right angles to everything else, and Boot's rag rugs were laid down parallel. It looked like somebody's earnest try at making a funhouse maze to lose you. For an instant Whit thought *She's raving crazy. Nothing but lunatics live like this*. Still he said "Where's Boot?"

"Old Mama? In Heaven, I'm guessing. I don't see her here." Martha looked around herself.

"When did she die?"

"Whit, I can't remember. Sometime last winter or maybe the fall. I was in Rhode Island. Phipps sent me the key—you know poor Phipps. He had a bad stroke, can't speak a word; but he wrote me notes with his good left hand. Anyhow he sent me the news on a postcard and ended up saying 'Come on and get it. She left it to you.' I wasn't doing much in Providence but trying to keep my mind shut down. So the next time it snowed, I got on the bus—to see Mama's grave—and here I am. Funny thing about me, Whit, I need to see your *grave*."

He frowned. "Not yet."

"I don't mean you. I mean I can't put nobody out of my mind and dreams till I see their grave and pay my due." Her eyes shut and her face was quiet as a midnight field.

Before she could sleep Whit said "You working any?"

Martha looked, studied his face and then laughed. "You wondering how I buy my groceries?"

"I'm hoping you aren't running short, that's all."

"Excuse me, Whit—thank you. I'm doing pretty good. Boot left me a little, and I saved some in the bank up North. I been a *money*-maker since you knew me." She took her teeth off a low table, covered her mouth and slipped them in. Then she plumped the pillow in a rocking chair and motioned him down.

As he sat Whit saw a framed face on the wall, a light beige boy maybe six years old, in a sailor suit with wide eyes gazing straight at the lens. *Martha left here for a Navy town. Is this the boy?* He kept on looking, the boy's blank mouth began to frown, the eyes burned in. *Any trace of me?* Whit jerked back to Martha. "You planning to stay on here awhile?"

She had seen his face when he caught the picture, but she answered the question. "I got the sugar, bad. I ain't got long."

"You take insulin shots?"

Martha pointed to a corner. "I back my butt up against that wall so I can't run away. I hate a needle, Whit. Lot of days I think 'Martha, what's the damned use? You'd rather be beat than to take another needle, and you're more than half blind, so just let it *be*—stretch on out and die."

"Your eyes that bad?"

She smiled at last in his general direction. "I can tell you're here, but I can't see your eyes."

Whit said "Christ, I'm sorry."

"I enjoyed your eyes."

"Martha, I loved you—"

She'd known two other white men after Whit, but till now nobody had gone that deep. Her fine eyes frowned and her hand went up to stop him there. It struck her that hard, and words were something she really could stop. So she raised a hand to stop him.

"I swear I did."

Martha managed to smile. "Did. Leave it there, back yonder. And we'll both forget it."

Whit had spoken without calculation, but even now he had no regret. Still the next time he spoke, he said "Best of friends" and found that he meant it, here and now at least. Then he felt the locks all suddenly shut, on windows and doors. The air of the room began to compress, and soon Whit's throat was feeling the crush. *They mean me to stay here and see Martha through.* He thought it that way, not stopping to ask who *they* might be or what was the trial he must see this woman through. He did see this, *One debt at least I can still repay.* For the next few seconds, he was cold with fear. Then a warming ease moved on him from her face.

She smiled again and nodded toward the wall. "I noticed you studying that sweet child." Though she could only see the brass frame, her smile only broadened.

Whit said "Where is he now?"

"Up yonder with Boot, if God ain't crazy." She pointed as if the roof were a place.

"Gone?"

Martha nodded. "Right after that picture. That was taken the day he started school—first grade, Newport News. And the people that kept him said he got on splendid, could read whole sentences well before Christmas and helped with the adding around the house. But February 4th he caught a bad cold from some of the children, and it went to his heart. Then the rheumatic fever lasted all spring. Nothing could stop him; he kept going down. Didn't last to wear the sport coat I sent him for the Fourth—fine big buttons carved out of deer horn. They claim he saw it though and said it was sporty."

Whit could see and hear how deeply it cut her, but he had to press. "Where were you?"

"Laid out up North." Martha still faced Whit but the whole of her face was streaked with a mist.

Whit said "Was he mine?"

Martha turned slowly and again found the picture. When she

looked back to Whit, her face had firmed; and her eyes were bright. "He was *mine* and I left him."

"He had to have a father."

She sat far back in her chair and waited. The gust of anger had blown on through. "Could have been, Whit. It could have been."

"You didn't know that many boys, that early."

"You really think so?"

"I knew it," Whit said. "You were that fresh to touch."

Martha smiled in pained expectance. "You swear to that?"

Whit said "I can see you then, clear as tonight."

She nodded. "Keep on seeing, child." Her eyes had stayed dry, and her voice was strong. But she took another long look at the boy. Whit couldn't know, and she could barely see. But what she hoped now, hot as ever, was to meet no blame in the wide young eyes. "Mr. Tuck says you got a fine girl in Raleigh."

Whit said "You'd like her."

"I hope I could. We had our good time, you and me. Remember?"

"I told you I did."

She said "You feel like the same boy, don't you?"

Whit waited a moment, then laughed a little. "I hadn't thought about it—Lord knows, we were young. But sure, I can feel every pore of our skin." It was not a lie. In his mind he could feel the single skin they managed to be, on moonless nights.

The belt of Martha's old robe was in her hands. She was rolling it up and then letting it out with slow attention, as if that mattered. And she wolfed down every word of his answer. She thought she was hearing postponed justice, poured out at last. First time in her life. *He's not lying, is he?* Then once she believed him, she could bring her mind back. She looked toward Whit's present upright body, dressed and thicker. "And you got bad hurt."

"Tuck tell you about it? Believe me, hurt. The doctors say, for practical purposes, I was dead when they found me."

She smiled. "You were always practical, Whit."

"Every chance I got. The problem here lately is, deciding whether I want to live."

"You too?" Martha frowned again. "You live for that child. Die now and you'll never forgive yourself."

Whit wanted to hear it as one more credible sign of life. He said "All right." But he was also swamped by sadness. To come here, fishing in the past for a son and then find a dead boy, years underground. He had to ask it—"What did you name him?"

Her lips pressed together and her eyes narrowed. *What right has he got?* But she finally said "Wade."

"First name or last?"

"First—Wade Burton. I told Mama Boot and she said 'Then Martha, don't never bring him home.' She meant how people would treat him too mean and maybe they would. So before Wade even got old enough to talk, I changed and started calling him Dolphus, after some man's voice on the radio. And he liked that—Adolphus Burton. Right to this day though, you go to the courthouse in Newport News; and he named Wade in the book they keep."

"Who does the book say was his father?"

"I told the doctor it was 'known to God.' He laughed in my face so I don't know."

A sudden hard thud on the door startled Whit. He got to his feet. "I better leave."

"Stay down," she said. "Ain't nothing for you." She was already on her way to the door. And once she cracked it, a black and brown dog the size of a spinet piano stalked in.

He caught sight of Whit and stopped in his tracks, head cocked to the side. Then he cranked a slow growl. If he charged he could take out a wall of the house.

Martha said "Don't kill him yet, Doc. He's a family member." She pressed down hard on Doc's broad skull; and he fell to the floor with another thud, still watching Whit. Then she went to her chair.

Whit said "He's down here from Rhode Island too?"

"He's a native, no. He was Boot's last friend, left waiting for me. To tell the truth, I come on down here mainly for him. I knew he wouldn't eat for nobody else."

Whit said "I can see he's back on his feed."

"Twelve years old and eat all I give him, his and my food both. I can't seem to eat."

"Something preying on your mind?"

Martha took it seriously. She thought it through and laughed. "No, Lord. That's the whole trouble, Whit. My mind is bad as my eyes someway. That wine they sell up North burnt me out. I sit in this empty house by myself; and most of the time, I don't think *nothing*. Just seems like every three weeks or so, I wake up long enough to know I'm hurting. Then I tune out again. It ain't so bad."

"You seeing a doctor?"

She nodded. "Get my needles from him—Dr. Bowles in Sidney. He's blind as me but he ain't got nothing to help my mind."

"What bothers you most?"

That also slowed her—*He thinks I blame him*—but she looked up at last. "Whit, why you taking this interest in me?"

"I already told you."

If he'd really said it, it had left her mind. "You saying you told me tonight, here now, or five hundred years ago when we were too young to see this far?"

Whit's chest was burning high again. "Tonight, just now."

"You saying you loved me?"

"Now. Now too." Astonished as he was, Whit thought *Somehow I mean it, no lie at all.* And somehow he did, though in ways their world could never admit, much less contain. He also wanted to stay and make some gesture toward her. Not that he wanted to lie beside her or touch her close. Except in her mind, she was no more kin to the girl he'd known than he was now to the boy he'd been. But strong as he felt for this present woman, there had to be some way to state it better than words. In this white glare though, with Doc at his feet, he couldn't think what or where it might lead when daylight came and the world formed round them again at the windows.

Martha managed a genuine smile, the first she'd enjoyed since the German surrender.

In Whit's sight it swept off her age and sadness. And one more time she sat there, fine as she'd ever been by the river, years back, or late last Monday on the road past Tuck's, looking nineteen again. Coal-glossy skin, every line of her face swept up again—slant eyes, lips, cheekbones.

She finally said "Don't get me wrong, it sounds so right it hurts my ears. But Whit, you'd do better talking to Doc. Doc needs love *now*. I'm liable to die and leave him again. But me, love can't mean no more to me than the hair Doc sheds all over this floor. You're a grown white man with a tall brick house full of tame white women. Mr. Tuck's got you-all's picture in the kitchen. I seen it too many times already. You're down here now for an hour or so; you been sick as me, so your mind's looking back at the past and thinking it's real. Maybe we *were* real, Whit—the best of friends, like you used to say and lovely as God—but we been dead and dust, millions of years. Don't reach back now and try to touch em, child. They ain't there to touch. Go home and don't try." Her eyes shut down as if they never meant to open.

Whit had the grace to know she was right. She was aimed as true as the angel in France that tried to reclaim him. Without understanding he guessed she'd taught him some good thing. *Hold it in, every word she said, and weigh it alone.* More than ever he knew he couldn't touch her now. He reached behind and brought out his wallet. "Can I help you some?"

Martha pressed slowly back in her chair; and when her eyes opened, they were clear again. "Help Doc. Like I said, Doc needs steady help." Her bare foot went out to scratch Doc's back.

"You still can't say any more about Wade?"

Her eyes were unblinking. "I can say I grieve for him all night long. That's near-bout all I know some nights."

So Whit laid a twenty-dollar bill on the table and pressed it down with a white river rock that was lying near. He'd handed the same white rock to Martha a thousand years ago, a souvenir of the times they touched. Not that he recognized it now. It was just a heavy thing close at hand.

Martha didn't know either; the rock had stayed here all the years she roamed the North. And as Whit stood to leave, she didn't stand. She leaned though, to hold Doc safe on the floor. And when he snarled she said again gently "Family member, old son. You tame on down." And as Whit's feet passed, she said "I'll meet you in Glory, all right?"

Whit said "All right," though again as he moved, a bitter rush of loss filled his mouth. He'd come here, meaning to find a child. He was leaving with nothing but one more ghost to hang in his mind and the sight of this woman, half blind and dying, whom he'd known at the crest.

But even as long as two hours later, bathed and fed and ready to sleep in a clean room in Greenville, he heard her last promise and hoped she was right. As he drifted off he even tried to picture the Glory she'd finally promised. *By rights it ought to be a torture chamber where Martha's the manager and gets her own grim chance after all. Her chance to pay back each human soul, and God Himself, for the harm they did her—her and Wade. But maybe it'll be nothing better than bliss—all rest and music, all flesh healed and young.*

The instant before he was deep asleep, Whit saw how she'd look, even the dress she'd get to wear—a tall young creature, no longer a woman but surely no man. Hot to the eye but cooled by the breeze that moved her skirt, a light blue cotton dress, fine as the sky.

FRIDAY

11 MAY 1945

MOST OF FRIDAY was smooth enough—light hail damage to tobacco near Greenville and an ancient gentleman out from Lucama who had slashed his mother's portrait to ribbons, then invented a gang of "nameless rogues" and claimed the loss. The local agent briefed Whit and gave him directions for finding the place. The house was at the absolute end of a narrow dirt trail. Once you were on the right road and persisted, you were there. The road stopped at the tall gray steps as if it were a driveway. The shadow of the house fell east like a twin to the actual house, a well-kept old two-story place with a green tin roof. It was just after two.

Like Tuck, the man here lived alone, only this one had servants. But it took awhile to rouse somebody at the open screen door. Finally a decrepit, very light Negro woman limped across the central hall, fifteen yards ahead.

Whit shouted to her.

When she came, she locked the screen before checking his eyes. "You kin to us?"

Whit laughed. "I'm sorry to say I'm a stranger. I came to see Mr. Frank Drake's picture that got cut up."

"Too late." She turned to her former errand.

Whit laughed again. "I understand it's ruined. I'm the insurance man."

She nodded. "Good. I burned it up—let me see—bout a month ago. When was Easter? Easter Monday I took it out back here and burned it. Mr. Frank don't know so don't you tell him—Easter Monday while he took his nap."

Whit said "Could I speak to Mr. Drake please?"

Her slack face tightened and, as she narrowed her scrutiny on him, Whit saw that her eyes were the palest blue. She said "You saying you doubt my word?"

Whit said "No no, but he filed the claim."

She debated the point in her own slow time, then unhooked the door. "Step on in here and wait in the parlor. I'll see can I find him." As Whit moved in, she also said "You ain't hungry, is you?"

"No thank you. I ate in Wilson."

"You be out dead by supper then." But she waved in the general direction of a tall door and retraced her path back down the hall. Then as if from the moon, Whit could hear her shouting his business to someone. "—Man drove out here looking for you. Want to see your mama's picture you ruint—when was it?"

"New Year's Eve." It was a young man's voice, a pleasant tenor.

"You thought it was New Year, cept you were wrong."

"By just a few months, no harm in that. Nobody keeping time on us."

"Get on out there and tell him yourself." She plainly had more urgent work.

"Where is he?"

"In the parlor, less he grabbed something precious and lit out already. Didn't look all that trusty to me."

Whit waited through sounds of coughing, foot scraping and a squeaky drawer opened. Then when no one appeared, he roamed the dim parlor. It was huge, maybe thirty by twenty with twelve-foot ceilings and the suffocated perfection of a thing untouched, under glass for years. At the four tall windows, there were giant heavy draperies, dozens of yards of red-wine velvet. Whit could see at once that the merest tap of a curious finger would bring them down in a landslide of dust. The walnut tables, good slave-made cabinetry, were bare of the usual trinket clutter. But the walls were swarmed with deep-framed pictures. Men, women, children, soldiers and one big family group with two dozen people, cradle to grave, posed out front here on a Turkish rug laid down in the dust. Whit craned up to study the clear strong faces. In the center, between the knees of a bearded patriarch, was a six-year-old boy. Tow-headed and rigged in a complicated suit with a Lord Byron collar and a low-slung belt, he was daring the camera to pick the lock of his shut face.

"Don't turn around yet."

The young man's voice was near Whit's back. It startled him cold but he didn't turn around.

"That child was me." When Whit had looked longer, the voice said "Now"—it had moved farther off.

So Whit turned slowly and a neatly dressed man was already waiting in a chair by the hearth. He was many years older than the voice but still firm and fit. He wore clean khaki trousers with knife-edge creases and a white shirt, buttoned tight at the collar with a gold collar-stud.

"Rest yourself here, son." The voice was this old snow-haired man.

Whit crossed what felt like five miles of floor and offered his hand. "Whitley Wade, Mr. Drake. I'm Fidelity's adjustor for this part of the state."

Mr. Drake waited; then his black eyes flared. "I thought fidelity came in one size, like it or not."

The opposite chair looked as old as the draperies, but Whit moved toward it and risked sitting down. It bore him amply so he faced Mr. Drake across five yards of space. *He wants to play*. Whit said "No sir, we offer all sorts. We'll insure your wife and send her to Borneo. Any dogs you've got, we'll insure against bears. I'll write you a hidebound policy now on this fine velvet." He pointed to the curtains.

Mr. Drake grinned at last. "Please don't. All this mess was my dead mother's. I'm praying to outlive it."

Whit said "Who's winning? That's mighty strong velvet."

"It is, finest Belgian. Nearly killed my father, paying the freight. Ever paid to ship a ton of velvet, from Ghent to here by sailboat freight?"

"How long ago?"

"Well-back before steam, when I was a boy." Mr. Drake sat deeper, then the eyes lit slowly. "When you think that was?"

Whit was generally a good judge of age. He was still confused by the youthful voice. But for all the sparse white hair and seamy skin, the eyes were bright enough for sixty-five. *Flatter him, underestimate*. Whit said "Maybe sixty." And when he heard Mr. Drake's high laugh, he knew he'd either hit dead-on or missed it wide.

"How old was I when the War Between the States passed up this road and walked in the door?"

"Mr. Drake, I'm trusting you weren't even born."

"*Born?* I was nine damned years old, and I answered the door. March 1865, cold as a son of a bitch in the heart—that same door you just walked through. Three men rode up the avenue yonder on the tallest horses I'd ever seen. Behind them on the road were untold soldiers on foot with rifles. I stood at this window and said to myself 'Start counting, Frank; you're dead.' I knew they'd shoot me if I answered the door. And if I didn't they'd call up the men and burn it down with me still in it. But the three men suddenly stopped and talked. Then the oldest two turned tail and left, just rode on back. But the young one came on. When he got to the gate and tied his horse, I could see his face. Then I *knew* it was fire. His hair was bright as a red-hot iron, and his eyes wouldn't blink—they just never shut. I thought 'All right. I've had nine years.' And since the past four had all been war, I felt ready to go. Then I saw his rank, a very young captain. He came to that door you just walked through and knocked politely. I gave him my right hand and said I was ready. He said 'Well, lad, I'll tell you—I'm *not*. Can you find some cool water and a place to rest?' Swear to God, that was it! He left the whole Yankee army back at the road to rest with me. Turned out to be a very first-rate gent, two years at Princeton before signing up. I showed him in here, brought him cold water and a hardboiled egg. He sat in the chair I'm in this minute. I sat over there on the stool by you. And we talked Latin for nigh on an hour, when he dozed awhile."

"You didn't try to kill him?"

"Kill him?—great God! I was nine years old, but I'd learned my manners. I sat still and watched till he woke back up."

"Then he ransacked the place?"

Exasperated, the bright eyes shut. "I said he was a scholar. Hell no, we talked some more. Cicero, Horace, Caesar, Catullus. My father had already helped me through Catullus's dirty words, the parts translators still leave in Latin. So I had the pleasure of telling the gent what Princeton neglected. I also recall he was weak in the fifth declension."

"You were that smart already?"

The eyes were still shut. "I was born speaking tongues."

Whit said "I believe you" and thought *Now here comes today's big loon.* "Anybody else in the house that day?"

The eyes sprang open and looked to the ceiling. "My sainted mother, weak in the head, was upstairs yonder with what few Negroes had stayed past the Freedom. They were sewing her pitiful bits of jewelry into petticoat hems and putting them on her. By the time the captain rode on off—I gave him a ham; I had three hid—Mama looked like a goddamned St. Bernard dog, padded and sent to succor the lost." The eyes drifted back down and found Whit's face. "She never forgave me."

"For what?"

"Being smart enough to save her hide and keep a good roof over all our heads and some food she could swallow."

Whit said "Maybe she just wanted to die."

Another grin, the widest yet—there were no teeth back of the four in front, top or bottom. "Of course she did. Well, she got her revenge. And I lived to learn why."

Whit knew he was meant to say "Tell me."

The grin was stuck; it couldn't fade. "She had lost my first and second brothers. Pa was in a prison just out from Chicago. And the morning of the day the Yankees came, she got a long letter saying five of her first cousins died in one battle—all brothers, all sons of her Uncle Jayce. It was that hard a world." Mr. Drake killed the grin and sat back silent.

Whit said "And it hasn't got that much softer, not in eighty years—has it?"

"You speaking of this thing they've got on now, this fracas abroad on other people's land?"

Whit said "Oh yes," very quietly.

Mr. Drake bore in with both eyes slowly. "You've been in it, ain't you?"

Whit nodded. "And died."

"I knew it, right off." He was watching Whit's face with fixed attention, and whatever he saw there raised a faint smile.

Whit said "How did you know?"

Mr. Drake held off till he understood. "You look like me—that old, that impressed. It may have been distant and no local danger, but it got your attention."

Whit said "You've been here eighty-nine years?"

He nodded. "Barely left. Oversaw it for Mama, then married a cousin barren as the Gobi, buried her at thirty and sat down to wait."

Whit said "Couldn't think of anything else to do?"

"Didn't need to, son. Didn't want to at all. I'm a very rich man, can't halfway spend what Papa's money earns. He made it all back—see—after the war. I went to France a time or two, spent a summer on the Rhine but always came on back down here. Seen one race of men, you've seen them all. I've been right here since nineteen-and-twenty, trying to spend my annual interest. I adopt young orphans, by proxy of course—farm them out to honest homes. I pay my help so well they despise me. From every year's tobacco crop, I keep my expenses; give the rest to my tenants. But I never could buy a friendly soul to share my bed. Nobody wants me—greatest curse God sends, inherited wealth."

"But still you want money back for your picture?" In his tour of the room, Whit had noticed a huge frame, empty and staring from a dark corner. "Who do you think these 'nameless rogues' were?"

Mr. Drake gave a hoot. "*Me*, son, me. I never called the sheriff; you're bound to have noticed."

"But you filed a claim."

"Did I? May be. Then it got me an afternoon visit at least. And I'm grateful to you—first white man I've seen this month."

Whit laughed. "I've enjoyed it."

Mr. Drake showed plain delight to hear him. "I'm enjoying the hell out of it. And not one reason on Earth to stop. I've got three empty beds, two cooks in the kitchen, big smokehouse full of the finest pork, chickens, three fresh cows. Move in for a month; send for your sweetheart—you're bound to need a long country rest."

Best offer I've had and no way to take it. Whit consulted his watch. "I'm due in Raleigh for supper."

"Your sweetheart?"

"Thank you. Do I look that young? I'll accept the compliment but set you right. My wife awaits—a wife and daughter, two fine women."

"They haven't helped you though."

Whit said "Beg your pardon?"

"You said you died, somehow in service. But I already saw it."

Whit tried to smile. "Everybody else I've met this week seems to think I'll make it."

Mr. Drake said "Oh, I don't doubt you will. Never hinted you'd fail. I've made it to here, fifty-six years older than Christ got to be. That's no such glorious deed to admire; who's proud of age? No famous person in all known history lived to a hundred. I defy you to name one."

Whit racked his mind for a good exception—Methuselah and that crowd probably didn't count. But all he could find were youthful corpses, like Joan of Arc and Stonewall Jackson. Then again his own dead friends pressed forward, close to his chair and blocking the light. *Hell, he's right. Why pray for life?* Whit hoped the thoughts had spared his face, and he reached for his papers to stand and go. "I surrender," he said. "The good die young." *Good and bad, white, black, tan, yellow.* To free himself from the useless past, Whit forced his eyes to see this room. "I think you've got a sweet world here—tastes good to me."

Mr. Drake followed suit and raised himself. It took a good while; and once he was up, he seemed blind and lost. Both hands went out before him like rudders. "It *has* been better with Mother's face gone. Ought to pay you for detouring way out here."

Whit said "My pleasure. I learned a lot."

Mr. Drake stopped still and really faced him. "*Learned?* You want to say what exactly?" It had to be only the second or third time any white man took him seriously.

Whit hadn't lied but of course he couldn't say what he meant. He knew anyhow he meant real thanks. The twenty minutes had passed like years and had built on further mute rooms in the house of whatever life was left him. A scared old boy with a mind like a blade, pushing ninety and ready for more, out here in the beautiful lonesome sticks with broke-down help to feed and tend him. Whit shook the cool frail hand extended, then moved toward the door, stepped out and shut the screen.

Mr. Drake was behind him, step for step. As Whit turned to wave, Mr. Drake said "*What*, son? Say one thing you learned out here."

Whit reached in the air with his mind and said the first words that came, "I learned how to walk from here on in—here to Heaven or Hell, whichever I get—on spider silk, the way you do."

Whit looked up—there! On the porch post, fresh as good news beside him, a spider the size of a melon seed hung in the midst of a web. Complex as a plan for future worlds. Here was a live and thoughtful creature, not sitting but waiting for the world to love his silk-thread trap. *Ready to wait till the sky sends food.*

Whit thought it resembled the whole world. A complicated beautiful trap that would hold and use him till the promised end—whatever fire and light would end us. All the rest, all week, had been kind thoughts—sweet cheer, maybe lies. Here was the secret visible truth. The world was real for a while to come, people and webs. It would hold him here and use him up for its own private need. It would take him back in. He'd lie back and live.

All that had taken no more than five seconds. Then Mr. Drake answered Whit's last speech, "I'm glad we helped." He waved round behind him, "The house and me in it."

Whit said "Don't mock me."

One bright eye winked. "Next time I won't. I solemnly promise. But *walk*, goddammit, and thank your kin."

At four Whit stopped on the far side of Smithfield to check a handmade map the local agent sent him. If the map was right, this had to be it. Another old trailer. It was parked in an open field, a broad wheel of ground—thick with tan broomstraw and rimmed with pines. Whit rummaged his briefcase to find the right papers. Then some force pressed his head back to rest on the seat. He'd take a minute to taste his luck so far, all week. He still felt good from leaving Mr. Drake; but whatever moved inside him now, he said in his mind *Shut your eyes, Bo. And wait for the spirit.* That was Holy Roller talk, not Whit's style at all. He still felt good but his head wouldn't rise from the warm seatback. *O Spirit, pour down.* He embarrassed himself.

But then he recalled how the Spirit had blown through the room like tongues of fire on all the disciples once Christ disappeared. Now in this field, inside Whit's car, the wound in his chest burned upward hot like lit gasoline in the depth of his mind, with the same blue whoosh, the inward suck. *What the hell? Am I dying or losing my mind? Am I more of a saint than anybody guessed?*

Inside the flame that wrapped his body and poured from his chest, Whit laughed in his heart, his whole new mind. What should have been pain was better, gladder to feel, than love—any love he'd known, in bed, on Earth or with young Martha on the warm ground at night. *I'm dead or crazy or, if anybody sees me, they'll shoot on sight or call the Law.* He tried to look round, his eyes stayed shut, but he thought he was smiling. *Take me now, on out of this car—I'm ready again—or let me stand up and pay this man in the trailer for what he's lost.*

*

It was one more burglary claim, weeks old. The war had swept most petty felons off the streets into action—housebreakers, pick-pockets, youthful rogues. So the company had recently sent out a brochure, advising adjustors to view such claims with healthy suspicion. Whit had saved them five hundred dollars just now, on Mr. Drake's portrait. He might be able to go easy here, depending on what he found in the trailer.

There seemed to be no particular path, just thick broomstraw right up to the door. For an instant Whit held back—the straw could hide things. But wading hip-deep through its feathery dryness reminded him of afternoons that summer at Tuck's, hid in such fields, chewing sweet grass, watching the sky, trying to reach his dead father's mind and draw his watchful love back down. In the space of ten yards, he'd walked himself deep into that past. And for then and there, he was young and taut in every cell.

The trailer was painted the same powder blue as Juanita's on Monday. It seemed a little longer though, with no sign of dogs. So far, so far. No sign of life or even smoke, though a chill was rushing through the afternoon. And when he finally got to the entrance, there were no steps up. Just a door hung three feet off the ground with a dirty window blocked by cardboard and a screaming-eagle decal at the bottom. The sight of the eagle's wind-forced beak, or something unseen in the vacant day behind him, suddenly said that Whit should leave. *I wish to Christ this wasn't the place, but the map says Yes*. The local agent had said the client worked at home and would surely be there.

Whit took a step back and called out strongly "Mr. Carle Towns, please." When twenty seconds passed with no answer, he came up again and beat on the door. The old steel boomed and, for one bad moment, Whit thought the trailer shook on its pilings but surely not. "Mr. Towns, I'm here about your insurance." Nothing still.

But then a tall man was on him, too close. Just materialized with no sound or stir from around the far corner. A tall head of black hair, straight as bristles and again blue eyes, light dawn-blue with pin-dot pupils. *Has every crank from here to the ocean got blue eyes? Is it one more sign?* The fellow stood maybe six foot four in bib overalls. Bare feet and arms, bare chest but clean, in the afternoon chill. *In one good stride he could reach my mouth.* Whit guessed he managed to hide the fright, but he had thought *Mouth—he could reach my mouth* and he wondered why. "Are you Mr. Towns?"

The man nodded. "Who in hell sent you?"

It eased Whit and he managed to laugh. "Nobody in Hell, just the insurance company. I hear you were robbed a few days back."

The overalls were too big for Towns. So he thrust both long arms inside them, halfway down his flanks. "I been robbed every damned Sunday they have church anywhere near me."

Whit laughed again. *They always cut loose the loonies on Friday.* But despite the shock of Towns condensing silent beside him, there was surely no threat. "You live in this trailer?"

"If you call it living." A smile tore across Towns's face like a slash. He strode forward, reached up with no strain and opened the door. Then with both palms pressed to the high sill, he raised himself in an unbroken move, inside and standing. He turned back to Whit. "You think you can do it?"

Whit had guessed at that before he knocked. His arms wouldn't do it. He hugged himself and said "The muscles on my right side are still weak."

So Towns squatted, dropped both long arms and easily lifted Whit through the air.

It was one room with a makeshift kitchen, an unmade bed and what looked like a world of magazines. Mostly *Life* and *National Geographic*, flung down anywhere. In the dimmest corner a double-barreled shotgun leaned against a wall with a peacock feather in one of the barrels. Otherwise the walls were bare except for a taped-up magazine cover of Ava Gardner in sloe-eyed splendor (she was from Smithfield, a local girl) and what seemed an actual painting of Mary. Whit stepped toward that.

She was dressed in her usual prim blue and white; but with boneless hands she flaunted her real and beating heart in the midst of her breast, all fire and blood. The kitchen was buried beneath stacked pots, but at least they smelled clean. No sign of clothes but what Towns wore, no boots in sight. Still it bore no threat. Except for Mary and her gory heart, it might have been most any college boy's room.

Towns swept a clear spot on the only piece of furniture, an old car seat converted to a sofa. Then he motioned Whit toward it. And when he was seated, Towns dropped to the floor, all but touching Whit's feet.

Whit searched his papers and found the relevant line in the claim. "Your radio's covered, the oriental rug and the cut-glass bowl. But I need to know more on these 'four precious coins.' "

Towns's eyes almost shut with the pain. "They're the only real thing. You can have the rest."

"Mr. Towns, I'm not the robber, remember? I well understand you've lost precious things. But just what were they—family heirlooms, cash, Confederate money?" He was straining to be serious.

And Towns was working to calm his face. But even tranquil, he looked worse off than most men strapped in the electric chair. "Don't talk that baby-shit to me, sir. I pay my premiums the day they fall due."

Grin now, Whit. And get out *of here.* "You're a first-rate client, a perfect record and the company's grateful. But your policy just doesn't cover money. Were these silver dollars, some present currency, foreign coins or what? You claim four hundred dollars here—"

"Four old Greek coins, 330 B.C. Alexander the Great."

Alexander was a boyhood favorite of Whit's. Years before his father died, he'd given Whit *A Boy Rules the World*. And that brief story—young Alexander winning the known world (with nothing but his mind, a few thousand men and outrageous courage); then dying young, so lonely and sick—had cut a deep groove in Whit's sense of life. *Better to burn out early but bright than dim and pale through eight decades.* Whit said "You got any pictures of the coins, any bill of sale?"

Towns swallowed hard. "I got them in France, the week I was hurt."

"A purchase, a gift or—what's the word—booty?"

Towns said "That's nobody's goddamned business, not down here anyhow, not till I'm dead."

Whit smiled. "Then whose business is it?"

Towns's eyes were burning. "God's. At the gate."

Whit took out his pen. "Mr. Towns, as I said, you don't have any rider to cover ancient coins. So I'm sorry to say, they constitute money. And again, money's not covered in your theft insurance."

Towns had never moved back from his nearness to Whit, and now he thrust his long face closer. The pupils of his eyes were lighter still, barely blue at all. "I thought they were covered or, Christ, I'd never have bled my pitiful pension to feed you leeches. You tell me nothing till it's too late to know."

Whit smiled. "I feel like that about life." But then he saw Towns's eyes go narrow. *No jokes. Keep moving.* "Mr. Towns, I sympathize with your loss. When I was a boy, I wanted to be Prince Alexander—"

Towns sneered. "Some chance."

"But old or new, coins are money in the eyes of your policy."

Towns waited another hard ten seconds. Then his whole face flushed a dangerous purple. Both hands reached out and took

Whit's ankles. "*Money?* You ever try spending a coin that's more than two thousand years old, with the face of a man wearing lion skin?" He pointed to the door as if Alexander might stand there now. "You'd be on the chain gang before dawn Sunday."

By then the hands on his ankles had loosened and Whit stayed put. He said "I understand your problem. I've lost a lot I'll never get back. And I'll be glad to write you a policy on whatever coins you've still got left. But for now that's the rules—it's in your fine print."

Towns sprang up and spoke to the unshaded window. "My whole life's down in the fine print, bud."

Whit said "Don't I know. So's mine, up to now."

"You shirked." Towns had spoken as if to the field, gazing out.

Whit wanted to write the check and leave. *Shirked* was a word he'd dreaded for months and, till now, never heard. And even here in the mouth of a crazy, he would not take it. "I beg your pardon."

Towns turned to face him, smiling. His smile was a good deal sicker than his frown. "What's your story, ace?"

Don't give him a word. Hold tight and leave. This fool is strong. "My story is really no part of this." Whit opened the checkbook and wrote the date. "*Carle Towns*—is that how you want it?" *Oh God, he's crying.* Whit kept on writing.

Enormous tears streaked down the long face and hit the floor. "I can handle myself round most anybody they throw at me—see?—but a goddamned shirker with your white hands—" Towns turned back and pressed his forehead to the window. "I think I'm asking you to leave right now."

Shut in as he was with this big a man, Whit felt no fear. Since Normandy, with all the pain and the blank walls before him, fear had seldom touched him. If he'd learned one thing that day in the pasture, he'd learned that he could take the worst. All they could do was kill you someway. And he'd survived that. *Bring on your next body blow. I'm ready.* He carefully tore the check from his book, shut his pen and stood.

Towns was still at the window, facing out.

Whit said "I'll leave it here on the counter. I gave you fifty dollars for the coins, the best I can do."

Towns still looked out. "I'm glad to give you a chance to do something."

Why take this, Whit? You did not *shirk.* He set a hand on the cold door handle; his voice was level. "I took a whole pound of steel in my chest. Right here—feel, Carle." Whit scrubbed at the covered scar and beckoned to Towns.

Towns stayed at the window but shook his head.

"In France," Whit said. "The same as you, June of last year." Then he opened the door and poised to jump.

Towns was on him in a single stride, those frozen eyes not a foot away. "I call you a liar."

Whit jumped, landed upright and walked ten yards, not running but quick and straight for the car.

"You're lying, right?" Towns hung in the door frame, both arms braced.

So as Whit stopped and turned, he saw the cartoon of crucifixion—one more human, racked up for good. He said "Carle, I'm sorry but no, it was every word true."

Whit had gone another five yards before Towns called. "They left you your mind though. You know day from night."

So that's been it. Whit could finally smile but he held it back. He turned again and raised his voice. "Matter of fact, Carle, no I don't. Is it day or dark?" And at once he believed himself. He shut his eyes and groped out around him. "They took my eyes, my mind, my whole heart—Christ Jesus, *all.* I'm hard-up as you, Carle, maybe worse. Far worse. Or have been till lately." It felt as true, this instant, as ever. Whit was not pretending to cover his pride. Nor mocking one other pain on Earth.

And Towns understood. He said "What helped you?"

Doctors, good women, prayer, what else? But Whit's hands were brushed by the dry broomstraw as wind combed through it. He looked out slowly at the field, the woods, then back to the homemade Jesus in the door. Deep in his mind, in the place that held Carle, he asked the Spirit for help to give. Whit waited a moment, then said what came. "What helped? All this. I wanted all this." He took big handfuls of straw and wrung it up, dry as it was. "And I wanted it too much to do something easy as dying young. Easy and cheap and hard on my kin." For the first full time since France and death, he had said a true thing to someone but Liss. Truthful, useful but surely unheard. *No good to him though. Go now or he'll shoot.*

But Towns didn't move. He held in place, nailed up on the rushing shadows behind him. His mouth spread open, a bigger wound than Whit now showed but no words came. Then he shut his eyes and nodded.

Who's he got? Ava Gardner, the Virgin Mary and mice in the walls, no radio. Not even a dog to meet his eyes. And I can't give him a pitiful thing.

When Whit had carefully stowed his papers, cranked and moved, Towns was still upright—for now, a piece of the place itself. A perch for birds, a rack of bones for the wind to pick. If he chose to stay.

And though Whit had got to the main road and signaled a right turn to Raleigh, Towns stayed in place maybe three more minutes—not posing, not meaning to make a sign—till two small boys from back in the woods came up and stood on the ground beneath him. The redhead was older and spoke out first, "Carle, we found you a whole new thing. Miss Amma Edwards—you know, our teacher—she said she well remembered you and that you could have her *Reader's Digests*, going back years, if you come haul em out of her attic."

At last Carle opened his eyes and smiled, then reached behind for his jar of change. He threw each boy a dime and they thanked him.

"She says there may be snakes up there, in her attic and all. But I said you weren't scared of no snake, not strong as you been." The talking boy was ten years old. "I'll help you tote em."

Towns nodded. "Do. Bring your big wheelbarrow here Saturday morning."

The younger boy said "Can you wait till then?"

"I'm trying, ain't I?"

The boys faced each other a moment, then laughed awhile. Then the redhead snapped to attention and saluted.

Both Towns's arms stayed hung above him.

So the boys ran off. Back in the winter he'd told them a secret, "Come here every day and see if I'm live. If not, come on in and call the sheriff. I'll give you a dime every day I'm alive." The only thing he dreaded now was lying here days on end, once he did it. Cold and blue, unfound, unburied. Or found by his mother, with that much blood beneath him on the floor, when she came by after church on Sunday to bring his clean towel—all the help he'd take, though she offered more. Through every trial he'd never been cut, never borne a wound except in his mind. So he knew how much blood waited to pour. These were good little fellows—what was their name? They'd handle him neat. They knew he'd left them all his magazines and the whole change jar.

Whit rode five miles toward the falling sun, with no thought but home. Then on the outskirts of Clayton, that changed.

Help—he heard the one word, clear as a shot in the car behind him. It chilled his mind and even his foot eased off the gas before he knew. It was Carle Towns's final question again—"What helped?" And for the first time, Whit understood what he'd tried to answer. The actual world had called him back—people, objects and the thing he prayed to—and now he'd obeyed. *That's about as much use as lukewarm spit to any boy hurt as bad as Carle.* Whit filed through the faces of every boy he recalled from all the hospital wards he'd known. He couldn't hear one other voice say *Help.* Everything else from *Fuck* to *Food* but no other *Help. Nobody asked me till now, today. And I tucked tail and ran when I heard it. He'll kill himself.*

Whit knew it, sure as he knew that the blazing ball ahead in the sky was setting now. *Turn, go back.* He checked in the mirror and the road was clear; the car on his tail had just turned off. The shoulders were wide. His arms could swing left and turn him easy. And he slowed again. *But our war's over, Carle's and mine.* Whit pulled to the right and stopped on the shoulder.

That's a lie and you know it. This war will last long as any man breathes that knew it first-hand. I'm praying to make my own truce now. But what word or sign could I give Carle? He's heard every one and he'll fight to the death. Whit found his mouth really saying what came—"Die easy, soon." The words surprised him and he waited to turn them over again. *Die? Who?* Then he knew he meant Carle. Carle would die by morning. *So go on home, Whit. Now before dark. Go where they can use you.* He understood they could last without him. They'd miss a few days and then move on. But he sat till a knot of cars had passed. Then he drove ahead.

It was five-fifteen, still pale daylight. So he had no reason to expect bright windows. But Whit was worried the house was dark, not even a glow at the kitchen window. He'd somehow pictured a winter homecoming—black night and both high stories of the house lit like a pleasure ship riding the deep. He knew he'd need to drive downtown for razor blades before bedtime. So he parked out front and unloaded his things, more than half waiting for Liss or June to come out to meet him. He hated being seen off on trips—too big a risk of real farewells, leaving for good—but a glad homecoming could justify the trip, a whole tired week.

The door was locked. Whit let himself in. No lights or noise but no sign of trouble. He paused in the dining room, set down his bag and spoke out firmly "Anybody live?" *Goddamn, Bo,* hush. *Talk about bad luck!* "June? Elissa?" He walked to the basement door in the hall, unlocked it and craned to see down the steps—June's car was gone. He'd promised to be here sooner than now so this was strange. Without ever saying so, June had made a point lately of having a peaceful life underway as he pulled in from trips. *She's left me a note.* But the kitchen blackboard, her usual note place, said nothing but *Matches* and *Eye drops.* No food laid out, a cold stove.

He called upstairs and when it was silent, he reached to phone the nearest neighbor. Anything to spare himself finding blood. His mind had already lunged on and found them, killed on the floor in separate rooms. *Ease back, Whit. This is normal somehow. June forgot to get butter. She's run to the store. But Liss?* He looked to the ceiling and bellowed her name. Seconds, years of empty silence.

Slowly he walked to the breakfast table and took the fourth chair, the one for guests. For whatever reason he sat in the dim light and spread both hands before him on the wood. His long fingers splayed and he actually spoke, not knowing why—"Don't do it please." When he wondered at his meaning, his mind saw the bottom of his sock drawer clearly. His dead father's pistol from the First World War.

Once he was home from the last hospital, Whit had checked the pistol's whereabouts. He'd been amazed that June had not only left it there but had cleaned and oiled it, which she'd seen him do. Whit seldom thought about prayer in daylight, but now he said *You don't want this. I know You don't. So help me quick.* Then he stood.

A woman's high voice—"Sorry, friend. We're finally back."

Whit sat again to calm himself.

And fifteen seconds later Liss found him there. She'd put out a hand to switch on the light when her eye snagged on him in the dim breakfast corner, so she left them half dark. "Whoa, stranger! You *got* me." She bent down laughing. Her left arm hung in a clean white sling. Then she came toward him.

"What's the matter? Break something?"

"Hug me first."

Whit rose to obey. And the smell of her hair—dry, electric, almost burnt—took his mind like fire in a field.

June was on them and joined the embrace. Then she went to the stove and opened a pot. "How long have you been here?"

"Ten minutes maybe."

"And you knew we were dead. Don't say you didn't." June checked his eyes and smiled. "I told you, Liss—we owed this particular man a note."

Whit shook his head. *No, never mind.*

June had to explain. "Liss came home at four, nursing a bad left arm from gym class. She wanted to leave it but I—"

Liss said "It's sprained pretty bad. But nothing's broken so end-of-story. A week of sling time and I'll be perfect."

He thought *You are. Stay right here for good.* She was still close in the crook of his arm. But even as he thought it, she slid away.

Standing at the sink Liss looked him over. "I'd know you, I guess."

Whit said "Beg your pardon."

"Anywhere—in jail, in the dark of night, I'd know your face in a long line-up."

June said "You've seen one movie too many. Go put on your blue jeans and help me now. This gentleman's starved."

Liss looked again. "Looks well-fed to me."

June said "Go" and stirred the pot. Without looking over she said "I scared you. I'm sorry, Whit. But I bet you'll live yet, years to come."

"You scared me all right. I headed for the gun." He'd seen the pistol in his mind, surely; but had he meant to use it? He waited. *Don't worry. She missed it. She didn't even hear.*

June kept on stirring. "Let's move that pistol."

Good girl. I couldn't get a blond gnat past those eagle eyes. He said "Where to?"

"How about the bottom of the goldfish pond?" Whit had dug a small pool out back for Liss's goldfish.

He nodded. "I appoint you the demolition squad."

"You think I don't trust you?"

Whit said "I think you don't know a good goddamn about me, old girl."

Though she still didn't look, June heard his smile. So first she laughed. "Caught again—all right, I plead ignorance. How many more years will I need in this school?"

"School?" Whit said.

"The Whitley Wade Code-Breaking Academy. You say I don't know a g-d thing after eighteen years."

Whit found he could also muster a laugh. "No, darling, you do." His voice went low. "You showed me last Sunday."

Instinctively June looked round for Liss, then heard the thump of a foot upstairs. She said "I missed you every minute this week." But she moved to the counter to peel an onion.

"How about *one* look, to be sure it's me?"

"I looked. Don't I get credit for my hug? You're fine as ever.

Just dogeared a little round the ears, from the road." She'd finally talked herself into looking. Whit was standing still, far back by the table. Sunset had reached the window on his left, and that whole side of his face and neck was a gold that looked too hot to touch, at the melting point. *Will he ever get back? Will he want me here?*

Yet his eyes held firmly to hers, unflinching.

And in the instant they stood on, silent, June thought she saw a final glimpse of the boy deep in him. Quick as it was, he was plainly the one she'd loved on sight. The only boy that had chosen her and asked her, in church, to give him all she had or would get and to take all of his, till they both gave out and went to whatever rest they'd earned. Bliss or torment or endless sleep—she'd never been sure. She said a quiet "Oh" at the sight. Then it made her grin; her eyes and throat filled. "I know you, boy."

Whit nodded slowly and also smiled. "*Boy*, still? Still not a man?"

"Oh God, yes. I never meant tha—"

But he moved on toward her and, since they could still hear Liss upstairs, he folded June as near to his heart as arms could bring her. The crown of her head was under his chin. So he did an old trick, digging at the roots of her fragrant hair with a stubbly jaw.

Her arms were pressing as near as his. But after a while she had to say "You'll break through into my brain any minute."

Whit said "Good news" but stopped the rubbing and stepped back to see. As always here in the past ten years, he worked to hide how much she'd changed. Almost nothing of the old June Green was left to see except the eyes, so brown they seemed like caves in the Earth. They were here, unmarred. And when they bore his look as now, they let him see through her whole shut mind, to near the midst.

The midst was where June lived alone. The place where she was born and would die, the meat of her soul which no man could touch. But next to that Whit saw the space where he'd always hoped she waited for him. Now he could see she was still there, standing with both hands out, not begging but ready. In the dimming kitchen he said "June Green, you take this man?"

"June Wade. I *took* him."

Whit said "Shame *on* you." Then he said "Thank God." In his arms she seemed entirely possible. No miracle, nor burden, but good for a lifetime. So he said "Any war news?"

She said "What war?"

"The World War, lady—the second half. You and Liss went to church at halftime, remember? Now we finish Japan."

June said "My war quits the day you get home." Whit nodded again on the crown of her head and tightened his arms. But then they heard Liss clatter downstairs. *Ah, we're grown. We made this child an equal partner and here she stands.*

Whit turned to see her in the door, a little edgy. Never till now had she looked so much like her mother long since. That clear-eyed gaze that said *I'm fit for all they send me.* But easy to ruin as a day-old bird. Her useless arm, though healing fast, gave her even more strength in Whit's eyes now. From the day she was born, he'd known her to be the grandest hostage he'd given to time. And here she hung—outside, excluded.

June had also seen her but made no sign.

Liss said "I forgot to ask, who hit your car?"

June said "Oh no."

Whit said "Dumb me. A tire blew out and rolled me over, last Tuesday night."

June pulled back to see him. "You look just fine." Then she saw the light scratch in his hairline and touched it.

Whit caught her hand. "I *am* fine—end of pointless story."

Liss said "Well, maybe you'll paint it now. Black cars depress me." And though she said it in a childish whine, she stood there lonely, grown and adrift.

So to bring her in, Whit said "Does that arm mean you can't make tea?"

Liss waved the sling. "Tea? Tonight?"

"For supper tonight and for good, spring and summer."

Liss said "I'll make it, long as I'm here. That's six more years. Then I'll be gone."

Whit thought *She's counted. She's waiting to leave.* But tonight someway, that was not hard to hear. He pressed his chin on June once more and said "No rush. No rush now at all."

For that one moment, all three believed it. They'd worked for this, it was here, it could last—in three minds anyhow, as long as they lasted if not for good. The sun was down, the room nearly dark. The neighborhood, tame by day as a fireside pet, had vanished now and would hide till dawn, if dawn returned.

Whit stepped over and switched on a light.

June said "Liss, please set the dining-room table. Let's splurge tonight."

Liss said "Ma, what kind of splurge is fish?"

"They're nice fresh blues, that's what, with my coleslaw."

Liss crossed her eyes and frowned at Whit. Then she slogged a path, with evident pain, to the cutlery drawer.

Whit said "Ma, let's eat the blue fish tomorrow."

"—And all die of ptomaine, writhing on the floor? Not me, thank you kindly." June sensed a quick conspiracy against her, they'd eaten fish every Friday for years, Whit loved fish and was partial to blues. And he'd said more than once how, all through England, he could taste her coleslaw with celery seed when all else failed—the memory of even her speaking voice or the pitch of her laugh. She couldn't face Liss; the anger would show. But she turned to Whit. "You want a steak, don't you?"

He said "Fair lady, I want to *thank* you." And he made a stiff bow.

The instant it happened, it cut no ice. But once June saw him flinch at her question, she recalled he'd gone to the end of a place she'd still never found, the outskirts of death. Now he'd been sent back. Or had chosen to come back now tonight. She didn't dissolve in tears or grins. She'd worked and waited a lot too long to respond that quickly. Finally she said "Far be it from June Green Wade to stand in the path of a free steak dinner with tossed salad and no pan to scrub."

Liss said "Waa-hoo!" and hopped a war dance. "Fried onion-rings—can I just have that?"

Fried onion-rings were new in the South like cold tossed salads. And throughout Raleigh they could only be found at Proescher's Steak House out past the fair grounds halfway to Cary. So the die was cast. Whit checked both women's eyes a last time. And when he saw no serious objection, he said "Everybody get clean and gaw-jous. I'll call right now and get us a room."

Even on Fridays in those lean years, before ten million fathers returned from Europe and Asia, you could get a whole private room for the family, if luck was with you. And it was, that night. The hostess led the three of them down the long center-hall to a room on the left—fifteen by twelve—and gave them each a tall white menu with black letters big as an auction sign.

Whit had taken the chair at the head with his back to the door. The women sat to his left and right with eight clear feet of the table beyond them. They all took glasses of water, so cold it could cleave strong molars, and drank while they sorted the menu as if it mattered like deathbed wishes.

The two women ate Delmonico steaks, well-done and gray as shingles. Only Whit had the nerve to eat rare beef in those last days before freezers pushed south from factories in Utica; and beef could cross state lines in safety, raw but sweet. They'd each consumed every leaf of an individual basin of salad greens with blue-cheese dressing, an equal third of the platter of onions and slices of a pecan pie so rich their minds were affected till near bedtime. But they said next to nothing. Little moans of pleasure, even from June who thawed completely before the pie came.

When Liss spoke of course it was all self-concerned, monumentally hand-sized school events that loomed for her like the nuclear blasts that were still three months off, hid from all but two dozen men, two hundred and fifty miles northeast in Washington, and ten or twelve more scattered elsewhere to the west.

Before the pie came June thought she could ask Whit the news of his week. Her delay had not been caused by interference. He had trained her, a good ten years ago, not to put him back through business trips and make him rehearse the drumming boredom of country hotels and cold-grease meals. She never held a jealous suspicion for more than an hour and had been right to do so, so she'd honored his wish.

But this one Friday—because of his phone call, the cast of his eyes, the lift in his voice, her dark recollection of Sunday night and her sense all evening that she was finally back again with the boy she'd loved and that now he'd stay—with that much knowledge June knew she could ask. "Darling boy, what happened that was good?"

Liss frowned at her mother in baffled annoyance.

And Whit said "Good? Am I that transparent?"

June nodded and smiled. "To your oldest friend."

But he no longer knew if the week had helped. He'd had quick sightings, since late Monday morning, of people living in this world now. Juanita and her weird dogs, Tuck and Tray, Beck and Martha and the picture of Dolphus, Mr. Drake as live as a burning coal on the hearth rug, Mr. Drake's old cook. And Carle Towns, lost in his door by a broomstraw field as fine as anything west of Normandy and that one all-but-lethal pasture—a burst of light that flooded Whit's chest and then the angel of death or light, signing him on or backward to life.

But in this room now, near his best kin, he recalled no more than his sight of the spider on Mr. Drake's porch, a famished spider and its homemade net. *Endless rounds of hunger and food.* He didn't quite say it that plain in his mind, but it came to that. All these last few years he'd starved. Now he was fed. It wouldn't last but it felt safe now to trust it awhile. So only three seconds after June claimed his friendship, he faced her and said "If you see through me, it's because I've let you." Then he beamed a broad and helpless grin.

Liss said "Shoot, I've seen through him right along. He never fooled me." She'd said it to June but winked at her father.

He rasped his chair well back to stand. Then he held out the check to figure the tip. "Here, young scholar, what's the damage toll? I'm still feeble-minded and I need trained help."

Liss put out her hand.

But June took the check. "It's eighteen dollars and eighty-eight cents."

Liss said "Magic number," an unplanned joke, and hoped nobody would ask her why. When they paid no notice, she tried again. "Give the waitress two dollars. She'll think we're famous."

Whit said "We are, in the Great Gold Book." With solemn mien he pointed to the sky. But he also smiled more easily than at any earlier point in the year.

So both women also stood to go.

As Whit paid the check at the desk out front, June fished for pennies and bought three chocolate mints in tinfoil and Liss disappeared. When her parents were ready, they looked at each other's eyes and thought *Where in God's name is she?* For once Whit didn't suspect disaster, despite June's frown. So while she paused to clear her mind with one of the mints, Whit moved on a hunch and checked the room beside the cashier.

It was ten feet square and dim as a dugout. The only light was a winking neon sign for beer. There was one unused pinball machine and, in the corner, a big contraption with a girl leaning over. *Liss? Sure, Liss.* "What have you found—a slot machine?"

"Pa, come look at this."

"Oh yes, I know. I saw it last week."

Liss said "*Boo,* it's brand-new to me."

"It's just a toy recording machine."

"*I* know what it is. But I never saw one." She read the lighted instructions aloud, " 'Insert half dollar or two quarters. At green light, speak to the horn. Talk two minutes till red light shines. Stopwatch shows time elapsed. To pause press WAIT. When finished, your record will drop through slot. Play on any Victrola. LIVING MEMORIES.' " It had captured Liss. She was brighter than Whit had seen her in months.

Whit said "Sounds too complicated for me," but he pulled out his change and found two quarters. "What will you say?"

June was with them by then.

Liss said "Not me. You and Ma make it for me."

June said "Fine—directions for combing Elissa Wade's hair." She reached for the child's unruly head.

"Ma, my hair's too young to lie down. No, you and Pa say something to me, some kind of surprise. I may not even play it for years. Then when I'm grown and everything's changed, I'll have you to keep. Just don't preach sermons." She had caught herself on the brink of trouble and hadn't said "I'll have it when you're dead." The practical beat of her voice burnt off all trace of sweetness.

Even June could agree, though she said "You'll play it by bedtime tonight."

Whit said "All right. You wait in the lobby."

As she went Liss said "Don't be dumb now. This is costing good money."

Whit said "It's my money. You just vamoose." And once she was gone, he drew June toward him. "You first," he said and fed the first quarter.

Her arm was around his back at the waist; she pressed him closer. "Hold up, let me think." It took a long moment; then she said "All right."

Whit fed the second quarter, cogs whirred, the green light.

June said "Old lady, this voice was your mother. If I'm gone now or you've moved off and already have your own child near, let him hear me now. This is for you both. Your mother and grandmother says 'Sleep *tight*.' "

Whit leaned forward quickly and said "Sleep *sober*."

June laughed, then realized she was done. She looked up to Whit and mouthed "Now you."

He let five heavy seconds pass. Then "Liss—Elissa—Elissa Anne Wade. Pa hopes you know the part you played in haling him back from his long trip. You and your mother are where I've landed. For now at least, the foreseeable future, this May the 11th, 1945. I enjoy the view of both you ladies and the world behind you. May you bypass places that steal your soul. May you find your own home base like me." He pressed the WAIT button, then "Love, Elissa—from Whitley Wade." He thought he was finished, but the stopwatch showed twenty seconds left. He looked to June. But what he saw was a face in the surf—Tim Grant last June. *Way past my help*. He pointed to the stopwatch and mouthed "You finish."

At first June shrugged, then knew her next words and nodded

Start. As the needle dropped, she began "Happy birthday," singing alone.

Dumb? Join her? Why the hell not? So Whit was with her by the second bar. They got it all in, in under eight seconds; then broke down laughing.

"Wait a minute! What have you nuts done?" Liss was there in the door. "Happy birthday?—that's August."

When they had calmed down, June said "My darling, your mother remembers."

Liss said "Dumboes. I knew you'd ruin it."

Whit said "You wait, Miss Flaming Perfection. Every August from here to the family grave, you'll have one birthday card at least." He'd forgot to press END. Now he finished the job.

More whirrs and clicks, then a five-inch record appeared in the slot in a yellow wrapper. June gave it to Whit.

He held it out in the air to Liss. "Happy lifetime, ma'm."

Her frown had relented but she stayed in place.

So one more time, Whit and June went toward her.

BACK BEFORE DAY

IF YOU HAD SAT anywhere near them in the bleachers, and were normally curious, you would almost surely have noticed the two. They were dressed a lot better than most fans at high-school basketball games, and their open faces and ease in one another's nearness were good to watch. The boy was five years old, named Brady, though nobody called him much but Brade. He had his mother's black hair and would get his father's body, compact and wiry. The man was his father and was thirty-six. He was named Dean Walker, a ginger-haired man with a face and body like a self-respecting ex-Golden Gloves champ. All through life, Dean had got cheap jokes about being the head of whatever school he was in at the time—"Dean Walker, can I get permission to smoke in the boys' bathroom? The doctor says it helps my fits." Dean always said "Sure" and rolled away smiling. He walked like a sailor, though he had been a foot soldier thirteen years ago.

He really liked school, right on through college and still, in the sixth year of this present job. It made him rare in his chosen profession, since he was a high-school football coach who taught crip courses—compulsory phys. ed. and "Your Valuable Body." The second course was Dean's invention and was strictly elective, but it always filled up with children who had already used their bodies more than he and still were baffled.

Tonight was the last home basketball game of the season. It set Dean's school, Don Watson High, against their arch rival from down the road, Lithia Springs. And as it wound down, with Watson losing by a shameful margin, it was not a finish anybody could watch with pride or interest, not even a fan of young male bodies. Everybody on the court was a hormone disaster of height and weight, and even the oldest and strongest were whipped. Yet the crowd of two hundred behaved itself, in expected fashion, as though its personal life was hanging by the thinnest thread.

Dean and Brade joined in, though Dean at least felt that he and his son were safe as granite in the walls outside. He had finished his football season in the black and was guaranteed for another year. When the basketball coach looked back at him now with pain and dread, at the last missed foul-shot, Dean gave a reassuring nod and a stout thumbs-up; but he thought *Aloha, Tex, that's it.* It was Dave's third loss in a row to Lithia, as nice a guy as Dean had known outside the Army but a piss-poor coach for teenage boys.

In the hall by the gym, Dean hung back to talk to Dee, the civics teacher that generally had a dumb question for him. She was new this term and more than attractive. But as she started to ask yet another, Dean heard what he thought was Brade's voice screaming. It came from Dean's right, and he looked that way—no Brade anywhere. He left Dee flat, pushed through the door and ran headlong into frozen air like a concrete wall.

There was Brade, hugging thin arms to his chest; he had just yelled out at the shock of the cold. An arctic front had been forecast and had slammed in on them while the game droned down.

Dean said an automatic silent *Thanks*, scooped him up, took a mock enormous bite from his neck and ran to the car.

It was nothing but a nine-year-old Corvette—even most student cars were newer and better—but in Brade's eyes, held sideways now, it looked like a silver rocket in the moonlight, something fast anyway and aimed away. He already knew the destination. Cold as it was, Dean had promised him a Nutty Buddy at the drive-in. Brade would make that last as long as he could; and like every child, he knew how to linger.

One thing Brade did not yet know, he stumbled on next. As they sat in the car, with the heater running, and finished their Buddies, Dean said "Sport, you ready for bed?"

Brade shook his head hard. "Took an extra-long nap."

At once Dean's hand went out to his forehead. Brade had had rheumatic fever last summer and spent five weeks mostly resting in bed. The doctor said he was doing fine now but should still rest an hour a day, after lunch. His forehead felt normal; Dean didn't want to scare him. He said "You felt like you needed some extra rest?"

By now Brade was chewing the ice-cream stick and gazing at the next car over. A couple were trying to swallow each other.

Dean knew the courting boy's neck on sight—Tim Timmons, left tackle. There seemed little hope of seeing the girl; she would likely be gone from Earth by morning, eat-up by Tim. So Dean said again "Brade, you been tired lately?"

Brade still did not turn; but he said "No sir, I wanted to get up but Flynn said wait." The boy had always called both parents by their names; Flynn was his mother, Dean's first and only wife.

Right off, it sounded wrong. Dean loved her too much, he always knew; so at first he told himself *Go easy*. He cranked the engine and got under way before he said "Did Flynn have a headache?"

"No sir, she—" Brade took a show-off deep long breath and began to whistle between his teeth, a skill he had only recently learned. The tune was meant to be the Don Watson anthem; his father was also teaching him that, "Golden Days."

But Dean had heard the unfinished business in Brade's last answer. He actually vowed not to press on the boy; but when they had cleared the lights of town and the dark woods began, Dean failed himself. He said "Was she punishing you for something?"

Brade had tried, ever since he mentioned the nap, to think of anything else—something good. And just before Dean mentioned punishment, the boy had managed to start his best story, the always unspoken movie in his head where he and Dean built a real canoe, of bent limbs and birch bark, and found a river that lasted a year and headed down it, through eagles and panthers. Now he must end it before it got far. He looked at the side of Dean's face and said "No sir. I behaved myself. Somebody knocked on the door to see her."

Dean bit hard at the lining of his cheeks. *I'll face this with Flynn.* But as the car drove itself on home, and the porch light showed up there ahead, Dean failed again. "Who was it, son?"

Brade's mind went a solid battleship gray; gray was all he could see. But he told the truth ."I think it was that guy we saw one time when I was a child, at White Lake—you know—in the leopard-skin trunks that you laughed at."

Dean's mind whooshed up like a gasoline fire, but his voice stayed calm. "Was his name Clyde Bowles?"

"I just heard *Clyde.*" Pure as his mind had managed to stay, Brade half-understood what that would cause. He even half-hoped it would mean he and Dean were truly alone from here on forever.

By the time they parked the car in the yard and aimed for the house, Flynn was there in the door behind screen wire. She smiled and gave her old bird-call, three falling notes that she always used to hale Brade in from the woods or the creek. Young as he was, he had five years of well-stocked memory of Flynn's good heart. So his mind relented and he skipped on toward her.

Dean came behind slowly, his customary pace.

Flynn could not yet tell how much he knew. *He wouldn't speed up if I burst into flames.*

Dean's cold mind was telling itself *Easy, easy. Don't break a-loose.* And when he had scraped his shoes on the top step and Flynn tipped her broad face to meet him, he even leaned and took her dry kiss on the edge of his jaw. But all he heard was his own mind saying what an uncle had told him the day of the wedding, *She's way too young for you, son; hold on.*

Once she got Brade settled in bed and came to find Dean, he was in bed too. He was turned to the wall and seemed asleep. But Flynn knew at once *My luck's not that good. Brade's bound to have told him.* She felt no fear but her own mind saw the same blank color that came over Brade when he had to say "Clyde." The headboard light on the bed was still burning, so she stripped off quickly and put on the clean old white cotton slip that Dean used to like. Then she stepped down the hall to brush her teeth. All those minutes, Flynn thought one thing—*Just tell him the truth and hope he believes you.* Dean had never so much as touched her in anger, though after that last time, he made a mean threat.

In the five minutes she spent in the bathroom, Dean seemed to have settled; he was breathing the way he breathed in sleep. Flynn thought *Lord God,* a quick thanksgiving—to the air; she barely believed in more. But then she knew *He's faking. Lie low.* She switched off the light, stretched out on her back and asked her mind to shrink her body. When she was a girl in bed with her brother, who hogged the space, she learned a way to all but vanish by narrowing down the eye of her mind to see herself as the smallest bird aimed west at sunset in a plumb-straight line.

The thing she must not think was *Clyde;* even the word would break her focus and start her growing till she crowded Dean and woke him now. For maybe ten minutes, she truly succeeded; and Dean was still turned away, still breathing easy. But then she faltered—not the name but Clyde's white patient face flashed up in her sight before she could down it. *If I gave him the word, he'd wait forever. As it is, he may still.* She frowned in the dim air, but it did not displease her.

Dean's back was still turned; but before he could risk her touch or smell, he said "I know about today."

Flynn said "I knew it."

Dean earnestly tried to hold himself in. He tried to think of his Aunt Pauline, the kindest person of all he knew. In his own big family, with all the razor tongues, still nobody ever faulted Pauline. From his early childhood, the sight of her face would generally ease him, whatever his pain—her hazel eyes that could find the horizon, wherever she stood, and gaze off at it. And any words she chose to speak were foolproof skeleton keys to his chest. Now though his mind could barely see her; Pauline was facing away from his mind, somehow refusing. *She won't be part of this mule shit here.* Even in thought, he could not swear around her. But the smell of Flynn was the strong prod now. He said to himself *I'm about to ruin things.* Then he said to Flynn "What did I tell you I'd do, the next time?"

"You said you'd leave me and Brady, here flat."

In the dark Dean nodded as though she could see. But then he said calmly "You got it wrong."

She was still not afraid, but sadness was swamping her; she could not speak.

"I said I'd leave *you*. Brade comes with me."

Flynn's throat closed down; for an instant she panicked and sat up for air. One of her long hands clawed at the space. When she had finally gasped a breath, she wadded her pillow and sat against the headboard. "Dean, do me one thing—turn here to face me."

Don't speak my name. But he thought it over and, though he stayed down, he rolled to his back and faced the ceiling. Their eyes were maybe twenty inches apart, but they saw only dark.

Flynn said "I don't know what Brade told you; all that happened was, Clyde stopped by here, driving to Durham. He was thirsty and tired, so he knocked on our door about one-thirty. Brade had finished his lunch and was already resting; I told him I'd shut his door awhile. Then I fixed Clyde a Coke and sat at the kitchen table thirty minutes while he drank it down and told me his news."

Dean was dressed in nothing but underwear with the sheet and blanket, but his entire body was scalded in fire. He heard his voice say "A glass or the bottle?"

"Beg your pardon?"

"The Coke—did he drink from the bottle or one of my glasses?"

Flynn said "Oh Dean, that's nothing but childish."

"Thank Jesus then. If the way you and Clyde are acting is grown, then I'll hang back with the waterhead babies. If Clyde Bowles drank from one of my glasses, I'll wreck the damned kitchen."

Flynn would not play that mean a game now or ever. She held her tongue for the next two minutes; then she said "He means this much to me" and snapped her fingers. In the damp still air, the sound was strong. And before it was gone, she knew she had lied.

Dean was still balked. Though his eyes were open, he could see very little. The weak hall-light that usually crept in and outlined objects was off tonight. Worse, he could not see forward in his life. The life he wanted with Flynn and Brade was stopped and dying in his mind, no hope. For the absolute first time since Brady's birth, Dean thought *They never let an orphan back in.* He was not an orphan, though his father had died six years ago. And he paused to wonder what he meant by *orphan;* it had shocked his mind. Maybe what he meant was *Life has walled me out.* He knew he was feeling sorry for himself; but Christ Almighty, who had a better reason in America anyhow this night now?

Flynn knew his mind almost entirely. She thought *Speak slowly; make every word true.* And then she began to obey herself, "Dean, you already know every word of this; and it's all still honest. Clyde Bowles loved me from high school on. Nobody much in my life till then had noticed me. So sure, I went with him nearly three years till you came back from Vietnam and were what I'd dreamed of without knowing how—a dignified nice-looking boy that claimed to need me. Clyde just disappeared from out of my mind and has stayed out, Dean. From the night you touched me that first time, I couldn't *see* Clyde when he walked through the door. He'd bow and scrape and my flesh would crawl. It nearly killed him; you well know it did. I couldn't help that; you were on my mind. So the years went by. And years after I swear-on with you, Clyde shows up twice in the past three weeks—just trying to be a friend to us all. He's so lonesome, Dean, he hurts to watch. I thought we could give him a little of what we've got a big surplus of, between us—"

"A slice of your butt?" The words flushed out and were strewn on the air now, no way to hide them.

Flynn could see them cut in the dark stale air; she read them over like a summons to grieve. At last she said "I'm going to try as hard as I can to gouge that out of my head forever."

"Gouge Clyde while you're at it."

"Dean, Clyde Bowles is nothing but a family friend. You and I, and Brade, have got more love than three people need—it may even be we've got too much. I thought we could dole out a crumb here or there."

Dean's eyes were still blocked, but he knew he could hear. He knew every word Flynn said could be true. And he almost thought they had the surplus of love she mentioned. All his life he had tried to trust that some things were true, from the face right on down to deep bedrock where they passed from sight. That was mainly why, in their years together, Dean had never asked what he asked her now. Still facing up, he tried to say her name. That would not come yet, so he said "Did Clyde ever touch your body?"

Flynn waited. "You sure you need to ask that?"

"I surely do."

"All right then, yes—long years ago."

Dean said "How much?"

Flynn said "Please don't head down that road. Then I'll have to start peeling skin off you—Sal Hawkins, Clarice, names I don't even know and don't need, Dean."

For the first time since touching her cheek on the porch, Dean put out his right hand and pressed her mouth—not hard, just to hush her. She hushed but he left his fingers in place; and in maybe ten seconds, the gray in his mind gave a heave and broke. He thought *In a minute there'll be some light.*

Flynn's hand came up, took his hand firmly and moved it down to her throat.

So if light stayed gone, at least Dean's skin began to warm—first his fingers and then, in a slow sweep, his whole cold body. He turned to face her.

She slid back down and rolled toward him. *He owes me better than this, Christ knows.* But she wanted to be where she was and she stayed.

Then for a burdened stretch of minutes, Dean felt her body like the blind man he was, hoping for aid; and Flynn held onto his warming shoulders and prayed this was it. *This'll break all ice; we'll both float free in a minute here.*

When his hand had readied her gently, Dean bent; then rode the distance up her secret way in one steady rise, far as he could, with the ease of falling. They both kept silent, no audible breath. Neither one of them felt immediate pleasure or gratitude; neither one of them looked toward pleasure as a goal. They were close as two people manage to get, short of skinning each other, eating the choice meat and wearing the hide. Yet though they could not have told you in words, their separate furious aims were alike. They each one wanted to forestall loathing or the need to seize one near human being and strike him or her in the brittle teeth or grind some former loved one to pulp and scrub his face, her hair and eyes, out of memory or notice.

As they worked, Flynn thought *I lived through a whole lot worse than now most days of my childhood.* She was thinking of her mother's early death, her life after that in a house with her father and three older brothers and soon with a stepmother worse than anything in books. At the thought she made a low moan, soft in Dean's hot ear. He seemed not to hear it, but still Flynn thought *I'll last and forget this day ever was.*

And with no refusal from inside Flynn, or her outer parts, Dean brought himself at a boy's slick speed to within clear sight of the lip of a hill he knew he would fling from, straight onto rest and a merciful dawn—not to speak of the surge in his haunches that rose by the instant to crest and spill and wash them both of the sickening faults of an ordinary day.

Flynn's voice amazed her own keen ears, when she whispered beneath him "*Trust* me, Dean."

The three words struck him at the pitch of his soar. Gut-shot, his body and mind tumbled from the crest of a thermal that had raised him near their best old height—his need for a lovely generous girl, her answering care, their mutual pardon—and he thudded down on her baffled skin, just short of his goal. The joint between their bodies was awful. Dean rolled back off her and turned away.

Flynn waited a long time. "Are you any better?"

He knew not to answer; the words would come wrong.

But in two more minutes, Flynn had to press. "Is it all right, Dean?" When no answer came, she asked again "Will it get all right?" *There I go, demanding a future from him.*

He wanted to say her name but could not. So he made a careful anonymous sentence. "I may know tomorrow. Now I'm trying to rest."

Flynn said to herself *He won't. Me either. The sky's breaking up.* Right or wrong, she thought she had caused it; and she knew that their life together would die. It might end slowly but *die* it would, from this night on and with Brade to stand watching. She also knew she was blameless as Brade. Then in her mind she saw Clyde's face as he was today, still hopeful as ever. In her mind he said what she knew Clyde would say in an instant when he heard this news, "I can make it up to you in a fine quiet home—you and Brade—from this minute on." But still in her mind, she tore at Clyde's tender grateful eyes till she thought *I'm crazy. This will all pass by. Lie still and see if the sun won't rise.*

A foot away, Dean was also trying for calm. Another smart thing his father told him was in his mind now, *Don't ever think of your troubles in bed; you'll just want to die or burn up the world.* So with spring practice only a few weeks off, Dean tried to run every new play in the book, seeing his tight neat diagrams lit in green on the air before him. But after three successful runs, Clyde Bowles's face kept butting up into the weaving trails of perfect players, running true.

So Dean switched games and tried a stunt he did in secret, more times than even Flynn could have guessed—he tried to picture each one of Brade's birthdays, how the boy had looked each step of the way, the clothes he wore, the presents he got and what he did or said when he saw them.

Dean prized him that much, not just as a son but as one real person with watchful eyes and a fine lot to say. His own mind moved on through the fourth birthday before it broke up the game and said *Your boy halfway understands Clyde Bowles. That slack-jawed face is in Brade's head too; and nothing I do will erase it now, except kill the boy*. The idea came, so wild and unmeant, that Dean shuddered hard and, before he knew it, was out of the bed and fumbling for his clothes.

Flynn said "What, Dean?"

He said "You sleep. I can't right now."

"I could fix you a sandwich—"

He said "You could but I couldn't eat it."

"Don't you go driving around in the night."

Dean was dressed by then. He stopped at the door, faced Flynn's direction and said what came. "You don't do anything I tell *you;* keep your orders to yourself." As the words spewed out, his mind was saying *Childish, childish;* but that was too late. He had no plan beyond removing his body from hers.

He walked past Brade's open door, no sound. Dean understood that he should not stop; he must not mire the boy in this any deeper than now. He went to the boxy living-room and sat on the couch he always hated, since the day he walked in and found it in place—mustard-colored and nubby.

It was dark here too, just leakage from the hall on the sparse belongings. *Everything that doesn't matter is mine*—a few cheap trophies, plaques so cheap he had secretly wanted to throw them back in the donors' teeth, a plaster bust of Sitting Bull he had owned as a boy and had now given Brade. He rolled his head back and tucked the palms of both cold hands between his legs. He knew Flynn's smell was still strong on them, and he rubbed them hard on his corduroy trousers. Then in what seemed help from the sky, three minutes later he was halfway asleep. It was not rest though but that kind of trance where your worries fly straight at your face in new forms, small and bumbling like bugs on a speeding windshield by night. You think *I'm solving each care as I go,* but the wakeful part of your mind knows better and poisons the rest.

When Dean came to, he stood upright at once. The wall clock said two minutes till midnight. His mother would just be yawning by now, alone in her old house, watching TV and fending off sleep. The last time he saw her, she said "I sleep maybe twenty-five minutes a month—if I'm tired." And she laughed but Dean knew the sorrowful reason. She forgot that she told him, six years ago as his father lay dead downstairs in the coffin, that whenever she took so much as a nap, she saw that still man's face as it was those grim last weeks when the stroke had left him speaking a language that might as well have been angel tongues—ferocious angels if not hateful demons.

Though she lived an easy hour west, Dean had not seen his mother since right after Christmas when he and Brade drove up to the foothills and spent a night with her. He went to the kitchen now, shut the swinging door and called her number. It rang till it scared him.

On the twelfth ring she answered with her usual words, "All *right,* Pat Walker."

Dean said "Beg your pardon. I woke you up."

"You did not, no sir. I'm just slowing down."

"But you're feeling O.K.?"

Pat chuckled. "K.O. would be more like it. I've had a chest cold," and she barked to prove it.

Dean said "What does Dr. Rogers say?"

"He hasn't," she said. "I'm dosing myself."

"With what?"

She said "Turpentine—mind your own business, son."

"Then see the doctor first thing tomorrow."

"Hush, Bean," she said. "I've run my own life sixty-two years; I'll run it on into the ground, thank you kindly." Pat always balked at calling him Dean. It was her ex-father-in-law's first name. And from the day her husband disowned her bed and body, when Dean was two, she called the boy Bean (even these days, she gritted her teeth just to write his full name on an envelope). Now she coughed again, a helpless seizure.

When she calmed a little, Dean said "Any fever?"

"I truly don't know. I bit my thermometer in two last winter, when I had those chills, and haven't replaced it. I don't feel hot."

"Are you staying in bed?"

Pat said "My darling, *forget* - my - trials. I'm a sensible soul; I'll be all right in a few more days. I know you aren't ringing up this late to feel my pulse. What's the news down there?"

He said "Things are normal. Brade drew a picture of you last week in kindergarten. He wants you to have it."

"Does it have horns and tail? If Flynn Walker helped him, I bet it does."

Dean dodged her ritual swipe at Flynn and thought two things, as ever on each new meeting with his mother. First, most people thought she was tough as shoe leather; so she played the part. Second, the tougher she tried to sound, the more his mind would reach out toward her with years of thanks. She had stuck by him through hard and easy with a strength no German shepherd could match, not to mention mankind. He wept about once every hundred years and mostly for joy, but his eyes stung now, and he knew not to speak.

His mother said "I dreamed about you last night."

"Was I misbehaving?"

"Not a bit. You had won that race you lost—when was it?—at the Labor Day picnic when you were seven. And you brought me the ribbon; I pinned it to my hat."

Dean laughed, "I think I was five; and to my certain knowledge, you never owned a hat."

"And you didn't bring me the ribbon, remember?" Then she laughed too, not her characteristic three rising notes but a deep long pleasure that became a coughing fit. It went on forever till she managed to say "Hang on. Let me drink some water."

Dean waited in what was sudden anguish. She had quit smoking five years ago, to spare her first grandchild the example. So this fit now was doubly unnerving.

At last she was back. "Excuse me, Bean. I was nibbling popcorn and inhaled a piece."

She often made late-night popcorn, but he thought she was lying. He made her promise to go in tomorrow to see Dr. Rogers; then he would phone her at noon for the verdict. They talked on a while about kin and the weather, her new used-car and more about Brade—how she noticed, when she saw him after Christmas, that he smiled on the left just like her father, whom Brade had never seen. "Ain't it wondrous," she said, "how it's all in there, just biding its time?—your smile and your faults, all ticking away like separate time-bombs."

Dean said "Is that so wondrous, you think?"

"Oh it is. You may need to be my age to see it."

"But what about family craziness and cancer?"

Pat just said "*Wondrous*—you mark my words." Then quietly she said "Let me go now, Bean. Here's a good-looking man on the Carson show. That'll heal me surely."

With a final repeat of the promise he extracted, Dean was ready to leave her. He said "I love you."

She waited and he thought *I've bowled her over;* but no, when she spoke her voice was level. "I've believed it since the first day you saw me, but I welcome it still and return the favor." Then her memory jogged her, "Oh son, do you know the sad news on Clyde?"

"Clyde?"

"Bowles—the only Clyde we know." She always assumed Dean had met nobody since he finished high school and left her house.

The name in his mother's mouth struck Dean almost as hard as it had in Brade's hours back. But Clyde's mother Essie lived two blocks from Pat, and the two women met at the grocery store every day or so. Now he said "I know Clyde still pines for Flynn. That's sad enough for me."

Pat said "Now you can ease your mind. Clyde's almost dead."

"Ma'm?"

"Liver cancer, no hope."

Dean said "Oh Jesus. How long has he known?"

"His mother told me this morning at the Laundromat. She said the doctors told Clyde last month. He kept it pent up inside him four weeks; then he called poor Essie the night before last and sobbed like a baby. Asked her if he could come home soon to die. You know she turned him out two years ago and said not to darken her door again till he gave up liquor."

Dean was split between pity, sick shame and the urge to stride in to Flynn this instant with the truth. He said "God, Mother, you say no hope?"

"You ever know anyone to beat liver cancer?"

"No." He thought *I ought to be glad* and waited to gloat in private. But all that came was the sight of Clyde Bowles eighteen years ago. Dean was an all-state senior quarterback when Clyde got cut from the jayvee team. Clyde's mother begged Dean to put in a word with the coach for Clyde; and when Dean said it would do no good, she looked him dead in the eye and said "My boy'll be rich when you're still playing these ignorant games." *She got my half of the future right anyhow.* And from that memory onward, Clyde's ninth-grade face and scarecrow body stood here in the kitchen, real as meat. *No hope, tonight or as far back anyhow as how he looked in the football showers, a white rack of bones with a curled-up dick like a dry blue nipple.* "Mother, where is he?"

"On the road, I guess—some motel or other. Essie said he's working till his strength gives out, to make all the money he can for her."

"The town, I mean; where is he tonight? If I call Essie, you think she'll know?"

"I guess but, son, Essie turns in at dark."

He said "I doubt she's sleeping this week."

"You may have a point. She's already lost a pound or two; her old turkey-neck looks worse than mine. You mean you want to call Clyde this minute?"

Dean said "I better think twice on that."

"Tell you what, I'll call Essie early tomorrow—before I head to see the doctor—and ask where he is. When you call me at noon, I'll give you the news." She took a long moment. "I'm glad you're feeling a change of heart."

"Clyde never set out to hurt me, I guess."

"Clyde Bowles never had a trace of harm in his soul. You and Flynn burnt his little dream down; he never built another." Her tears were even scarcer than Dean's, but her voice was thin.

Dean's tone went softer than he knew it could go. "I'll call you during my lunch hour then."

"Is Flynn asleep?" Pat seldom mentioned Flynn more than once per call—no anger, she thought, just an honest avoidance.

"She's trying," Dean said.

"Then spare her tonight—Clyde's news, I mean."

For an instant Dean felt compelled to say No and tell the tale of the past few hours; but then as quickly, he felt small and dry. He said "You're absolutely right. Now sleep."

Pat said "I love you more than you know."

"I very much doubt that but thanks anyhow." He meant he had always known she loved him, not that he doubted her. Pat gave no cause whatever for doubt.

She understood his answer. "Just wear your best suit at my funeral and *smile*—that's all I ask." She chuckled briefly, afraid she had scared him.

But he said "I promise."

A half hour later, Dean had drunk more coffee and looked at every picture of Clyde in his and Flynn's high-school yearbooks—pathetic credits like the Audiovisual Club, the band and the hiking team with Clyde in the back row every time, solemn as if he foresaw a future on the Federal bench and must not strew childish evidence behind him. In only one picture did he look bright and hopeful, the Left-Bank Ball in his junior year. There Clyde stood, with Flynn on his arm, in a white dinner-jacket, admitting to the lens how grateful he was for that night's luck. *How far did it go? Well, wherever, son, it won't come back. You're long gone now.*

Dean thought the one word *son* again. It had come to his mind as a big surprise. But he knew that, for now, he honestly felt a fatherly warmth run out toward Clyde, poor miserable loser. *Weeks, days to live.* Dean's heart that had been so choked in ice an hour ago—he might have killed Clyde if Clyde had knocked—split open to let in the hopeless fool. And the whole prospect of life with Flynn began to thaw and move in his mind.

He darkened that whole end of the house. Then he walked to Brade's door and listened—slow even breath—then on to his own bed and Flynn's small shape. In the shadows like this, she was smaller than Brade. *And as much my duty,* Dean thought as he moved to the bed again.

Something told him *Don't undress yet awhile.* But he shucked his loafers and lay on top of the cover, face up. He knew Flynn lay with her face turned toward him, but she sounded as deep asleep as Brade. So in less than three minutes, Dean had also sunk. For a while he floated or managed the speed and depth of his plunge. But then a central turbulence caught him; his mind and body spun dangerously. The sensible part of his mind could say *This is pretty damned trite, for even* my *dreams.* But as always the rest of his mind roared on. And he went deeper down than he had before, knowing as he went *This may be the last. I may be dead.*

All down the funnel, Dean passed vague faces in the thick brown water. Some were dead; some tried to breathe or scream. But the one face he knew was Clyde's of course—young Clyde, the face Clyde wore at school. And of course Clyde was smiling, though he spun even wilder than Dean or the others. *You tried to drown, every day of your life, pathetic loser. Now finally you made it.*

Then Clyde saw Dean and beamed even wider, but spindly arms came out from the face and reached for Dean. The sensible part of Dean's mind still thought *This is one dumb dream.* But fast as he and Clyde spun down through the thickening murk, Clyde's arms got stronger and managed to seize Dean's throat and clutch. As they grappled Dean in, he watched Clyde's helpless face grow mean. Soon the smile was a laugh, and then the teeth were pressing forward to Dean's bare throat.

Dean tore himself upward, badly shaken. It took a long moment to realize he was free and awake. Then he could see that Flynn was awake too, propped on her elbow there to his left. He raised both hands to scrub at his eyes.

Flynn took that motion as a chance to speak. She had lain

awake through most of the dream—Dean's moans and jerks—as always unsure of whether to end it. Now she said again "Are you all right?"

He sat up to raise his head above hers. "Clyde Bowles is dead."

Of all the answers she might have given, she only said "What time is it please?"

The glow of Dean's watch said one forty-five; so he rounded it off, "Nearly two o'clock." He stayed upright, both legs on the bed. And he thought *She's figuring out if I had time to kill him.* But his better judgment said *Give her* some *credit.*

Flynn propped herself back up on the headboard, then finally said "You don't want me to believe you killed him?"

It came from so far out of the blue that Dean missed the point. "I beg your pardon?"

"Clyde—you say he's dead. Who killed him?"

Dean said "God Above."

"Don't be sacrilegious. You care, if I don't." She honestly meant it, *Stick to your guns.*

He realized now that, dazed by the dream, he had made a bad mistake with the news. No way to turn back though. He said "Flynn, Essie Bowles has told my mother that Clyde's got liver cancer. That's a swift death-sentence."

"You're lying to me." Something in Flynn's nap had steeled her mind. Her voice was as hard as Dean's ever got.

Dean said "I wish."

She even laughed. Then she said "Start over and tell me the truth."

Dean propped his own pillow and leaned back against it. "I meant to wait till morning to tell you. But then it slipped out—I had a bad dream, and that brought it up. I apologize."

Flynn waited. "Clyde told me today how good he was doing—selling his pots and pans, minting money. He told me to picture my fantasy land, and then he said he could likely afford it."

Dean let the taunt lie. "Mother said he's working, long as he can, to lay up some kind of nest egg for Essie."

Flynn said "He looked fine and my eyes don't lie, not with somebody I've watched as long as Clyde. People with liver cancer turn a bad yellow."

Dean said "I guess I ought to hope you're right. But I don't know why my mother would lie."

Flynn laughed again, two bitter dry notes. "Pat Walker hates me."

"That's not so; you know it."

"Well, she's given a goddamned fine imitation of wishing a cancer would eat *me* fast and leave you to her."

Dean waited till he knew he meant every word. Then he said "I better tell you, you can go too far—in about five seconds, if you don't change the subject."

Under her breath but in a clear whisper, Flynn counted to five. She waited in a silence so cold she thought her teeth would crack. Then she said the worst sentence yet in her life, "He'd be well now if I'd done the right thing."

"Clyde?"

"Clyde Bowles, a decent man that loves me."

"And the right thing would be you marrying Clyde?"

"*Would* have been," she said, "if I'd known in time. But I got it all wrong."

Dean already saw where her tack would lead, so he felt no surprise. But he also was freezing by the instant. He felt what he had not felt since childhood, *Now. My life is ending now*—the life here with Flynn and Brade, that he loved and had worked so hard to earn. Then he thought *Don't speak. Any word will be wrong.* But at once he said "Brady Walker—I guess our son is just one more mistake?"

Flynn waited again. She was thinking this all through, finding these terrible facts in her path. She said "Brade's all I've got left now."

Dean said "There you're wrong."

When Dean had put Brade's socks and shoes on and wrapped the stunned boy in an oversized blanket, Flynn came to the door and said "You think you're leaving?" She was not sure what she meant at the moment—did she have the strength to try to stop him? Would it be with a knife or the loaded pistol Dean kept by the bed? Did she mean *If you both go, I'll kill myself?* Scared and mad as she was, she also knew that her combination of a gentle mind and the certain wish not to mark Brade Walker with fear left her no choice but to give Dean ground to circle in and then hope to calm him.

But as she stalled on the boy's threshold, Dean said "Brade and I are driving to Mother's. We'll take her in to the doctor first thing—she's got a bad throat. If you're still here, I'll try to call you by noon."

"You're skipping school." Flynn said it as the strangest fact of all.

Dean said "I'll phone my substitute from Mother's. He needs the money and'll jump at the chance."

Brade said "I need some money myself." They had thought he was only moving in his sleep, but for once he had managed to surface quickly. By now he could use Dean's favorite expression; he looked to his mother and said "What's the plan?"

Flynn meant to say "Ask your father" but could not. She pointed to Dean.

Dean said "Brade, your grandmother's got a bad cold. You and I are going to take her to the doctor."

At that Flynn noticed the clean clothes neatly piled by Brade.

Dean had got them out before he woke the boy; he must mean to dress him somewhere on the road or maybe at his mother's—just one change of clothes. She seized onto that as a pledge of hope. She said to Brade "You keep warm, hear? And I'll see you this evening."

The boy looked at her curiously, then pointed to his window—the coal-black sky. "It's evening now."

"It's early morning, angel." She wanted to smile to let him know one thing was sure. But then hot anger poured down from her head. She entered the room, sat on the edge of her son's hard cot and kissed the tangled crown of his hair.

Brade said "Can we have cheese weenies for supper?"

Her eyes glanced to Dean.

Dean said "You can have anything you want."

Flynn thought *You can get cheese weenies anywhere on Earth, I guess.*

Dean faced her at last and said "We'll see you in the funny papers." It was what his father had always said.

"By dark," Flynn said.

Dean said "If we can. Like I said, I'll call you."

She said "I went too far just now—what I said, you know."

Dean said "I think people say what they mean. I know I do." He hated the lie but he let it stand.

Flynn said "Well, your mind can change. You're a decent soul." She wanted him to hear the word *decent* from her. And she said in her mind, *He'd die in a ditch before he'd harm one flake of Brade's skin.*

Brade looked to his father and gave an order that he himself got from his mother daily, "You be sweet, hear?"

Dean gave a tight chuckle. "I'll work on it, ace. That's why I need you."

When he bent one last time to lift the boy, Flynn leaned again and kissed her son's hair. *Don't even* think *he's leaving for good.*

As they neared the door, Brade raised his head. "See you later, Head Waiter." He had loved rhymes lately and made them all day.

Flynn said "In a while, Mr. Smile."

With his own back turned, Dean waited for the moment it took the boy to curve his lips in a comic grin and fold his hand once like a soundless hinge, in a parting wave.

For all he knows, he's leaving me. Flynn would not wave back, but she also smiled until they were gone. Then she told herself *They will be here by dark,* though she knew how fast that single hope was burning every gram of the strength she had managed to store. As she heard Dean's motor crank and race, she told herself *Girl, all your life you have stood and let people walk off with what you love.* It was true enough to qualify as more than self-pity. She stood up and thought it was time for coffee. She could not imagine surviving the day, but she knew she would.

Dean had thought the boy would fall back asleep once the car warmed up. And he did stretch out in his quilt on the seat and lay his head on his father's lap. Brade knew this trip was entirely strange; but though his mother had seemed a little sad, the boy only registered the lack of a quarrel—Dean and Flynn got mad every few days lately; and each time, Brade would think *Here it comes. I'm an orphan now.* So lying there with the dashboard's green glow spread on his hands, he said "Big Dean, is it really Ma-Ma?"

Dean begged his pardon.

"You said we were taking Ma-Ma to the doctor? That's not the truth, right?" Both parents had warned him more than once that the word *lie* was a serious charge.

Dean drove a long mile before he answered, "Where would you rather go?"

Brade said "You guess—"

"That river run, that you've been planning?"

The sound of Brade's hope in his father's voice was almost too much, this deep in the night. The boy worked his fingers in the green light, trying not to smile. *I didn't know it was still in his mind. That means we're serious; we really are going.* Brade knew if he said the wrong thing now—even one wrong word—the plan would break to smithereens. He said "It's all up to you; you're the pilot."

So Dean made the sound he learned as a boy in the hot heyday of the war in Korea, the roaring plunge of a diving bomber.

Some boys young as Brade might shy at the scream. He had heard it more than once already, alone with Dean; and dazed as he still was, he joined his light voice onto the dive. It lasted so long, and his father's face was so excited, that Brade half-thought they were truly pouring through the sky, Earth-bound, with bombs for the enemy. Who would that be? There was nobody yet Brade feared or hated.

Dean broke off his roar and made the huge convincing boom of a phosphorus bomb, a whole town leveled but nobody dead. He smiled down at Brade as long as he could.

Brade also exploded and they rode in silence another few miles.

They were in deep country, a two-lane cement road with no center line; and on both sides, their lights brushed trees—black pines and cedars so old and knobby they could make you feel carefree and blessed, if you paid any notice and knew about trees. Neither Dean nor Brade even saw them now.

Brade slid back and forth in the boundaries of sleep—ten seconds of blank unconsciousness, then a minute of watching his father's chin or his two broad hands on the steering wheel. Young as Brade was, he still could think *I pick tonight as the best part ever* (long years ahead, he would still know that; still agree with his thought).

Dean lapsed into punishing sights of Clyde Bowles. There was Clyde on Flynn Walker—she said he had touched her—with his flat white butt hacking fast above her and a pitiful bright-red pencil-dick and bird-egg nuts. *Let him die slow and awful.* Dean bit at his tongue to punish the meanness; and to clear his mind, he started silently naming the bones of the human body, in order, crown to toe. It was too big a chore to impose on his students, but he had learned the names in college as a personal dare, and for years they had served as a kind of drug when his mind needed calm or like a curious kind of prayer.

Brade went on sleeping and waking in spurts. Whichever side of the boundary he roamed, he was skittishly aiming at one bright point, one fear and hope that he needed to test. Were he and Dean really on their own? What had happened to Flynn? Would they ever see her? Would she come and find them, if they ever stopped? And would he want that? Would Dean let it happen? Brade knew enough about the feeling in rooms to know that, in those minutes before they left his mother at home, there were knives between his father and mother—invisible blades, real as the ones Flynn had in the kitchen, that Dean kept sharp on the flat millstone which was their back step.

It was while the boy was thinking *knives* that Dean had to say a thing he regretted, "Son, sit up a minute; my leg's gone to sleep."

Brade heard him and understood completely, but he said "Just give me a minute please." What he would not say, even to Dean, was what he laid out next in his mind—one of the first real prayers of his life. *Please let me look out and see some magic that will help me know what I ought to do with Dean and Flynn. They need some help.* He shut his eyes hard, to clear them for what he knew would come (he was not a spoiled child, but he had no doubt that his wish would come). He looked to his father's chin and said "O.K., wake - your - leg - up." Then he sat up quickly. He was short, by an inch or two, to see past the dash; so before Dean could stop him, Brade climbed to his own knees and looked on past the reach of their headlights—the black empty world they had not reached yet and, he thought, never could. *It melts when we get there.*

Dean's right hand came out to brace the boy; and he said "Son, you're not safe, standing there."

Brade thought *I have never been safe in my life;* and at once some fifty yards ahead, beyond their lights, a trail of fiery sparks raced onward like a big match struck by a bigger hand. No sound at all, just the quick bright path. And though he cried "Whoa!" Brade thought *That's my wish* and knew he would need to think this through.

Dean gave a long low whistle. *Explosion.* He fully expected the great orange bloom of a gasoline fire; and he slowed to a crawl, then nearly a stop. There in the midst of the narrow road was a black motorcycle, skewed on its side, and a man in a dark suit climbing out from under. His head was bare and a helmet lay three yards behind him. Dean seemed to be speaking to himself, "Damn—a sailor. And still alive." Then he struck the steering wheel with both palms, looked to Brade and laughed. The streak of fire, and the rescued sailor, had made him that happy.

Brade's eyes burned; if this was his answer, how could he use it? But he rubbed both eyes and managed to laugh almost in time with his father's pleasure. "Who is it, Dean?" From Dean's bright face, Brade thought it was a friend. He generally liked meeting Dean's old friends and watching them act their childhood again; it mostly looked happy. "You know him, Dean?"

Dean said "I'm a stranger out here, sugar boy." The lighted trees were standard pines; but no, Dean couldn't place the spot, much less the sailor. Likely there were pines and sailors on Mars. But then as he pulled to the shoulder and stopped, Dean said "Oh

Jesus, that boy is bleeding." The sight was frequent enough for a coach; but in all his years, Dean had never got used to the shock of *red*—he always knew it meant the worst, a boy not seconds away from death and all Dean's fault. A *piss-poor job for a full-grown man, throwing boys on a field to beat each other down sooner than normal.*

By now the sailor had raised his cycle and was moving to the shoulder, in the headlights still.

Dean said "Son, sit right here in the warm; and I'll speak to him." He checked the gears, set the brake handle and, keeping the lights on, opened his door.

Brade scrambled to his knees, hoping to follow.

But Dean said "I mean it. This may be something you don't need to see."

Brade fell back, impressed, and covered his face.

Dean said "Try to rest," then shut the door gently. The sailor's back was turned and his head was down; both of his hands were loose at his sides. *You can die on your feet; I saw a man do it.* Dean had spent ten months in Vietnam, near the red snake-eye of that filthy storm; he saw a tall medic take a shot through the temple and stand in place for maybe four seconds, trying to think of the word for help. As he moved up now, he kept seeing that; and he thought *This boy may not have a face.* Dean pictured the sight of a faceless boy, one more time—he had seen that too.

And the sailor turned. You could tell from his eyes that he knew Dean was moving but could not see him (Dean was backed to the lights). Still he said "I'm fine, sir. You go on your way."

Dean stopped eight feet from the man and looked. *My God, Hunt Wilford—it's bound to be.* He said "Is it Hunt?"

The sailor's eyes went from baffled to stunned—a packed-down body, strong as a piling, and a broad honest face. "Hunt Wilford, yes sir."

So Dean went forward with his right hand out.

Hunt said "You don't want to shake this palm"—he showed it, scraped raw. Then as Dean got close and turned to one side, the light struck his profile; and Hunt said "*Coach,* you had me fooled."

"You think I was the Law?"

"Hell, I thought you were *God,* here to ship me to Hell."

Dean said "Not yet. What happened back there?" He thumbed behind him, the start of the skid.

Hunt said "Beats me. I was bombing along; next thing I know, my bike's scraping concrete and I'm airborne." He studied the bike again; both tires were whole.

Dean said "You must have hit some oil; I noticed a truck had been spilling oil. You really all right? That hand's scraped bad."

Hunt said "You've seen me worse off than this."

Sixteen years old, a fractured skull and a nose shoved over beside his ear. Dean said "How's your head?"

Hunt ran a hand through his hair. "Fine—no thanks to that wonderful helmet." The helmet was still where it landed, intact. Hunt stepped to get it and hung it from the handlebars.

Dean said "Look, I'm headed to my mother's; but I don't need to be there much before breakfast. So I'll run you in to the hospital now, get your hand strapped up, an X ray or two and—if you're O.K.—then I'll bring you back here, no charge at all. Your bike'll be fine; hide it in those trees."

Hunt thought *He ain't even mentioned his son. I'd sure mention mine.* Then he turned his right side to the light. The thick pants were shredded from hip to ankle. Hunt bent and pulled them up to his knee—a long mean scrape. He said "Don't matter" and looked up, grinning. "Coach, I'm glad to know you're still saving boys—somebody needs to—but I ship out of Norfolk at sunup. Got to hit the road."

Dean said "You already did that, notice. Use your head for something but *butting,* hear me?"

To his own surprise, Hunt thought again of the unmentioned boy. So he looked up, serious. "You hear I got me a real son too?"

At first Dean failed to understand; then he recalled Hunt had dropped out of school in his junior year—that straight-haired trashy girl down the road, some talk of a baby. "Seems I heard someway; how old is he now?"

Hunt's face was still serious. "Yes sir, a boy—be four years old this spring, a real rounder. I keep hoping he'll play for you awhile down the road and not crap out on you like his dumb dad."

Dean nodded but only said "Who was it you married?"

"It *was* Sue Galloway—soon will be again. She left me last Christmas like I was some cold dog's dinner on the stoop, claimed she couldn't stand my ways. I told her I had ways that she'd never seen, that she wouldn't let me show her. She didn't even laugh so I let her go, which cost me the boy. I been back though, these past two days, taking him a teddy bear bigger than me and saying goodbye. I'll be in the Persian Gulf in two weeks, if God and the Ayatollah agree. They won't say when we might get back."

Dean said "No way in the world will you *get* there unless you tend to that hand right now and be more careful on your second try." He heard a dull knock from straight behind him and looked to his car. Brade was still inside but leaning toward the windshield—waving, not smiling. Dean grinned, waved back and said "Hunt, come meet my boy." A surprising flush of pleasure moved through him.

"Thank you, Coach, I know you've trained him right; but all this blood would just upset him."

"He's a strong one," Dean said.

Hunt said "I bet." Then he waited a moment. "See, I just got over leaving Jesse; I better not see another child tonight."

"You can sit in the back then; we'll drive you in. My sick friend can wait."

"I thought you just now said it was your mother."

Dean frowned to think his mind had shifted from his mother to Clyde in less than an hour. And to his amazement, he said "You misheard me. It's a friend from way back with liver cancer; he's heading out fast." *What the hell do I mean?*

Hunt said "That'll do it—well, Lord have mercy." Something in the news of a stranger's ending and the sound of his own unlikely response made Hunt think of his cold body here. With no further word, he stepped past Dean and closer to the headlights. He stood there, apparently forgetting Brade, and studied his raw hand, his ankle and leg. Then he turned back to Dean. "Thank you, Coach. I can get myself to the doctor. You and your boy go see that man." He seemed to smile. "I'm glad not to know him, but I'll keep him in mind." Still without looking toward the boy, Hunt waved toward his window.

Dean said "Let's see if your cycle will run."

Hunt was moving back toward it. "This baby has plowed more dirt than most tractors—I've been a rough rider." For whatever reason, he gave a high whoop, mounted the seat and stabbed at the crank.

In the car Brade had watched every move in silence. Now as Hunt's engine fired, the boy thought suddenly *He killed himself*. It seemed as natural as a hundred such forecasts he made each day, most of them wrong and quickly forgot. This one came hard though and pressed itself deep. Not knowing the man, Brade still spoke up aloud in the car, "Bless *him*." Since he was three, he had said his prayers most nights with Flynn. She let him pick who and what to name—bless this one and that one, bless the lawn and the leaves.

Now he saw the cut man smile at Dean above the roar and hold his good left hand out to shake. Then he put the black helmet on again and faced toward Brade. The boy waved once but the man was moving. The cycle turned a wide slow circle and headed back the way they all came. Before Dean could climb in the car and tell him, Brade understood the grown men's mistake; and he thought he could help.

But Dean had made a quick explanation and driven onward another ten minutes before Brade thought of what to do. He was sitting firmly back on the seat, far over from Dean. He worked to be sure his voice sounded true. "We better go home."

"What?"

"You and me, now."

"You feeling bad, sport? Look here at your pa."

Brade already knew the way to look sick. He opened his eyes wide and narrowed his lips. By the time he turned, he was pale and blank.

Dean reached out and tested his forehead—no fever. "You're not homesick? Son, Flynn's all right; you'll see her at supper."

Brade knew he was well, but he also knew he must aim them back behind the cut sailor. He did not know why; at times like this, he mostly never did. All he understood was what they must do; they had no choice. Like boys in general, Brade got these sudden orders from his mind and tried to obey them. Twenty minutes ago he was warm and glad to be riding with Dean, far off for good—he knew Dean's mother was just their excuse. But since that trail of sparks came at him, he knew he and Dean must go back to Flynn's and wait for the old life to start up there. *This is a dangerous place in the night. That sailor is dead and Dean will be wild.*

Wild was what his mother called Dean's temper, mad or blue or even that night—awhile ago—when Dean was so glad to win a game that he picked them both up and whirled in a ring till they begged him to stop. Then they all three fell out laughing on the sofa Dean hated so much, that Flynn's father bought. Still facing his own father, Brade said "We can go to see Ma-Ma tomorrow. We need to go home."

Dean slowed a little but drove another mile, Brade watching him steadily. Finally he said "Son, tell the truth. You think I'm mad at your mother, don't you?"

Brade still knew how to cry on demand. But he knew not to do it. He held a hand palm-out toward Dean. "See, I think that friend of yours, he needs you."

So he overheard us speaking of Clyde. "I wish we could help him, Brade—nothing to do though."

"The sailor, I mean, that you used to know."

"Oh he'll be fine. They'll tape up his hand and X-ray his head. If anything's wrong, they'll keep him and fix it. I'll call in the morning and see what they did." Dean's foot unthinkingly pressed the gas.

And though Brade hated himself as they gathered, tears rose up. Knowing that if he touched his eyes, his father would see, Brade turned to hide.

But Dean understood. Until that moment, more than he knew, he had shared the boy's plot—to run, for good. *Hell, I made the plot. I told him about birch-bark canoes and endless rivers.* Again he slowed and reached for Brade's foot.

Brade scooted farther away toward his door and faced his own window, the moving dark.

Dean said "I'm taking you home right now."

The boy would not turn, but he said "You *stay* when we get there now—"

At the flat command, Dean went cold again. He said "Why's that?"

Brade's new voice was earnest. "I'm trying to tell you; but you won't listen—to help that sailor that you used to know, that played football when he was a child."

If Hunt had played for one more year and finished school, he might be safe in one piece tonight—not a motorcycle punk with a broken-up home, bound for dangerous waters at sunrise. But Dean pulled onto the next wide shoulder and turned the car home.

In five minutes Brade had sat back again, though he looked straight forward and worried his ear lobe.

And after a while the sight of that lean face, worried sick for an absolute stranger, made Dean begin to shift his own fear from his mother and Clyde to young Hunt Wilford. Despite her cough, his mother would likely outlast them all; if bravery counted she would outlast time. Clyde's time was up or numbered in days. What Dean hated now was thinking of Hunt Wilford as a hood, so he tried to picture the boy's good days.

They were halfway home before Dean found a curious pattern for Hunt in his mind—every one of the boy's best runs came in practice, when he wove like mercury poured downhill through the arms of his friends, with Dean Walker watching and struggling not to cheer. Actual rivals had cramped Hunt's style but not because they hated him personally or were smarter. The fact was, Hunt just hated to fight.

And now this morning they'll float him off to a maddog Iran that can burn his ass to cinders any second. Through the dark and cold, Dean went on hoping for Hunt's good luck, tonight and wherever. *Let him land back somewhere safe and calm down.* And by the time Dean could see Flynn's light on the porch ahead, Brade had dozed off. Brade's father though, bone-tired at last, was feeling the rightness of his son's strange claim—*That boy you used to know is dead.*

*

Flynn was up, in blue jeans, washing windows for the third time since Christmas. Without a word she stood by the door while Dean walked in with Brade, went straight to the boy's room, laid him back on his cot, took off his shoes, tucked him in and sat on the edge of his mattress till he slept. Then she came to Brade's door, reached for the light but left it dark. "Is he all right?"

Dean felt the boy's forehead again, still cool. "In the car he said he didn't feel good. But he'll be fine. I guess we scared him—"

Flynn snagged on that, then let the *we* slide.

"Funny thing," Dean said. "We saw a bad wreck, this long trail of fire lit straight up the road—" His voice refused, not tears, just the shock of the sight again.

"Did something explode?"

Dean nodded. "Not really. A motorcycle turned over fast and struck a long line of sparks up the road." He leaned then and pressed his lips to Brade's head. Dean was not a big kisser, but it seemed called for. Then he stood and said "Lady, would you know where there's some intravenous coffee?"

Flynn said "Five yards down the hall, my kitchen."

Separate as shy offended children, they headed there.

When they left, Brade rallied a moment and said "Dean, call that man." He thought he almost shouted the words but nobody heard him. And before he could try again, he was gone.

In twenty minutes, Dean had told the story—only one thing missing. He could not make himself repeat the fear that Brade and he had felt in the car. But the fear gathered strength as he lined out the details; and it swelled his mind when Flynn stirred in the facts she knew—that Hunt's wife Susie had cut Flynn's hair not three weeks ago at "The Gorgeous Box," a beauty parlor Dean called "The Short and Curly."

Dean thought *ex-wife*; then he thought *divorced widow. That son won't even get to sniff Hunt's insurance.*

And strangely Flynn said "Sue says she can't make herself divorce Hunt. She claims she prays for a change of heart and thinks he's bound to get it in Persia."

"It's Iran now, notice. You watch TV; what does Sue watch—the wall? There's not one crazier country on Earth, Flynn; and now it's aimed at Hunt Wilford."

Flynn waited and actually managed a grin. "I know your old players mean a lot to you, but I doubt those nuts feel all that personal about a local boy." She saw Dean's fingers splay, white on the table; then make white fists. She never once thought he meant to strike her, but she softened her voice and said "Hunt's run a charmed life till now."

"I doubt he's *run* much more than his dick, but I promised Brade I'll call the hospital and see how he did."

Flynn glanced at the clock—twenty past three. "Why don't you wait till just before seven? The nurses change then, you can catch the old shift, all his tests'll be in." She looked to Dean, who was watching his hands.

They were still fisted tight. Then the left hand eased, and those fingers worked the right hand open. He turned both palms upright between them and said "Flynn, things just break around me."

"That's because you're a rock. You could ease up, man—"

"Oh Jesus, no. I mean worse than that. Everywhere I've been, since my eyes opened, the good things break soon as I walk in."

She wanted to touch him, but she knew she must wait. "Anything you said to me here tonight, any hard thing, is already gone. And I said a lot more than I ever meant."

He met her eyes and nodded. "But *listen* to me. Look here just tonight—there's Brady and Mother, your Clyde and now Hunt, all breaking up round me."

"He's not my Clyde, never was and he's leaving. The rest are having normal lives, good luck and bad."

Dean's eyes stayed on her, though his head was shaking. "One time now, Flynn, try to see what I mean. I play the mean fool at the sound of Clyde's name and *slam* he's dead. I call my Mother to hear her voice in the bad part of night, and she can barely speak. Brade and I set out to keep her company, and *slam* a good old boy I coached nearly dies at my feet. I feel like I ought to get out now while you and Brade at least are breathing."

It flew through her skull before she could stop it, *Do. Get out now.* And she waited to know how much of her mind agreed with that.

Somehow Dean understood her silence; and now he never stopped watching her face, though he kept his eyes blank and tried not to force her.

At last Flynn said "I, for one, am asking no such thing. I know Brade wants you."

Dean said "I want all grades of goodness that I don't have and won't ever get—the money to give you and Brade what you need, better sense than to sit here one more year and teach dumb boys how to crush each other and a few more kids how to fuck and not die, not kill the fuckee. I've turned out less than average, Flynn—a D-plus well-intentioned slack boy—and I never meant that, never thought it would happen. You know how fine I planned on being—"

She knew; it was half of what kept her beside him, tonight and in general. Even when he got back home from the Army, he could quote Browning to her, that he learned in grade school—

A man's reach should exceed his grasp,
Or what's a heaven for?

After nearly a year of Vietnam, Dean's eyes had still been set high enough to wait while his lips said that and meant it. For all he told her, it was all he had learned that whole bad year. And she had been young enough, caught by his eyes, to think that she was meant by fate to be part of what he must always reach for, decent and fine.

It had not felt arrogant or foolish back then, as an aim at least; and still it did not. But all these years later here, what was she? *The same girl, eight more pounds on her hips, half a million miles on her mind and heart.* Flynn thought that was true; and she said to Dean, "I think we can take some reasonable credit. I doubt we need to be all that ashamed."

He even smiled but his meaning was hard. "You're speaking for *we*, like I said just now. I'm speaking for me. I don't like anything I know about me, except I'm half of what made Brady. And what you said about Clyde, before midnight, sounded truer than anything I've heard since. You were right, in the dark"—he pointed to the bedroom. "You picked the wrong horse, if you aimed to ride far."

If I'd picked Clyde, I'd soon be a widow. But she knew not to say it. She knew that Dean was in serious pain, prowling the oldest cellars of his mind. She never had known a remedy for him. Long ago he had said there was none. *He was hurt too early to let himself heal.* She could only do what she always did—make coffee, sit near, be her own best self and hope that the day would help him onward, just the light itself. Any blue sky brought Dean part-way back; he was that ever-ready to push on ahead. In sympathy though, she bent a little toward him and said "I've ridden as far as I planned, to this point—" When his eyes never blinked, she shied and faked a hillbilly voice, "You ain't throwed me yet, and now you ain't gonna."

Dean said "If the world turned honest at dawn, tell me what you think—would anybody give a plugged nickel to keep us here alive? You and me, I mean."

"Brade needs us completely. He's got his piggy bank; he might spare a dime. Your mother, my dad, the ladies I take hot lunches to—sure, they'd spare a nickel—the kids you've knocked good manners into. We might come up with thirty-five cents if they gave us till noon."

Dean said "You think old Clyde's asleep?"

"No." She shook her head very firmly.

"Why not? What soul did Clyde ever harm?"

Flynn said "I called him. He was wide awake."

Dean heard it as calmly as the weather report. "When?"

"When you and Brade left; you were still in sight."

Somehow Dean still felt almost peaceful, maybe too tired to care. "How'd you know where he was?"

"He gave me his itinerary when he left here today."

Dean actually smiled to himself. "In writing?"

"Well, mimeographed. He always sends it to his family and friends, in case they need him."

Dean said "Are you saying that, all these years, you've known where Clyde Bowles was every minute?"

Flynn could not smile now, but she shook her head. When she could speak, she said "Just today. I thought it was somehow creepy but I took it. He said 'Here, in case the Spirit moves you.' "

Dean said "So it did." He took it for granted that such things happened in lives no better than his at least.

Flynn was much less sure, but now she wanted to go with the drift. "That's what Clyde said when he heard my voice. I said 'Hey, friend' and he said '*Hallelujah*'—just a whisper but glad. Then he said 'The Spirit has moved at last.' I didn't ask him what that could mean. I prayed he didn't think I planned to run toward him."

Dean was peaceful as the table their hands lay on; except for exhaustion, he could not have believed it. *She said the word* prayed. *If she means that, then this thing is moving. Don't tip the boat*. "What did you say then?"

"I said your mother just told you the news—" Flynn's mouth clamped on her, though no tears came. Her hands and Dean's were ten inches apart; it seemed the distance from there to Peru.

Dean said "You told him we all were sorry."

Flynn waited awhile and then shook her head. "I said 'I want you to know the truth—' "

Dean said "You don't have to tell me this."

But her eyes flared open and she nodded hard. "I need to, please. I told him 'Don't stop me till I get this out; if you do, I'm sunk.' " Then I said 'Clyde Bowles, you and Coach Dean Walker weigh more with me than all the rest—grown people, that is.' "

Dean checked his mind. *No harm, I'm here, she's here in reach,* though he would not even think toward morning—how this would feel when their nerves woke up and they saw each other in natural light. He said "I guess that was just the truth."

Again she nodded as hard as if some power had asked her sole permission to keep Brade alive. When Dean smiled again, at the spoon in his hand, she could finally speak. "Clyde told me 'Flynn, if I thank you now, we'll both dissolve like two old snails.' Then he tried to laugh—he and I used to pour table salt on snails and watch them melt, outdoors I mean, when we were kids."

Dean said "Me too."

"Then he said 'I'm going to hang up now. I lie here and talk to God in the night.' And with no goodbye or see-you-soon, he hung up so quiet I waited on a while, still thinking he was there."

"He's dead," Dean said. "You did right by him and by your own self. You can let him go now, and he'll go a lot gentler."

Flynn despised that wiseman calm in his voice—*I'm not a teenage boy, Coach Walker*—but she held her tongue and tried to recall there was more here than this. Then she laid her palms together before her and brought her face down between them on the table. Her shoulders moved in the rhythm of sobs but no sound came.

Dean knew that any try to help her would break this peace. He had known that about her since the day they met, from her endless eyes. *She suffers on her own time; touch her and she'll strike.* He said "I'm going to the bedroom, hear?" He waited and, when she gave no sign, he stood and went quietly.

At Brade's door he paused and listened for the boy—absolute silence. He stood ten seconds in hopes of a breath; and when nothing came, he stepped to the cot, found Brade's body and turned back the cover. Then gently he reached inside the flannel jacket and felt for Brade's heart. It took awhile to find, and Dean was afraid the boy would wake. *He's warm, not hot. Leave him be.* But he had to keep trying, though gently as if this were some balky girl. Then suddenly he found it. It lurched out at him like a small trapped thing—a cornered squirrel. It was nearly too strong and Dean's hand jerked. Brade moaned and moved and Dean drew back. But peace continued so he leaned again and touched the edges of his son's warm hair. *I'd kill the world if that's what it took to see you through.* When he stood he frowned. *You're way out of order, Coach. Go on and rest.*

But in one swift turn, Brade rolled to his back and said "That man—"

Dean knew it was only a scrap of dream. Yet he stood awhile longer, then went to his own room and slowly undressed. *Two hours till day. I'll sleep like a bear.*

Twenty minutes later though, he still lay awake. For most of that space, he listened closely to Flynn in the kitchen. She washed the coffee pot and their cups, whatever else was left in the sink; then she dried them as if each object were precious and could not be replaced. There would come brief silences; Dean would think *She's finished.* But then he would hear the clink of a spoon laid back in the drawer, the chink of a glass. All his life, those sounds were a promise of safety. For now as he waited, he tried to think they meant the same as they meant on better days. Then one stretch of silence lengthened and deepened. *She's on her way back. We've cleared a deep trap.*

Her steps came down the hall a ways.

Three minutes in the bathroom; then she'll be here. But let her sleep, Dean. She's bound to be tired as me and sadder. He rubbed his hand over all her side of the bed, meaning to warm her sheet a little. *Eskimo squaw*—he always accused her of reptile blood; she wolfed up all the warmth in a room and spent the time from fall to spring, hugging her arms as if there were some private blizzard in progress over her lone head. But no water ran in the bathroom, no brushing.

Then he knew. She had done it once before, two years ago when they both yelled each other down about—what? Once more Flynn had laid herself down in Brade's room. If Dean were to creep out now and check, he knew he would find her. He also knew she was not on Brade's cot but hunched on the sheepskin rug beside it, under some old quilt with Brade's extra pillow. *She's guaranteeing I don't leave here again, not with the boy, not before day at least.* And he actually got to his elbows to find her. *Just be decent and patient. A boy her mind leaned on is leaving. Old Clyde, not even a quick clean death.* But tired as he was, the taste of that meanness offended Dean. He actually whispered "Bless his sad ass." And then tears came or as near to tears as Dean ever got. *Well, that makes three; now we've all boohooed, a perfect night. But if you mean to have any chance at day, pipe down and sleep.*

He rolled to his left side, facing Flynn's place, and set his head and both his arms at the necessary angles for causing sleep. *When Mother would make me wash my hands and I'd object, she'd always say 'Everybody's got to eat one peck of dirt in life anyhow. Don't go volunteering for more than your share.' What made me think that?* He halfway thought of the dirt he had forced down

Flynn and Brade in the past six hours—the shit he had strewn on poor Clyde's grave, the way he let Hunt Wilford leave—but again he was too dazed to feel regret or think of the several repairs he should make by sundown tomorrow. *Today. It's day already.* Sleep, *boy.*

He clamped both eyes till purple and gold rays shot through his mind. Then he started silently repeating his word, the one he picked out years ago when every hippie in the Army had a mantra and zoned out on it in trances Dean envied. His own word was *River* and, to this day now, he had never told a soul. Swear to God, he could be in a cold sweat of fear in the final play of a losing game or thinking of Flynn in somebody's hands; and if he could summon his good sense long enough, Dean could start saying the one word *River,* fast in his head; and his heart and mind would stretch right out and sweep him away or, at night like this, float him to sleep as if he were one boy sleep had waited for all these years.

But after the hundredth *River* now, a voice in Dean's mind stood up and told him *Hunt Wilford—you trusted his wild self to get help. And he didn't do nothing but pull off the road and let you pass him five minutes later. Then he lit out for Norfolk and points far east like a cutthroat hog.* The sight in his mind of Hunt's raw hand, pumping gas to an engine through six cold hours, woke Dean fully. *No hope on Earth till I know for sure.* He rolled to his back again. *Do it, fool.*

In the dark, he reached for the bedside phone. On some kind of deal at the savings bank, Flynn had got this whorehouse phone in mother of pearl with dim-lit buttons; so as quiet as he could, Dean dialed Information for the hospital number, the emergency room. A woman answered and, as he described Hunt's actual wreck, he realized how good he was at swift storytelling, a gift from his teaching. *You can lose a room of kids in under three seconds, if you don't hump it.*

But even so, the woman broke in. "Coach Walker, I'm Miriam Council, a nurse. I'm sorry to tell you, your friend has passed."

For an instant Dean heard it as "passed on his way." But then he heard the word she meant, the old reluctance to say "He's dead." And because she sounded rushed and would hang up, Dean said "*Hey!*" Then he begged her pardon. "I'm sorry, Mrs. Council, but when Hunt left me, he was just scratched up."

She halfway covered her end of the phone and told somebody, "Tighten the tourniquet on that drunk; he's *pouring* blood." Then calmly she came back to Dean in midstride. "Coach, we thought the same. The doctor on duty taped up his hand; I cleaned his leg. I whispered to him he was welcome to sleep on one of those couches in the lobby and wait for light—everybody else does—but he said he'd land in the brig if he did. So he gave me a big hug and walked through the door. I'd known him long before he could talk; his stepmother Maud is my first cousin. If you want to call Maud later on this morning, I've got her number." Again she was courteously trying to end it.

Dean said "I know her myself but please, what killed him?"

She waited awhile, then lowered her voice. "They're hoping to do an autopsy later; now all I know is, Hunt walked out of here, just a little slowed down. Then twenty minutes later, one of the orderlies stepped out back to smoke a cigarette; and, child, Hunt was lying there under his bike. He had managed to crank it, the colored boy said—his engine was running smooth as silk—but then he keeled over dead on the pavement. Looked like to me he died in midair, not even a bruise."

Dean said "You didn't X-ray his head?"

"The doctor didn't, no. That's not routine."

"He had a skull fracture and a bad concussion when he played ball for me—"

Her voice took a new defensive crouch. "Hunt didn't tell us a word about that."

Dean said, "Well, he wouldn't have, would he? He was hell-bent to go."

She waited again, then almost chuckled. "He *went* too, didn't he, wild to the grave."

Dean saw her last words, cut out on the air like an epitaph. It rubbed him wrong. But he thanked her, asked if Hunt left any bill—he would gladly pay it. No, Hunt had paid cash money on the spot. So he ended, "You know he left a son?"

"I do," she said. "And he loved the little fellow. But not enough, Coach."

"Ma'm?"

"Not enough to come back safe and be his dad."

In daylight, Dean would have fought for Hunt; but now there was no point in wrangling with a nurse who was tireder than he. *And may be right*. He thanked her for all she did to help. Then he asked her to be his guest at the first home-game next fall; and she accepted, for what that was worth.

His head had barely touched the pillow when he knew his plan. *Tomorrow night Brade and I will find Hunt's boy and take him something, a toy or some candy. Flynn will know what. And I can tell Sue the little I know*. Then he lay for a hard stretch, asking again if he was cursed; did he curse other lives? Something was causing pain all around him. But at last he could say *Dean, welcome to the club*. He meant the human race, everybody's old pain. By then anyhow it was so close to sunup he might as well dress and do his homework (though he knew the textbook, forward and backward, he still read through the day's lesson each time). *You'd wake Flynn and Brade. Let them rest at least*.

For a while he dreaded the last of the dark; he would lie here alone and taste every minute of the bitter night. He thought of saying *River*. But before he started, his ears heard something new in the air, a kind of busyness like kids talking at considerable distance. *Spring. Spring wind in the trees already*. It was wind all right, and the bare hardwoods in the grove by the house were stirred and clicking, but spring was still maybe three weeks off. The floor of the grove was silently heaving with one last frost, breaking on itself like ocean water.

As he lay, Dean understood all of that. He even pictured the rising ground, the sleeping creatures locked inside it, waiting for sun. He understood too that, in no time now, he must tell this further sadness to Brade and Flynn and help them take it. *Can Flynn take this much more? Of course.* He would need to know if his mother was better and then maybe drive there and make her be sensible, tell her she mattered, take her to the store and make her eat right.

With that much duty on his plate for morning, he halfway knew he ought to be worried or grieved at least. And he did take time to picture Hunt Wilford again at his peak, years past on the run, and Clyde Bowles happy for once at the prom, all spiffed in his dinner jacket, beaming hope. Both faces stood clear in his mind a long moment; but young as he was, Dean had a big stock of dead faces in his mind. So these two now began to fade as his last strength failed. By then Dean felt very little but thanks and a general peace in all his parts.

He was live above ground for this one minute of cold March dark. *I might even last a whole nother day. With a good-hearted woman next door near a boy that loves us both like the air he breathes, my chances are even.* Cold sun was due for the rest of the week. *I could live at the pole, if the sun would shine.* Dean rolled to his left side, stroked Flynn's place again and soon was telling himself an old story, a story he had long forgot he knew. It was nothing but the dream of perfect goodness he told himself so often in boyhood, when luck seemed more unlikely than courage; but he went through it now.

Two strong grown people in a house with a tight roof, a big oil furnace and deep woods behind, wild animals watching the house with respect. Upstairs in separate rooms of their own, two children, both boys born twelve months apart. They are each other's best friends but have their own games and keep close track of whose is whose. No voice ever rises except at Christmas or to say "Supper's ready." And no clocks tick anywhere in the house to age the people. They stay on calm and pass each other in rooms and hallways, peaceful as now, till God says "Stop," which He's known to do.

As his mind retold the ancient hope, it added more details of peaceful deeds like beautiful girls in slow-motion dances outside each window and all of them singing songs from a world where fairness is all life asks or gives. Even as he lay, Dean realized he had much less and would not get more—not short of a hairpin curve in Fate—but by the time the music reached him, he was well asleep. Fine as it sounded, he understood he was bound for day and the rest of a life that would be as strange as this dream or any, though harder to bear.

REYNOLDS PRICE

Reynolds Price was born in Macon, North Carolina in 1933. He was reared and educated in his native state, taking his A.B. from Duke University. In 1955 he traveled to Merton College, Oxford where he studied for three years as a Rhodes Scholar. He then returned to Duke and began the teaching which he continues as James B. Duke Professor of English.

In 1962 his first novel *A Long and Happy Life* appeared. It received the William Faulkner Award and has never been out of print. In ensuing years he has published seven more novels. In 1986 his *Kate Vaiden* received the National Book Critics Circle Award. He has also published volumes of short stories, poems, plays, essays, translations and a memoir, *Clear Pictures*. His television play *Private Contentment* was commissioned by American Playhouse for its first season, and in 1989 his trilogy of plays *New Music* premiered at the Cleveland Play House.

He is a member of the National Academy and Institute of Arts and Letters. His books have appeared in sixteen languages.

0 00 02 0513781 3
MIDDLEBURY COLLEGE